IRONHEART

IRONHEART

William MacLeod Raine

GUNSMOKE

First published in the UK by Hodder and Stoughton

This hardback edition 2009
by BBC Audiobooks Ltd
by arrangement with
Golden West Literary Agency

ISBN 978 1 408 46228 7

British Library Cataloguing in Publication Data available.

Printed and bound in Great Britain by
CPI Antony Rowe, Chippenham and Eastbourne

CHAPTER I

TURFING IT

A THIN wisp of smoke drifted up from the camp at the edge of the wash. It rose languidly, as though affected by the fact that the day was going to be a scorcher. Already, though the morning was young, a fiery sun beat down on the sand so that heat waves shimmered in the air. Occasionally a spark from the crackling cottonwood limbs was caught by a dust whirl and carried toward the field of ripe wheat bordering the creek.

Of the campers there were three, all of the genus tramp, but each a variant. They represented different types, these desert trekkers.

The gross man lying lazily under the shade of a clump of willows might have stepped straight out of a vaudeville sketch. He was dirty and unkempt, his face bloated and dissipated. From his lax mouth projected an English brier pipe, uncleansably soiled. His clothes hung on him like sacks, wrinkled and dusty, but not ragged. He was too good a hobo to wear anything torn or patched. It was his boast that he could get another suit for the asking any time he needed one.

"I'm a blowed-in-the-glass stiff," he bragged now. "Drilled from Denver to 'Frisco fifteen times, an' never was a stake man or a shovel bum. Not for a day, 'boes. Ask any o' the push about old York. They'll give it to youse straight that he knows the best flops from Cincie to Phillie, an' that no horstile crew can ditch him when he's goin' good."

York was a hobo pure and simple. It was his business in life. For "stew-bums" and "gay-cats," to use his own phraseology, he had a supreme contempt. His companions were amateurs, from his point of view non-professionals. Neither of them had any pride in turfing it, which is the blanket stiff's expression for taking to the road. They did not understand York's vocabulary nor the ethics that were current in his craft.

5

Yet the thin, weasel-faced man with the cigarette drooping from his mouth was no amateur in his own line. He had a prison face, the peculiar distortion of one side of the mouth often seen in confirmed criminals. His light blue eyes were cold and dead. A film veiled them and snuffed out all expression.

"Cig" he called himself, and the name sufficed. On the road surnames were neither asked for nor volunteered. York had sized him up three days before when they had met at Colorado Springs, and he had passed on his verdict to the third member of the party.

"A river rat on a vac—hittin' the grit for a getaway," he had whispered.

His guess had been a good one. Cig had been brought up on the East River. He had served time in the penitentiaries of three States and expected to test the hospitality of others. Just now he was moving westward because the East was too hot for him. He and a pal had done a job at Jersey City during which they had been forced to croak a guy. Hence his unwilling expedition to the Rockies. Never before had he been farther from the Atlantic than Buffalo, and the vast uninhabited stretches of the West bored and appalled him. He was homesick for the fetid dumps of New York.

The corner of his mouth lifted in a sneer. "Wot'ell would any one want to cross this Gawd-forsaken country fifteen times for unless he was bughouse?"

"If you read the papes you'd know that travel is a lib'ral ejucation. Difference between a man an' a tree is that one's got legs to move around with. You ginks on the East Side act like you're anchored to the Batt'ry an' the Bowery. Me, I was born there, but I been batterin' on the road ever since I was knee-high to a duck. A fellow's got to throw his feet if he wants to learn," York announced dogmatically.

There was obvious insult in Cig's half-closed eyes. " 'S at what learned you all youse know?" he asked.

"Don't get heavy, young feller," advised the blanket stiff. "I've knew guys to stay healthy by layin' off me."

The young man cooking breakfast barked a summons. "Come an' get it."

The tramps moved forward to eat, forgetting for the moment their incipient quarrel. Into tin cups and plates the cook poured coffee and stew. In his light clean build, slender but well-packed, was the promise of the athlete. His movements

6

disappointed this expectation. He slouched, dragging the worn shoes through the cracks of which the flesh was visible. Of the three, he was the only one that was ragged. The coat he wore, which did not match the trousers, was at the last extremity.

One might have guessed his age at twenty-three or four. If it had not been for the sullen expression in the eyes and the smoldering· discontent of the face, he might have been good-looking. The reddish hair was short, crisp, and curly, the eyes blue as the Colorado summer sky above, the small head well-shaped and beautifully poised on the sloping column of the neck.

Yet the impression he made on observers was not a pleasant one. His good points were marred by the spirit that found out-let in a sullen manner that habitually grudged the world a smile. He had the skin pigment of the blond, and in the un-tempered sun of the Rockies should have been tanned to a rich red-brown. Instead, the skin was clammily unhealthy. The eyes were dulled and expressionless.

York ate wolfishly, occasionally using the sleeve of his coat for a napkin. He talked, blatantly and continuously. Cig spoke only at rare intervals, the cook not at all. Within the silent man there simmered a nausea of disgust that included himself and all the universe in which he moved.

In the underworld caste rules more rigidly than in upper strata of society. The sense of superiority is everywhere an ad-mission of weakness. It is the defense of one who lives in a glass house. Since all of these men were failures, each despised the others and cherished his feeling that they were inferior.

"You 'boes turf it with York an' you'll always have plenty o' punk and plaster," the old tramp swaggered. "Comes to batter-in' I'm there with bells on."

Translated into English, he meant that if they traveled with him they would have bread and butter enough because he was a first-class beggar.

"To hear youse chew the rag you're a wiz, ain't you?" Cig jeered. "I ain't noticed you diggin' up any Ritz-Carlton lunches a guy can write home about. How about it, Tug?"

The cook grunted.

"Me, I can tell a mark far as I can see him—know whether he's good for a flop or a feed," York continued. "Onct I was ridin' the rods into Omaha—been punchin' the wind till I was froze stiff, me 'n' a pal called Seattle. Shacks an' the con tried to ditch us. Nothin' doing. We was right there again when the wheels began to move. In the yards at Omaha we bumps into a gay cat—like Tug here. He spills the dope that the bulls are layin' for us. Some mission stiff had beefed on me. No guy with or without brass buttons can throw a scare into old York. No can do. So I says to Seattle, says I—"

York's story died in his throat. He stood staring, mouth open and chin fallen.

Two men were standing on the edge of the bluff above the bed of the creek. He did not need a second look to tell him that they had come to make trouble.

CHAPTER II

"DE KING O' PROOSHIA ON DE JOB"

To Reed came his foreman Lon Forbes with a story of three tramps camping down by Willow Creek close to the lower meadow wheatfield.

The ranchman made no comment, unless it was one to say, "Get out the car." He was a tight-lipped man of few words, sometimes grim. His manner gave an effect of quiet strength.

Presently the two were following the winding road through the pasture. A field of golden wheat lay below them undulating with the roll of the land. Through it swept the faintest ripple of quivering grain. The crop was a heavy one, ripe for the reaper. Dry as tinder, a spark might set a blaze running across the meadow like wildfire.

Forbes pointed the finger of a gnarled hand toward a veil of smoke drifting lazily from the wash. "Down there, looks like."

His employer nodded. They descended from the car and walked along the edge of the bank above the creek bed. Three men sat near a camp-fire. One glance was enough to show that they were hoboes. Coffee in an old tomato can was bubbling over some live coals set between two flat stones.

The big man with the bloated face was talking. The others were sulkily silent, not so much listening as offering an an-

8

noyed refusal to be impressed. The boaster looked up, and the vaporings died within him.

"What you doing here?" demanded Reed. His voice was curt and hostile.

York, true to type, became at once obsequious. "No offense, boss. If these here are private grounds—"

"They are," the owner cut in sharply.

"Well, we'll hit the grit right away. No harm done, mister." The voice of the blanket stiff had become a whine, sullen and yet fawning.

His manner irritated both of his companions. Cig spoke first, out of the corner of his mouth, slanting an insolent look up at the ranchman.

"Youse de traffic cop on dis block, mister?"

Lon Forbes answered. "We know your sort an' don't want 'em here. Shack! Hit the trail pronto! No back talk about it either."

Cig looked at the big foreman. "Gawd!" he jeered. "Wotcha know about that? De king o' Prooshia on de job again."

The bluff tanned Westerner took a step or two toward the ferret-faced man from the slums. Hurriedly York spoke up. He did not want anything "started." There were stories current on the road of what ranchmen had done to hoboes who had made trouble. He knew of one who had insulted a woman and had been roped and dragged at a horse's heels till half dead.

"We ain't doin' no harm, boss. But we'll beat it 'f you say so. Gotta roll up our war bags."

Reed did not discuss the question of the harm they were doing. He knew that a spark might ignite the wheat, but he did not care to plant the suggestion in their minds. "Put out the fire and move on," he said harshly.

"De king o' Prooshia an' de clown prince," Cig retorted with a lift of his lip.

But he shuffled forward and began to kick dirt over the fire with the toe of his shoe.

Reed turned to the youngest tramp. "Get water in that can," he ordered.

"I don' know about that." Up till now the tramp called Tug had not said a word. "I'm not your slave. Get water yourself if you want to. Able-bodied, ain't you?"

The rancher looked steadily at him, and the longer he looked, the less he liked what he saw. A stiff beard bristled on the sullen face of the tramp. He was ragged and disreputable

9

from head to heel. In the dogged eyes, in straddling legs, in the half-clenched fist resting on one hip, Reed read defiance. The gorge of the Westerner rose. The country was calling for men to get in its harvests. His own crops were ripe and he was short of hands. Yet this husky young fellow was a loafer. He probably would not do a day's work if it were offered him. He was a parasite, the kind of ne'er-do-well who declines to saw wood for a breakfast, metaphorically speaking.

"Don't talk back to me. Do as I say. Then get out of here."

Reed did not lift his voice. It was not necessary. As he stood on the bank above the sand bed he conveyed an impression of strength in every line of his solid body. Even the corduroy trousers he wore folded into the short laced boots seemed to have fallen into wrinkles that expressed power. Close to fifty, the sap of virile energy still flowed in his veins.

The fist on Tug's hip clenched. He flushed angrily. "Kind of a local God Almighty on tin wheels," he said with a sneer.

York was rolling up his pack. Cig, grumbling, had begun to gather his belongings. But the youngest tramp gave no evidence of an intention to leave. Nor did he make a move to get water to put out the still smoldering fire.

The rancher came down from the bank. Forbes was at his elbow. The foreman knew the signs of old. Reed was angry. Naturally imperious, he did not allow any discussion when clearly within his rights. He would not waste his force on such a spineless creature as York, but the youngest tramp was of a different sort. He needed a lesson, and Lon judged he was about to get one.

"Hear me? Get water and douse that fire," the ranchman said.

His steel-gray eyes were fastened to those of Tug. The tramp faced him steadily. Forbes had a momentary surprise. This young fellow with the pallid dead skin looked as though he would not ask for anything better than a fight.

"Get it yourself," the hobo flung back.

The right fist of the ranchman lifted swiftly. It did not move far, but it carried great power back of it. The tramp's head snapped backward. His shoulders hit the sand. He had been caught on the point of the jaw by a knockout punch.

Tug came back to consciousness under the impression that he was drowning in deep waters. Cig was dipping a can in the creek and sousing its contents over his head. He sat up dizzily.

His uncertain gaze fell on some one who had arrived since his exit from activity.

She was a young woman on horseback. He noticed that she was slender and had a good seat. Her dark eyes watched him. Who was she? What the dickens was she doing here? Where was he anyhow?

His glance swept the scene. York was stamping out the last embers of the fire. There was a bruise on Cig's cheek and one of his eyes was rapidly closing. From the fact that Forbes was examining abraded knuckles it was an easy guess that he had been in action.

The rancher, hands in coat pockets, relieved his mind in regard to the youth he had knocked out. "You're a good-for-nothing loafer, not fit to live in a country that treats you too well. If I had charge of wastrels like you, I'd put you on the rock-pile and work you to a frazzle. What use are you, to yourself or any one else? When you were needed to fill a uniform, I'll bet a dollar you were a slacker. You still are. A worthless, rotten-to-the-core hobo. Now get up and get off my land or I'll give you that thrashing you need."

Tug got up, swayed unsteadily on his feet, and lurched forward. In his eyes, still dull and glazed from the shock his nervous system had endured, a gleam of anger came to life. He was a slacker, was he? All right. He would show this arrogant slave-driver that he could stand up and take all he had to give.

His rush was a poor leaden-footed shuffle, for he was shaky at the knees and weights dragged at his feet. The blow he aimed at Reed missed the brown face half a foot. It was badly timed and placed. The ranchman's counter caught him flush on the cheek-bone and flung him back.

Again he gathered himself and plunged forward. Clinton Reed belonged to the old fighting West. He had passed through the rip-roaring days of Leadville's prime and later had been a part of Cripple Creek's turbid life. Always he had been a man of his hands. He punished his dazed opponent with clean hard blows, most of them started at short range to save his own fists from the chance of broken or dislocated bones.

The tramp fell into a clinch to get time for recovery. Reed jolted him out of it with a short arm left below the chin and followed with two slashing rights to the face.

The hobo was in a bad way. In ring parlance, he was what is known as groggy. His arms moved slowly and without force back of the blows. His knees sagged. There was a ringing in

11

his head. He did not seem able to think clearly.

But the will in him functioned to push him to more punishment. He attacked feebly. Through a weak defense the ranchman's driving arms tore cruelly.

Tug went down again. He tried to rise, but in spite of the best he could do was unable to get up. The muscles of the legs would not coöperate with the will.

Some one in khaki riding-breeches flashed past him. "That's enough, Dad. I don't care if he was impudent. You've hurt him enough. Let him go now."

The figure was the boyish one of the equestrienne, but the high indignant voice was feminine enough.

"S'pose you try minding your own business, Bess," her father said quietly.

"Now, Dad," she expostulated. "We don't want any trouble, do we? Make 'em move on, and that's enough."

"Tha's what we're doin', Betty," explained the foreman. "It ain't our fault if there's a rookus. We told 'em to light out, an' they got sassy."

Tug rose with difficulty. He was a badly hammered hobo. Out of swollen and discolored eyes he looked at the ranchman.

"You quite through with me?" he snarled.

It was a last growl of defiance. His companions were already clambering with their packs out of the wash to the bank above.

"Not quite." Clint Reed took his daughter by the shoulders and spun her out of the way when she tried to stop him. "Be fresh if you want to, my young wobbly. I reckon I can stand it if you can." He whirled the tramp round and kicked him away.

"Oh, Dad! Fighting with a tramp," the girl wailed.

Tug swung round unsteadily, eyes blazing. He took a step toward the rancher. His glance fell on the girl who had just called him a tramp, and in saying it had chosen the last word of scorn. Her troubled, disdainful gaze met his fully. The effect on him was odd. It paralyzed action. He stopped, breathing hard.

She had called him a tramp, as one who belongs to another world might do—a world that holds to self-respect and decency. He had read in her voice utter and complete contempt for the thing he was. It was a bitter moment. For him it stamped the low-water mark of his degradation. He felt beneath her eyes a thing unclean.

12

What she had said was true. He was a tramp. He had ridden the rods, asked for hand-outs, rough-housed with hoboes, slept with them. He had just been thoroughly thrashed and kicked before her. What was the use of resenting it? He had become declassed. Why should he not be kicked and beaten? That was the customary way to treat his kind of cattle.

Tug swung heavily on a heel and followed his companions into the willows.

CHAPTER III

ONE OF THE LOST LEGION

AMONG the lost legion are two kinds of men. There are those who have killed or buried so deep the divine fire of their manhood that for them there seems no chance of recovery in this world. There are those in whom still burns somewhere a faint candle that may yet flame to a dynamic glow of self-respect.

The young tramp slouching along the bank of Willow Creek drank deep of the waters of despair. The rancher had called him a slacker, rotten to the core. It was a true bill. He was a man spoiled and ruined. He had thrown away his life in handfuls. Down and dragging, that's what he was, with this damned vice a ball and chain on his feet.

There was in him some strain of ignoble weakness. There must be, he reasoned. Otherwise he would have fought and conquered the cursed thing. Instead, he had fought and lost. He could make excuses. Oh, plenty of them. The pain—the horrible, intolerable pain! The way the craving had fastened on him before he knew it while he was still in the hospital! But that was piffling twaddle, rank self-deception. A man had to fight, to stand the gaff, to flog his evil yearnings back to kennel like yelping dogs.

His declension had been swift. It was in his temperament to go fast, to be heady. Once he let go of himself, it had been a matter of months rather than of years. Of late he had dulled the edge of his despair. The opiates were doing their work. He had found it easier to live in the squalid present, to forget the pleasant past and the purposeful future he had planned.

But now this girl, slim, clean, high-headed, with that searing contempt for him in her clear eyes, had stirred up again the devils of remorse. What business had he to companion with these offscourings of the earth? Why had he given up like a quitter the effort to beat back?

In the cold waters of the creek he washed his swollen and bloodstained face. The cold water, fresh from the mountain snows, was soothing to the hot bruised flesh even though it made the wounds smart. He looked down into the pool and saw reflected there the image of himself. Beneath the eyes pouches were beginning to form. Soon now he would be a typical dope fiend.

He was still weak from the manhandling that had been given him. Into an inside coat pocket his fingers groped. They brought out with them a small package wrapped in cotton cloth. With trembling hands he made his preparations, bared an arm, and plunged the hypodermic needle into the flesh.

When he took the trail again after his companions, Tug's eyes were large and luminous. He walked with a firmer step. New life seemed to be flowing into his arteries.

Where the dusty road cut the creek he found the other tramps waiting for him. Their heads had been together in whispered talk. They drew apart as he approached.

Taking note of Cig's purple eye and bruised face, Tug asked a question. "Was it the big foreman beat you up?"

"You done said it, 'bo," the crook answered out of the side of his mouth.

"I reckon you got off easy at that," Tug said bitterly. "The boss bully did n't do a thing to me but chew me up and spit me out."

"Wotcha gonna do about it?" Cig growled significantly.

The young fellow's glance was as much a question as his words. "What can I do but take it?" he asked sullenly.

Cig's eyes narrowed venomously. He lifted his upper lip in an ugly sneer. "Watch my smoke. No roughneck can abuse me an' get away with it. I'll say he can't."

"Meaning?"

"I'm gonna fix him."

Tug's laughter barked. "Did you fix him when you had a chance?" he asked ironically.

14

"Call that a chance? An' the big stiff wide as a door. 'F I'd had a gun I'd 'a' croaked him."

"Oh, if!"

"De bulls frisked me gun in Denver. But I'll get me a gat somewheres. An' when I do—" The sentence choked out in a snarl more theatening than words.

"Sounds reasonable," Tug jeered.

"Listen, 'bo." Cig laid a hand on the sleeve of the young fellow's coat. "Listen. Are youse game to take a chance?"

Eyes filled with an expression of sullen distaste of Cig looked at him from a bruised and livid face. "Maybe I am. Maybe I ain't. What's on your mind?"

"I'm gonna get that bird. See?"

"How?"

"Stick around an' gun him. Then hop a freight for 'Frisco."

There was in the lopsided face a certain dreadful eagerness that was appalling. Was this mere idle boasting? Or would the gangster go as far as murder for his revenge? Tug did not know. But his gorge rose at the fellow's assumption that he would join him as a partner in crime.

"Kill him without giving him a chance?" he asked.

Again there was a sound like the growl of a wild beast in the throat of the Bowery tough. "Wotcha givin' me! A heluva chance them guys give us when they jumped us. I'll learn 'em to keep their hands off Cig." He added, with a crackle of oaths, "The big stiffs!"

"No!" exploded Tug with a surge of anger. "I'll have nothing to do with it—or with you. I'm through. You go one way. I'll go another. Right here I quit."

The former convict's eyes narrowed. "I getcha. Streak of yellow a foot wide. No more nerve than a rabbit. All right. Beat it. I can't lose you none too soon to suit me."

The two glared at each other angrily.

York the peacemaker threw oil on the ruffled waters. " 'S all right, 'boes. No use gettin' sore. Tug he goes one way, we hit the grit another. Ev'rybody satisfied."

Tug swung his roll of blankets across a shoulder and turned away.

CHAPTER IV

BETTY RIDES

BETTY REED had watched unhappily the young tramp shuffle into the willows and disappear. She felt depressed by a complex she could not analyze. In part it was shame, for her father, for this tramp who looked as though he were made for better things, for the whole squalid episode; in part pity, not wholly divorced from admiration at the boy's insolence and courage. He might be a wastrel, as her father had said. He might be a ne'er-do-well. But by some sure instinct she knew that there had been a time when he fronted with high hope to the future. That momentary meeting of the eyes had told her as much.

Something had killed him as surely as a bullet fired through the heart. The boy he had been was dead.

Lon Forbes chuckled. "They'll keep going, I reckon, now they've found out this ain't no Hotel de Gink. You certainly handed that youngest bum his hat, Clint. I'll say you did."

Now that it was over Reed was not very well satisfied with his conduct. The hobo had brought the punishment on himself. Still—there was something morally degrading about such an affray. One can't touch pitch without paying the penalty.

"We'll begin cutting this field to-morrow, Lon," he said shortly. "Hustle the boys up so's to finish the mesa to-day." Across his shoulder he flung a question at the girl. "You going to town, Bess?"

"In an hour or so. Want me to do something?" she asked.

"Call at Farrell's and see if he's got in those bolts I ordered."

The ranchman strode to the car followed by Forbes. The foreman was troubled by no doubts. His mind functioned elementally. If hoboes camped on the Diamond Bar K and made themselves a danger to the crops, they had to be hustled on

16

their way. When they became insolent, it was necessary to treat them rough. That was all there was to it.

Betty swung to the saddle and rode back to the house. She was returning from an inspection of a bunch of two-year-olds that were her own private property. She was rather well off in her own right, as the ranch country counts wealth. The death of her uncle a year before had left her financially independent.

As Betty cantered into the open square in front of the house, her father and the foreman were getting out of the car. A chubby, flaxen-haired little lass came flying down the porch steps a-quiver with excited delight.

"Oh, Daddy, Daddy, what d' you fink? I went out to the barn an'—an'—an' I fink Fifi's got puppies, 'cause she—she—"

"Thought I told you to stay away from the barn," the ranchman chided.

His harsh voice dried up the springs of the child's enthusiasm. She drew back as though she had been struck. From the winsome, wee face the eager, bubbling delight vanished, the enchanting dimples fled. The blue eyes became wells of woe. A small finger found the corner of the Cupid's-bow mouth.

Clint Reed, ashamed and angry at himself, turned away abruptly. Little Ruth was the sunshine of his life, the last pledge of his dead wife's love, and he had deliberately and cruelly wounded her.

Swinging from the saddle, Betty ran to the porch. Her arms enfolded the child and drew her tenderly close. "Ruthie, tell big sister all about it," she whispered gently.

"D-d-d-daddy—" the sobbing little girl began, and choked up.

"Daddy's worried, dear. He didn't mean to hurt your precious little feelings. Tell Betty about Fifi's puppies, darling."

Through her tears and between sobs Ruth told her great news. Presently she forgot to weep and was led to the scene of Fifi's amazing and unique triumph. She gave little squeals of delight when Betty handed her a blind little creature to cuddle in spite of the indignant mother's protesting growls. The child held the warm white-and-brown puppy close to her bosom and adored it with her eyes. With reluctance she returned it at last.

Ruth's happiness was quite restored after her sister had given her a glass of milk and a cookie and sent her out to play.

The young woman waved her a smiling good-bye and went to work.

She had some business letters to write and she went to the

17

room that served her as a library and office. The sound of the typewriter keys drifted out of the open window for an hour or more.

The girl worked swiftly. She had a direct mind that found fluent expression through the finger-tips. When she knew what she wanted to say, it was never any trouble for Betty Reed to say it. A small pile of addressed and sealed letters lay in the rack on the desk before she covered the machine.

These she took with her.

Clint Reed she found tinkering with a reaper that had gone temporarily out of service.

"Want anything more, Dad? I'm going now," she said.

"You've got that list I left on the desk. That's all, except the bolts."

The sky was a vault of blue. Not even a thin, long-drawn skein of cloud floated above. A hot sun baked down on the dusty road over which Betty traveled. Heat waves danced in front of her. There was no faintest breath of breeze stirring.

The gold of autumn was creeping over the hills. Here and there was a crimson splash of sumac or of maple against the almost universal yellow toning. It seemed that the whole landscape had drunk in the summer sunshine and was giving it out now in a glow of warm wealth.

The girl took a short cut over the hills. The trail led by way of draw, gulch, and open slope to the valley in which Wild Horse lay. She rode through the small business street of the village to the post-office. Here she bought supplies of the store-keeper, who was also post-master.

Battell was his name. He was an amiable and harmless gossip. Wild Horse did not need a newspaper as long as he was there to hand tobacco and local information across the counter. An old maid in breeches, Lon Forbes had once called him, and the description serves well enough. He was a whole village sewing circle in himself. At a hint of slander his small bright eyes would twinkle and his shrunken little body seem to wriggle like that of a pleased pup. Any news was good news to him.

"Mo'ning, Miss Betty. Right hot, I'll tell the world. Ninety-nine in the shade this very minute. Bart Logan was in to get Doc Caldwell for his boy Tom. He done bust his laig fallin' from the roof of the root house. Well, Bart was sayin' your paw needs help right bad to harvest his wheat. Seems like if the gov'ment would send out some of these here unemployed to

18

work on the ranches it would be a good idee. Sometimes Congress acts like it ain't got a lick o' sense."

Betty ordered coffee, sugar, tobacco, and other supplies. While he waited upon her Battell made comment pertinent and impertinent.

"That Mecca brand o' coffee seems to be right popular. Three pounds for a dollar. O' course, if it's for the bunk house —Oh, want it sent out to the Quarter Circle D E. How're you makin' it on your own ranch, Miss Betty? Some one was sayin' you would clean up quite a bit from your beef herd this year, mebbe twelve or fifteen thousand. I reckon it was Bart Logan."

"Is Bart keeping my books for me?" the girl asked dryly.

The storekeeper cackled. "Folks will gossip."

"Yes," she agreed. "How much is that corn meal a hundred?"

"Cost you ten cents more'n the last. Folks talk about cost of livin' coming down. Well, mebbe 't is an' mebbe 't ain't. I told Bart I would n't believe you'd cleared any twelve or fifteen thousand till I heard you say so. That's a lot of money, if any one asks you."

Apparently Betty misunderstood him. "Yes, you're high, but I'll take two sacks. Send it to the Quarter Circle and charge it to me."

Betty stopped at the railroad station to ask the agent about a shipment of goods her father was expecting, and from there went to Farrell's to find out about the bolts.

It was well on toward noon when she took the road for home. At Four-Mile Crossing it intersected the railroad track. A man with a pack on his back was plodding along the ties in the direction of Wild Horse. The instant her eyes fell on him, the girl recognized the tramp her father had beaten. The pallid face was covered with wheals and bruises. Both of the sullen eyes were ringed with purple and black.

They met face to face. Full into hers his dogged gaze challenged. Without a word they passed.

Betty crossed the grade and followed a descent to a small grove of pines close to the road. The sun was so hot that she decided to dismount and give the pony a breathing spell.

From the saddle she swung, then trailed the reins and loosened the cinch.

A sound brought her head round sharply. Two men had come over the brow of a little hill silently. One of them was almost at her elbow. A twisted, malevolent grin was on his lips.

He was the hobo Lon Forbes had thrashed two or three hours ago.

"Welcome to our city, goil," he jeered in choice Boweryese. "Honest to Gawd, you knock me dead. Surest thing you know. We'll treat you fine, not like your dad an' that other big stiff did us. We'll not tell youse to move on, m' dearie. Nothin' like that."

The girl's heart felt as though drenched in ice-cold water. She had not brought with her the small revolver she sometimes carried for rattlesnakes. Both instinct and observation told her this man was vile and dangerous. She was in his power and he would make her pay for what her father had done.

She trod down the fear that surged up in her bosom. Not for nothing had she been all her life a daughter of the sun and the wind and wide outdoor spaces.

"I stopped to rest my pony from the heat of the sun," she explained.

"You stopped to see old Cig," he corrected. "An' now you're here it'll be him an' you for a while. The hop-nut don't belong to de same push as us no longer. I shook him. An' York don't count. He's no lady's man, York ain't."

The slim girl in the riding-suit could not quite keep the panic out of her eyes. None of the motives that swayed the men she knew would have weight with him. He was both base and bold, and he had lived among those who had small respect for a woman.

Betty's glance moved to York. It found no comfort there. The gross hobo was soft as putty. He did not count, as his companion had openly sneered.

"No. I won't stop," she said, and made as though to tighten the loosened cinch.

"Won'cha? Think again, miss. Old Cig ain't seen a skirt since he left li'l' old New York. Sure as youse is a foot high he's hungry for a sweetie of his own."

He put his hand on her arm. At the touch her self-control vanished. She screamed.

The man's fingers slid down to the wrist and tightened. His other hand clamped over her mouth and cut off the cry.

She writhed, twisting to free herself. In spite of her slenderness she was strong. From her lips she tore his hand and again called for help in an ecstasy of terror.

The crook of his arm garroted her throat and cut off the air

20

from her lungs. He bent her body back across his hip. Still struggling, she strangled helplessly.

"Youse would, eh?" His voice, his narrowed eyes, exulted. "Forget it, miss. Cig's an A1 tamer of Janes. That's de li'l' old thing he's de champeen of de world at."

He drew her closer to him.

There came a soft sound of feet thudding across the grass. The arm about Betty's throat relaxed. She heard a startled oath, found herself flung aside. Her eyes opened.

Instantly she knew why Cig had released her. The man stood crouched, snarling, his eyes fixed on an approaching runner, one who moved with the swift precision of a half-back carrying a ball down a whitewashed gridiron.

The runner was the tramp whose face her father had battered to a pulp. He asked for no explanations and made no comment. Straight for the released convict he drove.

Cig had not a chance. The bad air and food of the slums, late hours, dissipation, had robbed him of both strength and endurance. He held up his fists and squared off, for he was game enough. But Tug's fist smashed through the defense as though it had been built of paper. The second-story man staggered back, presently went down before a rain of blows against which he could find no protection.

Tug dragged him to his feet, cuffed him hard with his half-closed fist again and again, then flung him a second time to the ground. He stood over the fellow, his eyes blazing, his face colorless.

"Get up, you hound!" he ordered in a low voice trembling with anger. "Get up and take it! I'll teach you to lay hands on a woman!"

Cig did not accept this invitation. He rolled away, caught up York's heavy tramping stick, and stood like a wolf at bay, the lips lifted from his stained yellow teeth.

"Touch me again an' I'll knock your block off," he growled, interlarding the threat with oaths and foul language.

"Don't!" the girl begged of her champion. "Please don't. Let's go. Right away."

"Yes," agreed the young fellow, white to the lips.

York flat-footed forward a step or two. "No use havin' no trouble. Cig he did n't mean nothin' but a bit of fun, Tug. Old Cig would n't do no lady any harm." The tramp's voice had taken on the professional whine.

Tug fastened the girth, his fingers trembling so that he could

21

hardly slip the leather through to make the cinch. Even in the reaction from fear Betty found time to wonder at this. He was not afraid. He had turned his back squarely on the furious gangster from the slums to tighten the surcingle. Why should he be shaking like a man in a chill?

The girl watched Cig while the saddle was being made ready. The eyes in the twisted face of the convict were venomous. If thoughts could have killed, Tug would have been a dead man. She had been brought up in a clean world, and she did not know people could hate in such a soul-and-body blasting way. It chilled the blood only to look at him.

The girl's rescuer turned to help her into the saddle. He gave her the lift as one does who is used to helping a woman mount.

From the seat she stooped and said in a low voice, "I want you to go with me."

He nodded. Beside the horse he walked as far as the road. "My pack's back there on the track," he said, and stopped, waiting for her to ride away.

Betty looked down at him, a troubled frown on her face. "Where are you going?"

A bitter, sardonic smile twitched the muscles of the bruised face. He shrugged his shoulders.

"Looking for work?" she asked.

"Maybe I am," he answered sullenly.

"We need men on the Diamond Bar K to help with the harvest."

"The ranch where I was kicked off?"

"Father's quick-tempered, but he's square. I'll talk with him about you—"

"Why waste your time?" he mocked mordantly. "I'll not impose on him a good-for-nothing loafer, a worthless rotten-to-the-core hobo, a slacker, a wastrel who ought to be on a rockpile."

"Dad did n't mean all that. He was angry. But if you don't want to work for him, perhaps you'd work for me. I own a ranch, too."

He looked up the road into the dancing heat waves. She was wasting pity on him, was she? No doubt she would like to reform him. A dull resentment burned in him. His sulky eyes looked into hers.

"No," he said shortly.

"But if you're looking for work," she persisted.

"I'm particular about who I work for," he told her brutally.

She winced, but the soft dark eyes were still maternally tender for him. He had fought for her, had saved her from a situation that held at least degradation and perhaps horrible despair. Moreover, young though he was, she knew that life had mauled him fearfully.

"I need men. I thought perhaps—"

"You thought wrong."

"I'm sorry—about Father. You would n't need to see him if you did n't want to. The Quarter Circle D E is four miles from the Diamond Bar K."

"I don't care if it's forty," he said bluntly.

Her good intentions were at an *impasse*. The road was blocked. But she could not find it in her heart to give up yet, to let him turn himself adrift again upon a callous world. He needed help—needed it desperately, if she were any judge. It was written on his face that he was sailing stormy seas and that his life barque was drifting toward the rocks. What help she could give she must press upon him.

"I'm asking you to be generous and forget what—what we did to you," she pleaded, leaning down impulsively and putting a hand on his shoulder. "You saved me from that awful creature. Is n't it your turn now to let me help you if I can?"

"You can't help me."

"But why not? You're looking for work. I need men. Would n't it be reasonable for us to get together on terms?" Her smile was very sweet and just a little wistful, her voice vivid as the sudden song of a meadowlark.

Under the warmth of her kindness his churlishness melted.

"Good of you," he said. "I'm much obliged. But it's no use. Your father had the right of it. I'm not any good."

"I don't believe it. Your life's got twisted somehow. But you can straighten it. Let me help. Won't you? Because of what you did for me just now."

Her hand moved toward him in a tentative offer of friendship. Automatically his eyes recorded that she wore a diamond ring on the third finger. Some lucky fellow, probably some clean young man who had given no hostages to vice, had won her sweet and gallant heart.

She was all eager desire and sympathy. For a moment, as he looked into the dusky, mobile face that expressed a fine and gallant personality, it seemed possible for him to trample down

23

the vice that was destroying him. But he pushed this aside as idle sentiment. His way was chosen for him and he could not go back.

He shook his head and turned away. The bitter, sardonic smile again rested like a shadow of evil on his good-looking face.

CHAPTER V

TUG IS "COLLECTED"

TUG followed the rails towards Wild Horse.

He groped in an abyss of humiliation and self-disgust. Slacker! The cattleman's scornful word had cut to the quick. The taste of it was bitter. For he had not always been one. In war days he had done his share.

How was it McCrae's poem ran?

> "We are the Dead. Short days ago
> We lived, felt dawn, saw sunset glow,
>   Loved and were loved, and now we lie
>   In Flanders fields.
>
> "Take up our quarrel with the foe:
> To you from failing hands we throw
>   The torch; be yours to hold it high.
>   If ye break faith with us who die
> We shall not sleep, though poppies grow
>   In Flanders fields."

Yes, he had kept the faith in France, but he was not keeping it now. The obligation was as binding on him in peace as on the battle-field. He knew that. He recognized it fully. But when the pain in his head began, his mind always flew to the only relief he knew. The drug had become a necessity to him. If the doctors had only let him fight it out from the beginning without help, he would not have become accustomed to the accursed stuff.

But what was the use of going over that again and again? He was done for. Why send his thoughts forever over the same treadmill?

The flaming sun poured down into the bowl of the valley and baked its contents. He moved from the track to the shade of a cottonwood and lay down. His racing thoughts grew more vague, for the hot sun had made him sleepy. Presently his eyes closed drowsily. They flickered open and slowly shut a second time. He began to breathe deeply and regularly.

The sun passed the zenith and began to slide down toward the western hills. Still Tug slept.

He dreamed. The colonel was talking to him. "Over the top, Hollister, at three o'clock. Ten minutes now." He shook himself out of sleep. It was time to get busy.

Slowly he came back blinking to a world of sunshine. Two men stood over him, both armed.

"Must be one of 'em," the shorter of the two said.

"Sure thing. See his outfit. All rags. We'll collect him an' take him back to the ranch."

There were cowboys or farmhands, Tug was not sure which. He knew at once, however, that their intentions were not friendly.

"What do you want?" he asked.

"You," the short, stocky one answered curtly. He wore a big broad-rimmed hat that was both ancient and dusty.

"Interesting. You a sheriff? Got a warrant for me?"

The little man raised the point of his thirty-eight significantly. "Ain't this warrant enough?"

"What's the trouble? What d' you want me for?"

"Tell him, Dusty," the lank cowboy said.

"All right, Burt." To the tramp he said roughly: "We'll learn you how to treat a lady. Get up. You're gonna trail back to the Diamond Bar K with us."

"You've got the wrong man," explained Tug.

"Sure. You're jus' travelin' through the country lookin' for work," Dusty jeered. "We've heard that li'l spiel before. Why, you chump, the ol' man's autograph is writ on yore face right now."

Tug opened his mouth to expostulate, but changed his mind. What was the use? He had no evidence. They would not let him go.

"I guess you hold the aces." He rose, stiffly, remarking to the world at large, "I've read about those three-gallon hats with a half-pint of brains in them."

Dusty bridled. "Don't get gay with me, young feller. I'll not stand for it."

"No?" murmured the hobo, and he somehow contrived to make of the monosyllable a taunt.

"Just for that I'll drag you back with a rope."

Dusty handed his weapon to the other cowboy, stepped to his horse, and brought back a rope. He uncoiled it and dropped the noose over the tramp's head, tightening it around his waist.

The riders swung to their saddles.

"Get a move on you," Dusty ordered, giving the rope a tug. The other end of it he had fastened to the horn of the saddle.

Tug walked ahead of the horses through the sand. It was a long hot tramp, and Dusty took pains to make it as unpleasant as possible. If the prisoner lagged, he dragged him on the ground, gibing at him, and asking him whether he would insult another woman next time he got a chance.

The cowpuncher found small satisfaction in the behavior of the man at the other end of the rope. The ragged tramp neither answered his sneers nor begged for mercy. He took what was coming to him silently, teeth clamped tight.

At last Burt interfered. "That'll be about enough, Dusty. The old man's gonna settle with him. It's his say-so about what he wants done to this guy." He added, a moment later: "I ain't so darned sure we've got the right one, anyhow. This bird don't look to me like a feller who would do a girl a meanness."

"Hmp! You always was soft in the head, Burt," his companion grunted.

But he left his prisoner in peace after that. Burt had said one true word. Clint Reed would not want a half-dead hobo dragged to the Diamond Bar K. He would prefer one that he could punish himself.

Tug plodded through the fine white dust that lay inches deep on the road. A cloud of it moved with them, for the horses kicked it up at every step until they ascended from the valley into the hills. The man who walked did not have the reserve of strength that had been his before he had gone to the hospital. There had been a time when he could go all day and

26

ask for more, but he could not do it now. He stumbled as he dragged his feet along the trail.

They reached the summit of the pass and looked down on the Diamond Bar K. Its fenced domain was a patchwork of green and gold with a background of pineclad ridges. The green patches were fields of alfalfa, the gold squares were grain ripe for the mower.

Downhill the going was easier. But by the time the horsemen and their prisoner drew up to the ranchhouse, Tug was pretty well exhausted.

While Dusty went in to get Reed, the tramp sat on the floor of the porch and leaned against a pillar, his eyes closed. He had a ridiculous feeling that if he let go of himself he would faint.

CHAPTER VI

"NOTHING BUT A GAY-CAT ANYHOW"

WITH an unusual depression Betty had watched the tramp move down the dusty road to the railroad track after he had declined her offer of employment. An energetic young person, she was accustomed to having her own way. One of her earliest delightful discoveries had been that she could nearly always get what she wanted by being eager for it and assuming that, of course, the others involved would recognize her plan as best, or at least would give up theirs cheerfully when she urged hers.

But this ragged scamp, out of whose heart youth and hope had been trampled, was leaving her dashed and rebuffed. She liked to make conquests of people in bending them to the schemes she made for the regulation of her small universe, though she would have denied even to herself that she liked to manage her friends. In the case of this drear-eyed boy, the hurt was not only to her vanity. He might be five or six years older than she, but the mothering instinct—the desire to save

27

him from himself and his fate—fluttered yearningly toward him.

She did not blame him. There was at least a remnant of self-respect in his decision. Nobody wants to be done good to. Perhaps she had seemed smug to him, though she had not meant to be.

He was on her mind all the way back to the ranch, so much so that she blurted out the whole story to her father as soon as she saw him.

Clint Reed moved to prompt action. He did not see eye to eye with his daughter. What concerned him was that these bums should waylay and insult Betty. It was a nice state of affairs when a girl was not safe alone on the roads. He gathered his men and gave them orders to find the hoboes and bring them to the ranch.

The girl's protest was lost on Reed. It hardly reached his mind at all. Besides, this had become public business. It was not her personal affair. If hoboes needed to be taught a sense of decency, the men of the community would attend to that.

Betty went into the house dissatisfed with herself. She had not meant to make more trouble, but to enlist her father's sympathy in the cause of the young fellow who had saved her from the other tramp. As for the one who had attacked her, she did not care whether he was punished or not. She had much rather no hue and cry over the country was made about it. Though she did not say so, she hoped the vagrants would get away uncaught.

She busied herself with household duties. Under her direction and with her help, Bridget the cook was putting up half a dozen boxes of peaches. The two women worked into the middle of the hot afternoon before they had finished.

"An' that's that," Bridget said with a sigh of relief as she sealed the last jar. "Fegs, I don't mind a hotter day this summer. It's a b'iler."

She was an old family servant and was in part responsible for the bringing up of Betty. More than one rancher in the neighborhood had attempted the adventure of wooing Bridget Maloney, but none of them had been able to lure her from the Diamond Bar K to become the mistress of a home of her own.

"You'd better lie down and sleep an hour, dear," the girl advised.

"An' phwat would I be doin' that for wid all these kettles

28

an' pots to be cleaned up? Scat! Get ye out o' my kitchen now, mavourneen, an' I'll redd up in a jiff."

Betty found a magazine and walked out to the shade of a pine grove where a hammock hung. She settled herself comfortably and began to read. It was delightfully cool among the pines after the hot kitchen. She grew drowsy. Her eyes closed.

The sound of far-away voices was in her ears when she wakened. As her thoughts cleared, so did the voices. She heard Dusty's, strident, triumphant.

"It's up to the old man now."

The girl turned in the hammock and saw the squat cow-puncher go jingling into the house. Burt lounged on a horse, his right leg thrown round the horn of the saddle. Some one else, partly hidden from her by the ponies, was sitting on the porch.

She got up quickly and walked toward the house. The man on the porch, she saw presently, had a rope around his waist the other end of which was fastened to the saddle of Dusty's mount. An eyeflash later she recognized him.

"You!" she cried.

The tramp called Tug rose. He did not lift his hat, for he no longer had one. But his bow and sardonic smile gave an effect of ironic politeness.

"The bad penny back again," he said.

"What have they been doing to you?" she asked breathlessly.

He had been a disreputable enough specimen when she had last seen him. The swollen and discolored face, the gaping shoes, the ragged coat; all of these he had carried then. But there were scratches like skin burns down one side of the jaw and on his hands that had come since. His coat was in shreds. From head to foot dust covered every available inch.

"Your men have been having a little sport. Why not? The boss had his first and they had to follow his example. They're good obedient boys," he scoffed bitterly.

"What do you mean? What did they do?" she demanded sharply.

He shrugged his shoulders and she turned imperiously to the man on horseback. "Burt, you tell me."

The lank cowboy showed embarrassment. "Why, Dusty he —he kinda dragged him when the fellow lagged. Jus' for a ways."

29

"On the ground? That what you mean?" The dark eyes flashed anger.

"Well, you might say so. He sorta stumbled, an' he'd been right sassy to Dusty, so—" Burt's explanation died away. He felt he was not getting very far with it.

"So you acted like brutes to him—to a man who had just fought for me when—when—" A sob of chagrin and vexation choked up in her throat. She stamped her foot in exasperation.

"Don't get excited about me," the victim gibed. "I'm nothing but a gay-cat anyhow. What's it matter?"

Dusty strutted out of the house, his spurs making music. The girl turned on him with pantherish swiftness.

"Who told you to torture this man, Dusty? What right have you got to make yourself law on the Diamond Bar? You're only a drunken lunkhead, are n't you? Or did Father ask you to be judge and jury on the ranch?"

It was ludicrous to see the complacency vanish from the fatuous face. The jaw fell and the mouth opened.

"Why, Miss Betty, I figured as how he'd done you a meanness, an' I thought—"

She cut his explanation short with stinging ruthlessness. "What for? You were n't hired to think, but to obey orders. You'd better get back into the wheatfield before Father comes. Pronto."

The cowboy shut his mouth with a view to opening it again in self-defense, but Betty would have none of his excuses. She shooed him from the scene indignantly. While she was busy with Dusty, the lank rider quietly vanished.

The prisoner watched her, the rope still about his waist. His mind paid tribute to the energy with which she got results.

"Greatly obliged," he said with sarcasm. "I suppose your father won't have me hanged now."

"Take off that rope," she said.

"That's an order, is it?"

"I don't blame you for hating us all," she flamed. "I would in your place. The whole place is bewitched today, I believe. We're all acting like bullies instead of the quiet, decent people we are. Take Dusty now. He's a good little fellow, but he thought you'd attacked me. He would n't stand that. Men in the ranch country won't, you know. They look after us women."

"That's a peculiarity of the ranch country, I suppose."

30

She ignored the derisive gleam in his eyes. "No . . . no! Good men always do. I wish I could tell you—could show you —my thanks because you stood up for me. I'll never forget. It was fine, the way you fought for me."

"Nothing to that. I'd been saving a punch or two for him. Don't forget that I'm a good-for-nothing bum, on the authority of your own father. No need of getting sentimental. Don't make the mistake of putting me in a class with him and other such truly good men as your friend Dusty and the lamblike foreman who beat up Cig because he would n't apologize for being alive."

Voice and manner both fleered at her, but she was determined to accept no rebuff.

"Did Dusty hurt you? Can I do anything for you? Tell me. I'd be so glad to. Let me get you a drink."

Like a flash, she was off at her own suggestion to the kitchen. His impulse was to go at once, but he could not escape his past and be deliberately discourteous to a woman whose only desire was to help him. He waited, sullenly, for her return. Why could she not let him alone? All he asked of the Diamond Bar K was for it to let him get away and forget it as soon as possible.

When the girl came back, it was with a pitcher and a glass. The outside of the jug was beaded with moisture. From within came the pleasant tinkle of ice.

Betty filled the tumbler with lemonade.

The vagabond had no desire to accept the hospitality of the ranch, but he found it impossible to affront her churlishly again.

"Thank you," he said, and drank.

The drink was refreshing. Two fresh-beaten eggs had been stirred into it for nutrition.

"Another?" she begged, and poured without waiting for an answer.

The ghost of a smile crept into his eyes. It was the first hint of wholesome humor she had yet seen in him. He offered her, with a little bow, a quotation.

> " 'I can no other answer make, but thanks,
>   And thanks, and ever thanks.' "

The dimples broke into her cheeks as her smile flashed out in the pleasure of having broken the crust of his reserve.

31

"That's Shakespeare, is n't it? I'm dreadfully illiterate, but it sounds like him."

"It does a little, does n't it?" He raised the glass before drinking. "Happy days, Miss Reed."

"That goes double," she said quickly.

The sardonic mask, that had for a moment been lifted, dropped again over his face. "Many more like this one," he fleered.

"You may look back on it and find it a good day yet," she said bravely.

He handed back the empty tumbler. "Afraid I'm not an optimist. Now, if you don't mind, I'll be going. The ranch might change its mind about that hanging bee."

"But I do mind," she protested. "I don't want you to go yet. Please stay and meet my father. He's not really hard and cruel as you think."

Again she saw on his lips the dry, bitter smile.

"Think I'll take your word for it. I've met him once."

"No, you have n't met him—not to know him," she cried softly, giving rein to swift impulse. "You've not met my Daddy—the best man in Paradise Valley. You can ask any one about him. He's the squarest that ever was. The man you met was exasperated and—and not himself. Dad's not like that—really."

"Indeed!" His voice was a compound of incredulity and indifference. It put her out of court.

But her good impulses were not easily daunted. She had already learned that this young fellow wore armor of chain-mail to protect his sensitive pride. In her horoscope it had been written that she must give herself, and still give and give. The color beat through her dusky cheeks beneath the ardent eyes. She stabbed straight at his jaundiced soul.

"If it were my father only that you don't like—but it is n't—you don't find joy in anything. Your mind's poisoned. I was reading the other day how Mr. Roosevelt used to quote from Borrow's 'Lavengro': 'Life is sweet, brother—there's day and night, brother; both sweet things; sun, moon, and stars, all sweet things—and likewise there's a wind on the heath.' It's because he felt this in everything he did that they called him 'Greatheart.'"

It came to him that the name might not inaptly be applied to her. He thought of Browning's "My Last Duchess":

". . . . . She had
A heart—how shall I say?—too soon made glad,
Too easily impressed: she liked whate'er
She looked on, and her looks went everywhere."

He hardened his heart to her generous appeal to him. "It's a very comfortable point of view to have," he said with no spring of life in his voice.

"And a true one," she added swiftly.

"If you say so, of course." His skeptical smile made no concessions.

He turned to leave, but stopped to look at a cloud of white dust moving down the road toward them.

CHAPTER VII

TUG SAYS, "NO, THANK YOU"

THE advancing dust cloud rose from a little group of horses and men. Some of the latter were riding. Others were afoot.

"Lon's caught them," said Betty. "I'm sorry."

"Not so sorry as they'll be," returned the ragged youth grimly.

The foreman swung heavily from his horse. Though he was all muscle and bone, he did not carry his two hundred pounds gracefully.

"We got the birds all right, Miss Betty, even if they were hittin' the trail right lively," he called to the girl, an ominous grin on his leathery face. "I guess they'd figured out this was n't no healthy climate for them." He added, with a swift reversion to business, "Where's yore paw?"

"Not back yet. What'll he do with them, Lon?" the girl asked, her voice low and troubled.

Distressed in soul, she was looking for comfort. The big foreman gave her none.

"He'll do a plenty. You don't need to worry about that. We aim to keep this country safe for our women-folks."

"Oh, I wish he would n't. I wish he'd let them go," she said, almost in a wail.

"He won't. Clint ain't that soft." Forbes stared at the disreputable vagrant standing beside Betty. "What's he doing here?"

"Dusty dragged him back. That 's all the sense he has."

Lon spoke just as though the vagrant were not present. "Lucky for him he's got an alibi this time."

"Is it necessary to insult him after he protected me?" the girl demanded, eyes flashing. "I'm ashamed of you, Lon."

He was taken aback. "I reckon it takes more'n that to insult a hobo."

"Is a man a hobo because he's looking for work?"

The foreman's hard gaze took in the man, his white face and soft hands. "What would he do if he found it?" he asked bluntly.

"You've no right to say that," she flung back. "I think it's hateful the way you're all acting. I tell you he fought for me —after what Father did to him."

"Fought for you?" This was news to Lon. His assumption had been that the young fellow had merely entered a formal protest in order to clear himself in case retribution followed. "You mean with his fists?"

"Yes—against the thin-faced one. He thrashed him and put me on my horse and started me home. Then Dusty ropes him and drags him here on the ground and you come and insult him. He must think we're a grateful lot."

As they looked at the slim, vital girl confronting him with such passionate and feminine ferocity, the eyes of the foreman softened. All her life she had been a part of his. He had held her on his knee, a crowing baby, while her dimpled fingers clung to his rough coat or explored his unshaven face. He had fished her out of an irrigation ditch when she was three. He had driven her to school when for the first time she started on that great adventure. It had been under his direction that she had learned to ride, to fish, to shoot. He loved her as though she had been flesh of his flesh and blood of his blood. It was a delight to him to be bullied by her and to serve her whims.

"I renig," he said. "Clint never told me the boy done that. I had it doped out he was just savin' his own hide. But I'll take it all back if it's like you say. Shake, son."

The tramp did not refuse to grip the big brown hand thrust

at him. Nor did he accept the proffered alliance. By a fraction of a second he forestalled the foreman by stooping to knot a broken lace in one of the gaping shoes.

Cig, who had been edging closer, gave Tug a rancorous look. "I ain't forgettin' this," he promised. "I'll get youse good some day for rappin' on me."

"He did n't tell on you. Some of my men brought him here in the gather like we did you," Forbes explained.

"Wot'ell youse givin' me? He rapped. That's wot he done, the big stiff. An' I'll soitainly get him right for it."

"That kind of of talk ain't helpin' you any," the foreman said. "If you got any sense, you'll shut yore trap an' take what's comin'."

"I'll take it. Don't youse worry about that. You'd better kill me while youse are on the job, for I'll get you, too, sure as I'm a mont' old."

Reed drove up in the old car he used for a runabout. He killed the engine, stepped down, and came up to the group by the porch.

"See you rounded 'em up, Lon."

"Yep. Found 'em in the cottonwoods acrost the track at Wild Horse."

The ranchman's dominant eyes found Tug. "How come you here?" he asked.

The gay-cat looked at him in sullen, resentful silence. The man's manner stirred up in the tramp a flare of opposition.

"Dusty brought him here. I want to tell you about that, Dad," the girl said.

"Later." He turned to Tug. "I want a talk with you—got a proposition to make you. See you later."

"Not if I see you first," the ragged nomad replied insolently. "I never did like bullies:"

The ranchman flushed angrily, but he put a curb on his temper. He could not afford to indulge it since he was so much in this youth's debt. Abruptly he turned away.

"Bring the other two to the barn," he ordered Forbes. "We'll have a settlement there."

York shuffled forward, in a torment of fear. "See here, mister. I ain't got a thing to do with this. Honest to Gawd, I ain't. Ask Tug. Ask the young lady. I got respeck for women, I have. You would n't do dirt to an old 'bo wot never done you no harm, would you, boss?"

His voice was a whine. The big gross man was on the verge of blubbering. He seemed ready to fall on his knees.

"It's true, Dad. He did n't touch me," Betty said in a low voice to her father.

"Stood by, did n't he? Never lifted a hand for you."

"Yes, but—"

"You go into the house. Leave him to me," ordered Reed. "Keep this young man here till I come back."

Betty knew when the words were useless with her father. She turned away and walked to the porch.

The cowpunchers with their prisoners moved toward the barn. York, ululating woe, had to be dragged.

Left alone with the tramp called Tug, Betty turned to him a face of dread. "Let's go into the house," she said drearily.

"You'd better go in. I'm taking the road now," he said in answer.

"But Father wants to see you. If you'll wait just a little—"

"I have no business with him. I don't care to see him, now or any time." His voice was cold and hard. "Thank you for the lemonade, Miss Reed. I'll say good-bye."

He did not offer his hand, but as he turned away he bowed. There was nothing more for Betty to say except "Goodbye."

In a small voice of distress she murmured it.

Her eyes followed him as far as the road. A sound from the barn drove her into the house, to her room, where she could cover her ears with the palms of her small brown hands.

She did not want to hear any echo of what was taking place there.

CHAPTER VIII

A RIFT IN THE LUTE

In the cool of the evening Justin Merrick drove down from the Sweetwater Dam to the Diamond Bar K ranch. It was characteristic of him that his runabout was up to date and in perfect condition. He had an expensive taste in the accessories of life, and he either got the best or did without.

Hands and face were tanned from exposure to the burning sun of the Rockies, but he was smooth-shaven and immaculate in the engineer's suit which fitted his strong, heavy-set figure so snugly.

He drove with precision, as he did everything else in his well-ordered life. There was in his strength no quality of impatience or turbulence. He knew what he wanted and how to get it. That was why he had traveled so far on the road to success and would go a great way farther.

To-night he anticipated two pleasant hours with Betty Reed. He would tell her about the work and how it was getting along, his difficulties with the sand formation at the head gates and how he was surmounting them. Even before she spoke, he would know from her eager eyes that she was giving him the admiration due a successful man from his sweetheart.

Afterward he would pass to more direct and personal lovemaking, which she would evade if possible or accept shyly and reluctantly. She was wearing his ring, but he doubted whether he had really stormed the inner fortress of her heart. This uncertainty, and the assurance that went with it of a precious gift not for the first chance comer, appealed to his fastidious instinct, all the more that he was sure she would someday come to him with shining eyes and outstretched hands.

To-night Merrick found Betty distrait and troubled. Her attention to the recital of his problems was perfunctory. He was conscious of a slight annoyance. In spite of his force, Justin was a vain man, always ready to talk of himself and his achievements in a modest way to an interested and interesting young woman.

It appeared that her father had had a difficulty with some tramps, which had eventuated in insolence that had brought upon the vagrants summary physical punishment. From her account of it, Justin judged that Reed had not handled the matter very wisely. There was a way to do such things with a minimum of friction.

But he saw no need of worrying about it. The tramps had been given what they deserved and the affair was closed. It was like a woman to hold it heavily on her conscience because one of the ne'er-do-wells chanced to be young and good-looking.

"If you'd seen him," Betty protested. "A gentleman by the look of him, or had been once, fine-grained, high-spirited, and yet so down-and-out."

"If he's down-and-out, it's his own fault. A man's never that so long as he holds to self-respect."

This was incontrovertibly true, but Betty chose to be irritated. Justin was so obviously successful. He might have had a little sympathy for the underdog, she thought. Everybody did not have a square, salient jaw like his. Weakness was not necessarily a crime.

"He looks as though life had mauled him," she said. "It's taken something vital out of him. He does n't care what happens any more."

"If he can only mooch his three meals a day and enough cash to keep him supplied with bootleg poison," the engineer added.

They were walking up to the Three Pines, a rocky bluff from which they could in the daytime see far down the valley. She stopped abruptly. If she did not stamp her foot, at least the girl's manner gave eloquently the effect of this indulgence.

"He's not like that at all—not at all. Don't you ever sympathize with any one that's in hard luck?" she cried out, her cheeks glowing with a suffusion of underlying crimson.

"Not when he lies down under it."

She flashed at him a look resentful of his complacency. It held, too, for the first time a critical doubt. There was plenty to like about Justin Merrick, and perhaps there was more to admire. He got things done because he was so virile, so dominant. To look at the lines and movements of his sturdy body,

38

at the close-lipped mouth and resolute eyes, was to know him a leader of men. But now a treasonable thought had wirelessed itself into her brain. Had he a mind that never ranged out of well-defined pastures, that was quite content with the social and economic arrangement of the world? Did there move in it only a tight little set of orthodox ideas?

"How do you know he lies down under it?" she asked with spirit. "How do we know what he has to contend with? Or how he struggles against it?"

If his open smile was not an apology, it refused, anyhow, to be at variance with her. "Maybe so. As you say, I did n't see him and you did. We'll let it go at that and hope he's all you think he is."

Betty, a little ashamed of her vagrant thoughts, tried to find a common ground upon which they could stand. "Don't you think that men are often the victims of circumstance—that they get caught in currents that kinda sweep them away?"

" 'I am the captain of my soul,' " he quoted sententiously.

"Yes, *you* are," she admitted, after one swift glance that took in the dogged, flinty quality of him. "But most of us are n't. Take Dad. He's strong, and he's four-square. But he would n't have gone as far as he did with these tramps if he had n't got carried away. Well, don't you think maybe this boy is a victim of 'the bludgeonings of chance'? He looked like it to me."

"We make ourselves," he insisted. "If the things we buck up against break us, it's because we're weak."

"Yes, but—" Betty's protest died away. She was not convinced, and she made another start. "It seems to me that when I read the new novelists—Wells, Galsworthy, or Bennett, say—one of the things I get out of them is that we *are* modified by our environment, not only changed by it, but sometimes made the prey of it and destroyed by it."

"Depends on how solid on our feet we are," answered the engineer. "That's the plea of the agitator, I know. He's always wanting to do impossible things by law or by a social upheaval. There's nothing to it. A man succeeds if he's strong. He fails if he's weak."

This creed of the individualist was sometimes Betty's own, but to-night she was not ready to accept it. "That would be all very well if we all started equal. But we don't. What about a man who develops tuberculosis, say, just when he is getting going? He's weak, but it's no fault of his."

"It may or may not be. Anyhow, it's his misfortune. You can't make the world over because he's come a cropper. Take this young tramp of yours. I'd like to try him out and show you whether there's anything to him. I'd put him on the work and let him find his level. Chances are he'd drift back to the road inside of a week. When a man's down-and-out, it is n't because he does n't get a chance, but because of some weakness in himself."

Betty knew that in the case of many this was true. For a year or more she had been an employer of labor herself. One of the things that had impressed her among the young fellows who worked for her was that they did find their level. The unskilled, shiftless, and less reliable were dropped when work became slack. The intelligent and energetic won promotion for themselves.

But she did not believe that it was by any means a universal truth. Men were not machines, after all. They were human beings. However, she dropped the subject.

"He's gone, so you won't have a chance to prove your case," she said. "Tell me about the work. How is it going?"

The Sweetwater Dam project had been initiated to water what was known as the Flat Tops, a mesa that stretched from the edge of the valley to the foothills. It had been and still was being bitterly opposed by some of the cattlemen of Paradise Valley because its purpose was to reclaim for farming a large territory over which cattle had hitherto ranged at will. Their contention held nothing of novelty. It had been argued all over the West ever since the first nesters came in to dispute with the cattle barons the possession of the grazing lands. A hundred districts in a dozen States had heard the claim that this was a cattle country, unfit for farming and intensive settlement. Many of them had seen it disproved.

The opposition of powerful ranching interests had not deterred Justin Merrick. Threats did not disturb him. He set his square jaw and pushed forward to the accomplishment of his purpose. As he rode or drove through the valley, he knew that he was watched with hostile eyes by reckless cowpunchers who knew that his success would put a period to the occupation they followed. Two of them had tried to pick a quarrel with him at Wild Horse on one occasion, and had weakened before his cool and impassive fearlessness.

But he did not deceive himself. At any hour the anger of

40

these men might flare out against him in explosive action. For the first time in his life he was carrying a revolver.

Clint Reed was a stockholder and a backer of the irrigation project. He owned several thousand acres on the Flat Tops, and it was largely on account of his energy that capital had undertaken the reclamation of the dry mesa.

The head and front of the opposition was Jake Prowers, who had brought down from early days an unsavory reputation that rumor said he more than deserved. Strange stories were whispered about this mild-mannered little man with the falsetto voice and the skim-milk eyes. One of them was that he had murdered from ambush the successful wooer of the girl he wanted, that the whole countryside accepted the circumstantial evidence as true, and in spite of this he had married the young widow within a year and buried her inside of two. Nesters in the hills near his ranch had disappeared and never been seen again. Word passed as on the breath of the winds that Prowers had dry-gulched them. Old-timers still lived who had seen him fight a duel with two desperadoes on the main street of Wild Horse. He had been carried to the nearest house on a shutter with three bullets in him, but the two bad men had been buried next day.

The two most important ranchmen in the valley were Clint Reed and Jake Prowers. They never had been friendly. Usually they were opposed to each other on any public question that arose. Each was the leader of his faction. On politics they differed. Clint was a Republican, Jake a Democrat. There had been times when they had come close to open hostilities. The rivalry between them had deeped to hatred on the part of Prowers. When Reed announced through the local paper the inception of the Sweetwater Dam project, his enemy had sworn that it should never go through while he was alive.

Hitherto Prowers had made no move, but everybody in the district knew that he was biding his time. Competent engineers of the Government had passed adversely on this irrigation project. They had decided water could not be brought down from the hills to the Flat Tops. Jake had seen the surveys and believed them to be correct. He was willing that Reed and the capitalists he had interested should waste their money on a fool's dream. If Justin Merrick was right—if he could bring water through Elk Creek Cañon to the Flat Tops—it would be time enough for Prowers to strike. Knowing the man as he did, Clint Reed had no doubt that, if it became necessary in order to defeat the project, his enemy would move ruthlessly and without scruple. It was by his advice that Justin Merrick kept the dam guarded at night and carried a revolver with him when he drove over or tramped across the hills.

CHAPTER IX

UNDER FIRE

ALL day the faint far whir of the reaper could have been heard from the house of the Diamond Bar K ranch. The last of the fields had been cut. Much of the grain had been gathered and was ready for the thresher.

The crop was good. Prices would be fair. Clint Reed rode over the fields with the sense of satisfaction it always gave him to see gathered the fruits of the earth. His pleasure in harvesting or in rounding-up beef steers was not only that of the seller looking to his profit. Back of this was the spiritual gratification of having been a factor in supplying the world's needs. To look at rippling wheat ripening under the sun, to feed the thresher while the fan scattered a cloud of chaff and the grain dropped into the sacks waiting for it, ministered to his mental well-being by justifying his existence. He had converted hundreds of acres of desert into fertile farm land. All his life he had been a producer of essentials for mankind. He found in this, as many farmers do, a source of content. He was paying his way in the world.

To-day Reed found the need of vindication. He was fonder of Betty than he was of anything or anybody else in the world, and he knew that he was at the bar of her judgment. She did not approve of what he had done. This would not have troubled him greatly if he had been sure that he approved of it himself. But like many willful men he sometimes had his bad quarter of an hour afterward.

It was easy enough to make excuses. The Diamond Bar K had been troubled a good deal by vagrants on the transcontinental route. They had robbed the smokehouse only a few weeks before. A gang of them had raided the watermelon patch, cut open dozens of green melons, and departed with such ripe ones as they could find. Naturally he had been provoked against the whole breed of them.

But he had been too hasty in dealing with the young scamp he had thrashed. Clint writhed under an intolerable sense of debt. The boy had fought him as long as he could stand and take it. He had gone away still defiant, and had rescued Betty from a dangerous situation. Dragged back at a rope's end to the ranch by the luckless Dusty, he had scornfully departed before Reed had a chance to straighten out with him this added indignity. The owner of the Diamond Bar K felt frustrated, as though the vagabond had had the best of him.

He was not even sure that the severe punishment he had meted out to the other tramps had been wise. The man Cig had endured the ordeal unbroken in spirit. His last words before he crept away had been a threat of reprisal. The fellow was dangerous. Clint read it in his eyes. He had given orders to Betty not to leave the ranch for the next day or two without an escort. Yet he still felt uneasy, as though the end of the matter had not come.

It was now thirty hours since he had last seen the hoboes. No doubt they were hundreds of miles away by this time and with every click of the car wheels getting farther from the ranch.

He rode back to the stable, unsaddled, and walked to the house. Betty was in the living-room at the piano. She finished the piece, swung round on the stool, and smiled at him.

"Everything fine and dandy, Dad?"

His face cleared. It was her way of telling him that she was ready to forgive and be forgiven.

"Yes." Then, abruptly, "Reckon I get off wrong foot first sometimes, honey."

He was in a big armchair. She went over to him, sat down on his knees, and kissed him. " 'S all right, Dad," she nodded with an effect of boyish brusqueness. Betty, too, had a mental postscript and expressed it. "It's that boy. Nothing to do about it, of course. He would n't let me do a thing for him, but—Oh, well, I just can't get him off my mind. Kinda silly of me."

"Not silly at all," demurred Clint. "Feel that way myself— only more so." He cleared his throat for a confession. "Fact is, Bess, he's managed to put me in a hole. Or else I've put myself

43

there. It's that infernal quick temper of mine. I'd no business to let myself go. Of course, I was figurin' him just a bum like the others, an' for that matter he is a tramp—"

"He quoted Shakespeare at me," inserted Betty, by way of comment.

"I dare say. He's no ignorant fool. I did n't mean that. What was it he called me?" The ranchman smiled ruefully. "A local God Almighty on tin wheels! Maybe I do act like one."

"Sometimes," agreed Betty.

The smile that went with the word robbed her concurrence of its sting. It was tender and understanding, expressed the world-old superiority of her sex over the blundering male who had always claimed mastership. There were times when Betty was a mother to her father, times when Clint marveled at the wisdom that had found lodgment in the soft young body of this vivid creature who was heritor of his life and yet seemed so strangely and wonderfully alien to it.

"Point is that I did n't measure up to my chance and he did," Reed went on gloomily. "It don't set well with me, honey. After I'd thrashed him till he could n't stand, he goes right away an' fights for you because you're a woman. Makes me look pretty small, I'll say. I'd like to take him by the hand and tell him so. But he would n't have it that way. I've got to play my cards the way he's dealt 'em. Can't say I blame him, either."

"No, he had a right to refuse to have anything more to do with us after the way we'd treated him."

"Mostly we get second chances in this life, but we don't always, Bess. Oh, well, no use crying over spilt milk. What's done's done."

"Yes," she agreed. "Don't worry, Dad. I did my best to get him to stay—went down on my knees almost. But he would n't. There's something queer about him. What is it? He acts as though he does n't care what becomes of him, as though he's let go somehow. Did you notice that?"

"Going to the devil fast as he can, looked like to me."

This was probably accurate enough as a summary, but it did not explain why to Betty. She dismissed the subject for the moment, because Ruth came into the room followed by Bridget.

The child was in her nightgown and had come to kiss them before going to bed. She ran to her father, threw her arms around his neck, and gave him a great bear hug. Long since she had forgotten his harshness of the morning.

44

But he had neither forgotten nor forgiven himself. In the first place, he had been unjust. The injunction against going to the barn had not been a blanket one. It had applied only to that part of the building where the blooded stallion was kept in a box stall. He had hurt her feelings as a vent to his annoyance at what had taken place by the creek a half-hour earlier. It was pretty small business, he admitted, to take out his self-disgust on an innocent four-year-old.

He held Ruth close in his arms while Bridget waited smilingly and the little one confided to him plans about the puppies.

" 'N' I'm gonna have Lon make me a wagon, 'n' I'll drive it jus' like Betty does the team, 'n' I fink I'll call the puppies Prince 'n' Rover 'n' Baby Fifi 'n'—'n' everyfing," she concluded all in a breath.

"That'll be bully," the father agreed, stroking the soft flaxen curls fondly. He wondered reproachfully why it was that he could turn on those he loved, as he had done on the child this morning. He had never done it before with Ruth, and he resolved he never would again.

Ruth kissed Betty good-night and went out of the room in the arms of Bridget, held close to her ample bosom, kicking and squealing with delight because she was being tickled in the ribs.

As soon as Betty was in her own room, alone with her thoughts and the rest of the world shut out, her mind went back to the problem of the boy who had so early made such shipwreck of his life. She puzzled over this while she was preparing for bed and afterward while she lay between the white sheets, barred squares from the window frames checkering the moonlight on the linen. What in the world could cause a man, educated, clean-fibered, strong, to let go of life like that?

It could not be a woman. In spite of her youth, she knew this by instinct. A game man did not give up because of blows dealt to him from the outside. The surrender had to come from within. No wounds at the hands of another can subdue the indomitable soul. Young though she was, she knew that. Books of fiction might say the contrary, but she had a sure conviction they were wrong. What was it Browning said?— ". . . Incentives come from the soul's self." Well, the converse of it must also be true.

Somewhere in this boy—she persisted in thinking of him as a boy, perhaps because his great need so filled her with the desire to help him—there must be a weak strain. It was not, could not be, a vile one. She held to that steadily and surely, without any of the passionate insistence that doubt engenders. Ragged and dusty though he was physically, on the drift to destruction, cynically self-condemned, he was yet essentially clean and fine, a strain of the thoroughbred in him. That was her judgment, and she was prepared to wager all she had on the truth of it.

Betty did not sleep. Thoughts drifted through her mind as fleecy clouds do across a summer sky. The magnet of them was this youth who had already drunk so deeply of life's bitterness. He extraordinarily stimulated her interest.

It must have been near midnight that she heard quick voices and lifted her head to the cry of "Fire!" Sketchily she dressed and ran downstairs. The blaze was in the lower meadow where the wheat was gathered for the thresher. A great flame leaped skyward and filled the night with its reflection.

One of the men from the bunkhouse was running toward the unpent furnace. She caught up a saddle blanket from the porch and followed. In the lurid murk figures like marionettes moved to and fro. As she ran, she saw that there were three fires, not only one. This surprised her, for the distance between two of them was at least one hundred and fifty yards. It was strange that in this windless night a spark had traveled so far.

The roar of the conflagration reminded her of some huge living monster in a fury. Tongues of flame shot heavenward in vain menace to the stars.

"Stand back!" Forbes shouted at her. "All we can do is see it don't spread." He was flailing at a line of fire beginning to run in the dry stubble.

"How did it start?" she asked breathlessly.

"Fire-bugs."

"You mean—on purpose?"

"Yep."

"The tramps?"

"I ain't sayin' who." He shouted to make his voice heard above the crackle of the bellowing red demon that had been set loose. Already he spoke hoarsely from a throat roughened by smoke.

"Where's Dad?" she called back.

"Don't know. Ain't seen him since I left the house."

46

Dusty gave information. "Saw him runnin' toward the creek awhile ago."

Almost instantly 'Betty knew why. He, too, must have guessed that this fire had come from no chance spark, but of set design. No doubt he was trying to head off the incendiary.

"Just which way?" she asked the cowpuncher.

Dusty jerked a thumb to the left. The girl turned and moved swiftly in the direction of the fringe of bushes that rose as a vague line out of the darkness. She believed her father's instinct was true. Whoever had fired the stacks would retreat to the willows and make his escape along the creek bed, hiding in the bushes if the pursuit grew close.

Before she had taken a dozen steps a sound leaped into the night. It was a revolver shot. Fear choked her. She began to run, her heart throbbing like that of a half-grown wild rabbit in the hand. Faint futile little cries broke from her throat. A sure intuition told her what she would find by the creek.

Her father lay on a sand spit close to the willows. He was dragging himself toward the cover of some brush. From the heavy foliage a shot rang out.

Betty flew across the open to her father.

"Look out!" he called sharply to her. "He's in the willows. Down here." Reed caught at her arm and pulled her behind him where he lay crouched.

The automatic of the man in ambush barked again. A spatter of sand stung Betty's face. Almost simultaneously came the bull roar of the foreman's hoarse voice.

"You're shot, Daddy," the girl whimpered.

"Keep still!" he ordered.

A heavy body crashed through the bushes in flight. At the same time came the thump of running feet. Dusty broke into sight, followed by the foreman.

The wounded rancher took command. "He went that way, boys," he said, and pointed down the creek. "Lit out a minute ago. Hustle back to the house and get guns, then cut down the road in the car and head him off."

Forbes nodded to Dusty. "You do that. Take the boys with you. Hit the creek at the ford and work up." He turned to his employer. "How about it, Clint? Where'd he hit you? How bad?"

"In the leg. It'll wait. You get him, Lon."

The foreman pushed into the willows and disappeared.

Reed called him back, but he paid no attention. The ranch-

47

man fumed. "What's the matter with the dawg-goned old idiot? No sense a-tall. That's no way to do. He'll get shot first thing he knows."

Her father was so much his usual self that Betty's terror fell away from her. If he were wounded fatally, he would not act like this.

He had been hit just above the top of his laced boots. Betty uncovered the wound and bathed it with water she brought from the creek in Clint's hat. Around the wound she bound a large handkerchief she found in his hip pocket.

"Does it hurt much?" she asked, her soft voice mothering him.

"Some. Know I've got a leg. Lucky for me you came along. It must 'a' scared him off. You an' Lon too."

"See who he was?"

"Too dark."

"Think it was the tramps? Or Jake Prowers?"

"The tramps. Not the way Jake pulls off a job. He's no bungler."

She sat down and put his head in her lap. "Anything else I can do, Dad? Want a drink?" she asked anxiously.

Reed caught her little hand and pressed it. "Sho! Don't you go to worryin' about me, sweetheart. Doc Rayburn, he'll fix me up good as new. When Lon comes back I'll have him—"

He stopped. A rough voice was speaking. A foot struck a stone. Vague figures emerged from the gloom, took on distinctness. The big one was Lon Forbes. He walked behind a man who was his prisoner, his great hands clamped to the fellow's arms.

Betty stood up and waited, her eyes fastened on them as they moved forward. Her heart was going like a triphammer. She knew what she dreaded, and presently that her apprehensions were justified.

The foreman's prisoner was the tramp who called himself Tug.

CHAPTER X

"ONE SQUARE GUY"

FROM Betty's cheeks the delicate wild-rose bloom had fled. Icy fingers seemed to clutch at her heart and squeeze the blood from it. This was the worst that could happen, since she knew her father was not wounded to death.

Lon spoke, grimly. "Bumped into him down the creek a ways—hidin' in the willows. Heard a rustling an' drapped in on him onexpected. Thought he would n't come with me at first, then he changed his mind an' thought he would."

The tramp said nothing. His dogged eyes passed from Betty to her father. She thought there leaped into them a little flicker of surprise when they fell upon the ranchman sitting on the ground with his leg bound up.

"Have you taken his gun from him?" Reed asked.

"Could n't find it. He must 'a' throwed it away." The foreman passed an exploring hand over the body of the prisoner to make sure that he had not missed a concealed weapon. "No, sir. He ain't got a gat with him now, unless he's et it."

"Take him to the bunkhouse and keep him guarded. We'll 'phone for the sheriff. Soon as you get to the house call up Doc Rayburn and have him run right out. Then hook up a team and come get me," the ranch-owner directed.

From the fog of Betty's distress a small voice projected itself. "You're not going to send for the sheriff without making sure, Dad?"

"Sure of what?" The steel-gray eyes were hard and cold.

"Sure he did it. He has n't said so."

Reed's laughter was harsh and without humor. "Nor he ain't liable to. Right now he's trying to fix up his alibi."

"Are n't you going to hear what he's got to say?"

"He can tell it in court."

Betty turned from him to the prisoner. "Why don't you say something?"

She did not get past the defense of his sardonic smile. "What shall I say?"

"Tell him you did n't do it," she begged, seeking assurance for herself.

"Would he believe me? Would you?"

There came to her a conviction that she would—if he said it in a way to inspire confidence.

"Yes," she said.

The veil of irrision lifted from his eyes. He looked straight at her. "I did n't do it."

Instantly Betty knew he was telling the truth. A warm resurgent wave flooded her veins. His life was bound up with tragedy. It had failed of all it had set out to be. But she knew, beyond doubt or evidence, that he had not fired the stacks or shot her father. The amazing thing now, to her mind, was that even for a moment she could have believed he would kill at advantage in cold blood.

"I knew it! I knew it all the time!" she cried.

"How did you know all that?" her father asked.

"Because."

It was no answer, yet it was as good as any she could give. How could she phrase a feeling that rested only on faith in such a way as to give it weight to others?

"I'm one o' these Missouri guys," the foreman snorted. "He'll have to show me. What's he doin' here? What was he hidin' out in the bushes for?• How could he tell soon as I jumped him that a man had been shot?"

"He can explain that," she urged; and to the vagrant, "Can't you?"

"I can," he answered her.

"We're waiting," snapped Reed, and voice and manner showed that he had prejudged the case.

The young man met his look with one of cold hostility.

"You can keep on waiting—till the sheriff comes."

"Suits me," snapped the ranchman. "Hustle along, Lon. No use wasting time."

The foreman and his prisoner departed. Betty stayed with her father, miserably conscious that she had failed to avert the clash of inimical temperaments. None the less she was determined to keep the young man out of the hands of the law.

She began at once to lay siege to her father.

50

"I knew he did n't do it. I knew he could n't. It was that one they call Cig. I know it was."

"All three of 'em in it likely."

"No. They had quarreled. He would n't be in it with them. That Cig thought he had told you about his attacking me. He threatened this Tug. I think he'd have shot him just as he did you—if he'd got a chance."

"If he did shoot me. That's not been proved."

"Well, if this one—the one they call Tug—if he did it, why did n't he have a gun when Lon found him? Lon says he came on him unexpectedly. He had no time to get rid of it. Where is it?"

"Maybe he dropped it while he was running."

"You know you don't believe that, Dad," she scoffed. "He'd have stopped to pick it up. Don't you see he had to have that gun—the man that shot you did—to make sure of getting away? And when Lon found him he would have killed Lon, too. He'd have had to do it—to save himself from the hangman. The fact that this Tug did n't have a gun proves that he did n't shoot you."

"Say he did n't, then. Does it prove he was n't in cahoots with the man who did? What was he hiding here on the ground for?"

"You did n't give him a chance to tell. He was ready to, if you'd let him."

"I asked him, did n't I?"

"Oh, Dad, you know how you asked him," she reproached. "He's got his pride, same as we have. If he was n't in this— and I know he was n't—you can't blame him for getting stubborn when he's badgered. His explanations would have tumbled out fast enough if he'd been guilty."

This struck Reed as psychologically true. The fellow had not acted like a guilty man. He had held his head high, with a scornful and almost indifferent pride.

"What did I say, for him to get his back up so quick?" the ranchman grumbled.

"It's the way you said it, and the way Lon acted. He's quick-tempered, and of course he's fed up with our treatment of him. Would n't you be?"

"What right has he to travel with a bunch of crooks if he does n't expect to be classed as one?"

"Well, he has n't." Betty put her arms round his neck with a warm rush of feeling. Motives are usually mixed in the most

51

simple of us. Perhaps in the back of her mind there was an intuition that the road to her desire lay through affection and not argument. "I can't row with you now, Daddikins, when you're wounded and hurt. I'm so worried about you. I thought—a while ago—when I saw you lying on the ground and that murderer shooting at you—"

She stopped, to steady a voice grown tremulous in spite of herself. He stroked her black hair softly.

"I know, li'l' girl. But it's all right now. Just a clean flesh wound. Don't you feel bad," he comforted.

"And then that boy. I don't want us to rush into doing anything that will hurt the poor fellow more. We've done enough to him. We'd feel awf'ly bad if we got him into trouble and he was n't the right man."

Reed surrendered, largely because her argument was just, but partly, too, because of her distress. "Have it your own way, Bess. I know you're going to, anyhow. We'll hear his story. If it sounds reasonable, why—"

Her arms tightened in a quick hug and her soft cheek pressed against his rough one. "That's all I want, Dad. I know Clint Reed. He's what Dusty calls one square guy. If you listen to this tramp's story, he'll get justice, and that's all I ask for him." She dismissed the subject, sure in her young, instinctive wisdom that she had said enough and that more would be too much. "Is the leg throbbing, Daddy? Shall I run down to the creek and get water to bathe it? Maybe that would help the pain."

"No, you stay right here where it's dark and quit talking. The boys may drive that fellow back up the creek. My leg'll be all right till Rayburn sees it."

"You think he'll come back here again?" she asked, her voice a-tremble.

"Not if he can help it, you can bet on that. But if the boys hem him in, and he can't break through, why, he'll have to back-track."

The girl's heart began to flutter again. She had plenty of native courage, but to lie in the darkness of the night in fear of an assassin shook her nerves. What would he do if he came back, hard-pressed by the men, and found her father lying wounded and defenseless? In imagination she saw again the horrible menace of his twisted face, the lifted lip so feral, the wolfish, hungry eyes.

Would Lon Forbes never come back? What was he doing?

What was keeping him so long? He had had time long since to have reached the house and hitched a team. Maybe he was wasting precious minutes at the telephone trying to get the sheriff.

A dry twig crackled in the willows and Betty's hand clutched spasmodically at her father's arm. She felt rather than saw his body grow taut. There came a sound of something gliding through the saplings.

Betty scarce dared breath.

A patter of light feet was heard. Clint laughed.

"A rabbit. Did n't think it could be any one in the willows. We'd 'a' heard him coming."

"Listen!" whispered Betty.

The rumble of wagon wheels going over disintegrated quartz drifted to them.

"Lon's coming," her father said.

Presently they heard his voice talking to the horses. "Get over there, Buckskin, you got plenty o' room. What's eatin' you, anyhow?"

Forbes stopped on the bluff and came down. "Left the fellow with Burwell tied up in the bunkhouse. Got both the sheriff and Doc Rayburn. How's the leg, Clint?"

Reed grunted a "'S all right," and showed the foreman how to support him up the incline to the wagon.

Five minutes later they were moving back toward the ranch-house. The fired stacks had burned themselves out, but smoke still rolled skyward.

"Keller's watchin' to see everything's all right there," Forbes said. "I don't aim to take chances till we get the whole crop threshed."

"Might 'a' been worse," Clint said. "If that fellow'd known how to go at it, he could have sent half the crop up in smoke. We're lucky, I'll say."

"Luckier than he is. I'll bet he gets ten years," the foreman said with unction.

Neither father nor daughter made any answer to that prophecy.

CHAPTER XI

MR. NE'ER-DO-WELL

Tug walked to the bunkhouse beside the foreman, the latter's fingers fastened like steel bands to his wrist. If Forbes said anything to his prisoner during the tramp through the wheat-field, the young fellow scarcely heard it. His mind was full of the girl who had defended him. In imagination she still stood before him, slim, straight, so vitally alive, her dark eyes begging him to deny the charge that had been made against him.

The low voice rang in his brain. He could hear the throb in it when she had cried, "Tell him you did n't do it," and the joyous lift of her confident "I knew it—I knew it all the time."

The vagrant's life was insolvent in all those assets of friendship that had once enriched it. He had deliberately bankrupted himself of them when he had buried his identity in that of the hobo Tug, driven to it by the shame of his swift declension. It had been many months since any woman had clung so obstinately to a belief in him regardless of facts. He had no immediate family, no mother or sister with an unshakable faith that went to the heart of life.

But this girl who had crossed his path—this girl with the wild-rose color, the sweetness that flashed so vividly in her smile, the dear wonder of youth in every glance and gesture—believed in him and continued to believe in spite of his churlish rejection of her friendliness.

Though he was one of the lost legion, it was an evidence of the divine flame still flickering in him that his soul went out to meet the girl's grave generosity. In his bosom was a warm glow. For the hour at least he was strong. It seemed possible to slough the weakness that rode him like an Old Man of the Sea.

His free hand groped its way to an inner pocket and drew out a package wrapped in cotton cloth. A fling of his arm sent it into the stubble.

54

"What you doin'?" demanded Forbes.

"Throwing away my gun and ammunition," the tramp answered, his sardonic mouth twitching.

"It don't buy you anything to pull that funny stuff," growled the foreman. "You ain't got a gun to throw away."

Forbes turned the captured vagrant over to Burwell, one of the extra harvest hands, and left him at the bunkhouse while he went to telephone the doctor and the sheriff.

It was a busy night at the Diamond Bar K. The foreman drove away and presently returned. Tug heard the voices of Betty and her father as they moved toward the house. Some one chugged up to the house in a car with one spark plug fouled or broken.

Burwell went to the door of the bunkhouse.

"Get 'em, Dusty?" he asked.

"Not yet," the cowpuncher answered while he was loosening the plug. "But, y'betcha, we'll get 'em if this bird we done got caged did n't play a lone hand."

Presently Dusty drove away again, in a hurry to rejoin his companions. He had come back to find out whether anything new had been discovered.

The foreman showed up in the doorway. "The boss wants to have a talk with you, young fellow," he said.

Betty would have known without any explanation that the prisoner had no intention of running away. But Lon had no perception of this. He did not release his grip until the tramp was in the living-room.

The owner of the Diamond Bar K lay on a lounge and Betty was hovering close to him as nurses do in their ministrations.

Reed spoke at once. "Let's get down to brass tacks, young man. Put your cards on the table if you're in the clear. Come through clean. What do you know about this business?" The rancher's voice was crisp, but not unfriendly.

Tug sensed at once a change in attitude toward him. He had come expecting to be put through the third degree. It was possible that was being held in reserve for him. His mind moved cautiously to meet Reed.

"What do you mean come clean—confess?" he asked.

"Call it what you want to. You claim you did n't shoot me —that you were n't in to-night's job at all. Let's hear your alibi."

"If you'd care to tell it to us," Betty suggested gently.

55

The vagrant looked at her. "Why not? I don't fire wheat-fields and I don't shoot from ambush."

"All right. Let's have it," the wounded man said impatiently.

"When I left the ranch yesterday. I went to Wild Horse and camped a mile or so out of town. I did n't care to meet the fellows I'd been with. They blamed me for having them hauled back to the ranch here—thought I'd hurried back to squeal on them. But I was looking for work and I was n't going to run away from them. About noon I tramped it into town to see about getting a job. I saw this Cig in a store. He was buying a gun and ammunition for it. He did n't see me, so I passed by. Later I went back to the store and made sure, by asking the clerk, that Cig had bought the gun."

Betty broke in eagerly. "And you thought he meant to kill Father. So you followed him out here to-night," she cried.

"Not quite," the tramp answered with an edge of cold anger in his voice. "I would n't have lifted a finger for your father. He brought it on himself. He could look out for himself. I don't know what he did to Cig yesterday afternoon, but I know it was plenty. What would he expect from a fellow like Cig after he'd treated him that way? He's dangerous as a trapped wolf and just about as responsible morally."

"Very well. Say I brought this fellow and his gun on me by giving him what was coming to him. What next?" asked Reed brusquely.

"I could n't get him out of my head. If I could have been sure he'd limit his revenge to you and your foreman—But that was just it. I could n't. He might lie in wait for your daughter, or he might kidnap her little sister if he got a chance."

"Kidnap Ruthie?" the girl broke in, all the mother in her instantly alert. "Oh, he would n't do that, would he?"

"Probably not." He turned to her with the touch of deference in voice and manner so wholly lacking when he faced her father. "I thought of it because the other day we were talking of the Charley Ross case, and Cig had a good deal to say about just how a kidnapping ought to be done. The point is that I would n't trust him, after what your people have done to him, any more than I would a rattlesnake. His mind works that way—fills up with horrible ideas of getting even. And he's absolutely unmoral, far as I've been able to find out."

"So you trailed him out here—on the off chance that he might hurt Betty or Ruth. Is that it?" inquired the rancher.

"You see I can't mind my own business," the prisoner

jeered. "You invited me forcibly to get off your land and stay off, but I had to come trespassing again."

"No need to rub it in," blurted Reed by way of apology. "I got off wrong foot first with you. Not all my fault, though. You acted mighty foolish yourself. Still, you've got a legitimate kick coming. I'll admit that. Sorry—if that does any good."

He did not offer to shake hands. It was his judgment that this youth with the somber eyes so ready to express bitter self-mockery did not want to have anything more to do with him.

The vagrant offered no comment. His white face did not soften or its rigidity relax. Clearly he would make no pact with the Diamond Bar K.

Betty asked a swift question, to bridge the silence left by his rejection of her father's tentative acknowledgment of wrong. "How did you know when they were coming?"

"I knew they'd come after dark, and probably tonight." He corrected himself at once. "I ought n't to say 'they,' for I knew York would n't come. He hasn't the nerve."

"You're dead right there," the foreman said. "All we give him was a first-class chapping, an' he howled like he was bein' killed. That other guy, now, he's one sure-enough bad actor, if you ask me, but he's game."

"So I lay in the brush near their camp," the gay-cat explained. "York went down to the railroad yards. He's likely riding the rods for 'Frisco by this time. After dark Cig started this way and I followed. When he left the track, I trailed behind. The moon was n't up, and I lost him. I knew he could n't be far away, so I headed for the ranch, keeping close to the creek. For a while I did n't see or hear anything more of him. Just as I'd made up my mind to strike for the house, the fires flamed up. I heard two or three shots, then some one went by me on the run. Time for me to be going, I thought. Your Mr. Forbes was of another opinion. He showed up just then and invited me to stay."

Reed's cool, shrewd eyes had not lifted from the tramp while he was making the explanation. He was convinced that he had been told the truth. The man had come out to do a service for his children, which was equivalent to one for Clint himself. Again he felt the sting of self-reproach at having played a poor part in this drama that had been flung into the calmness of their quiet round of existence.

"Glad Lon did find you," the wounded man responded. "I'll go the whole hog and tell you straight I'm right sorry for the way I've treated you. That makes twice you've come through for me. I'll not forget it, Mr.——" He hesitated, waiting for the other to supply the name.

"Mr. Ne'er-do-well," suggested the white-faced tramp, and on his face was a grim, ironic smile.

Reed flushed. "You've a right to remind me of that if you want to. It's not the first time I've been a damned fool, and it likely won't be the last. But you can tie to this, young man." The steel-gray eyes seized those of the hobo and held them fast. "If ever there comes a time when you need Clint Reed, he'll be here waiting. Send for him, and he'll come. That's a promise."

"Will he bring along with him Dusty and Mr. Forbes and the rest of his outfit?" Tug asked, a derisive flash in his eyes.

"Say anything you've a mind to. I'll not blame you if you hold hard feelings. I would in your place. But don't forget the fact. If you're ever in trouble, Betty and I are here waiting to be called on."

The girl slipped her hand into her father's and gave it a quick squeeze. It told better than words how glad she was of the thing he was doing.

"I can count on that knock-out punch of yours, can I?" the prisoner asked ironically.

The girl came forward impulsively, a shell-pink flag fluttering in her cheeks. "Please don't feel that way. We're sorry— we truly are. We'd love to have you give us a chance to show you how we feel."

The hard lines on his face broke. An expression warm and tender transformed it. He turned his back on the others and spoke for her ears alone.

"An angel from heaven could n't do more for me than you've done, Miss Reed. I'll always remember it—always. If it's any comfort for you to know it, be sure one scamp will never forget the girl who out of her infinite kindness stretched down a hand to him when he was sinking in the mud."

"But won't you take the hand?" she whispered, all eager desire to help. "It's not a very strong one, I'm afraid, but it's ever so willing."

He took it, literally, and looked down at it where it lay in his. "I'm taking it, you see. Don't blame yourself if it can't pull the scalawag out of the mire.' *Facilis descensus Averni,* you know."

"Is your trouble so far beyond help?" she murmured, and in

58

her eyes he read the leap of her sweet and gallant soul toward him. "I can't believe it. Surely there can't be any sorrow or distress that friendship won't lighten. If you'll let me in where you are—if you won't shut me out by freezing yourself up—"

The honk of an automobile horn had drawn Forbes to the window, from which point of observation he was reporting progress to his employer.

"Reckon it's the sheriff an' Doc Rayburn. . . . Yep. They're gettin' outa the car an' comin' in." He turned to Reed. "What about this fellow here? What's the play we're makin' to Daniels?"

"That he came to warn us, but got here too late. I'll do the talking, Lon."

A fat little man with a medicine case in his hand bustled into the room. At his heels moved a big blond cattleman whose faded blue eyes were set in a face of brown leather.

"What's the trouble? What's the trouble?" fumed the doctor. It was his habit of mind and manner to effervesce.

"Some tramps set fire to my wheat and shot me up, Doc. Nothing worth putting in the papers, I reckon," answered the ranchman easily.

"Let's see about that. Let's see," the doctor said with his little touch of pomposity.

He stripped his automobile gloves for action.

CHAPTER XII

"IS THIS BIRD A PRISONER, OR AIN'T HE?"

WHILE Dr. Rayburn, with Betty and Forbes to wait upon him, made preparations to dress the wound, Sheriff Daniels listened to the story of the ranchman. The officer was a hard-headed Westerner who applied common sense to the business of maintaining law and order.

"Looks like that tramp Cig did it, unless this young fellow is passing the buck for an alibi," he said in a low voice.

Reed shook his head. "No, Frank. This boy's all right. I thought at first he might be in it, but I know now he was n't. He helped my girl out of a hole yesterday—licked this Cig because he got fresh with Bess. Even before that he had parted company with the other two. You'll go to barkin' up the wrong tree if you suspect him."

The sheriff looked at Tug. The vagrant was standing beside the piano glancing at the music piled on top of it. Ragged, dusty, and unshaven, he was not a prepossessing youth. Livid and purple bruises ridged his pallid cheeks. Daniels found in the face something not quite normal, and, since he was a clean outdoor man himself, an unhealthy variation from the usual stirred in him a slight feeling of distrust.

"By yore way of it, Clint, you beat up this hobo here for trespassing on yore land. I'd say from the looks of him you gave him a plenty. Does it look reasonable to you that he'd trail the other hobo for miles to protect you from him?"

"Not to protect me, Frank. He gave it to me straight it was n't for me. 'Seems he got to worryin' about what this Cig might do to the children. The fellow had been talkin' about kidnapping and how easy it could be pulled off. So this one— Tug he calls himself—followed Cig here. Looks reasonable to me. He's game. You'd ought to have seen him come at me with his legs wobbling under him. Well, a game man does n't make war on women and kids, does he?"

"Our kind of man does n't. But he's not our kind. Looks to me like a dope fiend. Expect he's got a lot of these anarchist ideas tramps are carryin' around the country nowadays. I don't say he's guilty. What I do say is that I'm not convinced he's innocent. Far as being game goes, this other man Cig is game enough, too, by what you say. Stood the gaff, and then bawled you out, did n't he?"

"He's game like a cornered wolf. I tell you this one's different. He's an educated man gone wrong. At first I did n't get him right myself."

"Sure you've got him right now?" the sheriff asked, smiling.

"Far as this business goes, I have. I'll admit he's got no cause to like me, but I've got a hunch he's white."

"I'd rather have facts than hunches."

The owner of the Diamond Bar K was a new convert to the opinion he was giving voice to, and he was therefore a more eager advocate of it. "Look at this from my point of view, Frank. I thrash him till he can't stand, and he pays me back by lookin' out for Bess when she's in trouble. One of my men hauls him back here at the end of a rope. He settles that score by tramping five or six miles to help us again. I'd be a poor sort if I did n't come through for him now."

"Well, I'll not push on my reins, Clint," the officer promised. "Very likely you're right, and I'm sure not aimin' to make trouble for any innocent man. This tramp of yours will have every chance in the world to show he's straight. I'll not arrest him unless I've got the goods on him."

Dr. Rayburn, ready for business, came forward fussily. "You quit exciting my patient, Sheriff. Quit it. And move on out of this sick-room. I don't want any one here but Miss Bessie and Bridget and Lon Forbes."

The sheriff laughed. "All right, Doc. It's yore say-so."

He walked out of the room, the vagrant by his side.

"Am I under arrest?" the latter asked.

"You're not under arrest, but I'd like yore word that you'll stick around till I've had a chance to size this thing up."

"If I'd fire wheat and shoot a man down from cover, what good would my word be?"

"That's so." The sheriff's eyes swept up and down him. "Still, I'll ask for yore word. Reed believes in you. I don't reckon you did this job. Will you stay where I can reach you for a few days? I might need you as a witness."

"Yes."

The sheriff was surprised, not at the promise, but at the sense of reliance he put in it. It came to him that, if this young fellow gave his word, he would keep it at any cost. Since this was scarcely reasonable, he tried to reject the conviction. He recalled his court experience in listening to witnesses. Some of the most convincing were liars out of whole cloth, while honest ones with nothing to conceal were at times dragged sweating through a tangle of incompatible statements.

"Better go to the bunkhouse and wait there. I'll fix it with Forbes so you can sleep there to-night," Daniels said.

Tug walked to the bunkhouse and sat down on the porch. After a time the car returned with the men. They had not been able to find any one hiding in the brush or hurrying to escape.

Daniels took charge of the man-hunt. "We'll tackle this job on horseback, boys," he said. "This fellow will make for the railroad. He'll jump a train at a station or water-tank if he can. We'll patrol the points where the cars stop."

The foreman came down to the bunkhouse. Evidently he

61

had his orders. "Boys, the sheriff's in charge of this job now. You'll do as he says."

Dusty spoke up. He and others had been looking with open and menacing suspicion at the paroled prisoner. That young man sat on the porch, chair tipped back on two legs, smoking a cigarette with obvious indifference to their hostility. The coolness of his detachment from the business of the hour was irritating.

"What about this bird here?" Dusty wanted to know. "Is he a prisoner, or ain't he?"

Forbes passed on further orders. He did it in a dry voice that refused responsibility. "He ain't. The boss says he's under obligations to him an' you boys will treat him right. An' he means every word of it. I would n't advise none of you to get gay with—with our guest."

"How is the boss?" asked Burt.

"Doc says he'll do fine if no complications occur."

"He's got the right idea, Doc has," Burwell grinned. "Always leave yoreself an alibi. Operation successful, but patient shy of vitality. No flowers, please."

"That's no way to talk," reproved Forbes. "The old man's all right. He's lying there on the chaste lounge chipper as a wood-chuck in the garbage barrel at a dude ranch. You got a con-sid'rable nerve to get funny about him, Burwell."

"I did n't aim for to get funny about him, but about the doc," apologized the harvest hand. "Looks like when I open my mouth I always put my foot in it."

"You put more ham an' aigs an' flannel cakes in it than any guy I ever did see," commented the foreman. "I been watchin' to see if all that fuel would n't mebbe steam you up for work, but I ain't noticed any results yet. Prob'ly you wear out all yore strength talkin' foolishness."

"That had ought to hold you hitched for a while, Burwell," Dusty chuckled.

"All right, boys. Let's go. Get busy," the sheriff ordered crisply.

They poured out of the bunkhouse to get their horses.

CHAPTER XIII

A JOB

BETTY rose at daybreak and got Justin Merrick on the telephone. After preliminary greetings she asked a question.

"Would it be convenient for you to come down this morning? There's something I want to talk over with you if you have time."

"I'll make it convenient," came the answer. "Anything serious happened?"

"That tramp Cig came back last night to fire the wheat. He shot Father. No, he's not badly hurt, but—"

"I'll be right down."

It was like Merrick that he did not wait for breakfast. He was at the Diamond Bar K as soon as his car could bring him.

Betty set out a breakfast for him in the dining-room and waited on him herself with the aid of Ruth, who trotted back and forth with honey, syrup, and butter for his hot cakes. Miss Ruth was not exactly fond of Merrick. He did not give himself out enough. But she appreciated him. He had some good ideas about bringing her candy, teddy bears, and dolls.

When Betty had reassured her fiancé about Mr. Reed and answered such questions as he put about the fire and the man-hunt, she came to the real reason for asking him to call.

"It's about that young man who was with the tramps," she explained. "You offered to give him work. I wish you would, Justin. You're so reliable. It might be a great thing for him to be under you—the very thing he needs."

Merrick was not especially pleased at being chosen as the agent to reform a vagrant. He was a very busy man. Also, he had a theory that every man must stand on his own feet. But he had made a promise. He did not make many, but he always kept those he made.

"Let's get this right, Beth," he answered, smiling. "I said I'd put him to work and see what he had in him. I'm willing to do that. It'll be up to him to make good. No special favors or sympathy or anything of that sort."

Betty met his smile. "I don't think you'd find it very easy to waste any sympathy on this young man. He's not that kind. If you'll give him work, that's all you can do for him. Good of you, Justin. I'll not forget it. I've got him on my conscience, you know."

"Did he ask for work? Will he take it?"

"I don't know. He did n't ask us for it. He's got his foolish pride. But he does n't know who you are. I mean—that I'm friendly with you or anything. Mr. Daniels wants him to stay in the neighborhood for a few days. I think he'd be glad to get a job with you if he felt you really needed him."

"Then he'll get a chance of one," Justin said. "Probably I can't put him on specialized work. Did he mention what his trade is?"

"No. He does n't look as though he'd had a trade. Maybe he was studying for some profession."

"Where is he?"

"I don't know. At the bunkhouse, maybe, or wandering about the place. Shall I send for him?"

"No; I'd better meet him by chance and bring the thing up casually, don't you think?"

"Yes, that would be better," she agreed.

Having finished breakfast, Merrick went out to run down his man. He found presently a ragged young fellow sitting on the tongue of an old wagon puffing nervously at a cigarette.

The engineer nodded a good-morning at him and stopped. "Not so hot as yesterday," he said by way of introduction.

"No," assented the ragged one gloomily.

"I've learned that Sheriff Daniels wants you to stay around a few days. I'm in charge of the Sweetwater Dam irrigation project. We need men. Want a job?"

"If it's one that suits me," answered the tramp, eyeing Merrick ungraciously. He recognized the man's strength and force. Every line of him, every glance, every inflection of the voice helped to bear out the impression of success he radiated. Clearly he was masterful and dominant, but the younger man did not like him less for that.

"What can you do? What's your line?"

"I'm an engineer."

"What kind?"

64

"I've done more bridge-building than anything else."

Merrick looked him over more carefully. "College man?"

"Massachusetts Tech."

"My name's Merrick."

The stranger hesitated a fraction of a second. "You can call me Jones."

"One of my men quit yesterday. Would you care to take a try at it? It's cement work."

The man who had given his name as Jones was suffering the tortures of the damned. He wanted a shot in the arm to lift him out of himself, and he had thrown away his supply of the drug. Just now everything else in the world was unimportant beside this ravenous craving that filled his whole being.

"I'd just as soon," he said without enthusiasm.

Ten minutes later he sat beside Merrick in the runabout. The car was taking the stiff grade of the road which climbed the Flat Tops to the hills.

CHAPTER XIV

ONE BAD HOMBRE MEETS ANOTHER

OLD JAKE PROWERS looked grimly down upon the Flat Tops from the Notch. He could see the full stretch of the mesa and below it one end of Paradise Valley. The windmill of the Diamond Bar K was shining in the sun, miles away, flinging out heliographic signals that conformed to no man-made code.

"Wonder how Clint is this mo'ning," he said in a high, squeaky voice that went congruously with the small, twisted figure and the wrinkled, leathery face.

His *fidus Achates,* Don Black, shifted in the saddle to ease himself and rested his weight on one stirrup. He was a black-bearded, fierce-looking man in blue overalls, faded flannel shirt, and run-down-at-the-heel boots.

"Did n't know he was sick," he said, chewing tobacco imperturbably.

"Fellow shot him last night, by jiminy by jinks, an' set fire to his wheat."

"Did?" Black shot one startled, questioning look at his employer.

Jake cackled with splenetic laughter. "No, sir. Don't you look at me thataway, Don. I had n't a thing to do with it. If I'd 'a' done it, it would 'a' been done right. This fellow was a tramp, they say. He did n't get any consid'rable amount of the wheat an' he did n't get Clint."

Fate had played a strange trick when it put the unscrupulous and restless soul of a Lucifer in the warped body of Jake Prowers, when it expressed that soul through a thin, cracked voice and pale-blue, washed-out eyes. To the casual observer he seemed one of life's ineffectives. Those who knew him best found reason to shudder at his mirthless laughter and his mild oaths, at the steady regard of his expressionless gaze. They seemed somehow to stress by contrast the man's dark and ruthless soul. There were moments when from those cold eyes flamed something sinister and blasting that chilled the blood.

Black had been living for weeks at an out-of-the-way cabin in the hills. He was riding herd on a bunch of Prowers's cattle feeding on the edge of the Government reservation. Consequently he had been out of the way of hearing the news of the community.

"What had this tramp got against Clint?" he asked, firing accurately with tobacco juice at the face of a flat rock.

"You know how high-headed Clint is. He beat up a bunch of tramps an' one came back to even up things. Last night he took a whirl at it. The fellow set fire to some wheat-stacks an' gunned Clint when he showed up, by the jumpin' Jehosaphat. But Clint's no invalid. He'd take right smart killing, an' all he got was one pill in the leg. Trouble with most of these here bad men is they ain't efficient. When you lay for Clint, Don, I'd advise you to spill about a pint of lead in him."

The little man grinned with broken-toothed malevolence at his henchman.

"I don't aim to lay for Clint," growled Black. He was not a humorist and he never knew when Prowers's jokes were loaded with dynamite.

Jake cackled. "O' course not. Clint, he's a good citizen if he did kick you off'n the Diamond Bar K once. What's a li'l' thing like that between friends."

"I don't claim him as any friend of mine. If you ask me,

66

he's too dawg-goned bossy—got to have everything his own way. But that ain't sayin' I got any notion of layin' in the brush for him. Not so any one could notice it. If Clint lives till I bump him off, he'll sure be a Methuselah," Black answered sulkily.

"That's fine," jeered the cattleman. "I'll tell Clint to quit worryin' about you—that you ain't got a thing against him. Everything's lovely, even if he did kick you around some."

The rider flushed darkly. "He ain't worryin' none about me, an' I did n't say everything was lovely. I like him same as I do a wolf. But all I ask is for him to let me alone. If he does that, we'll not tangle."

On the breeze there came to them from far to the left a faint booming. Prowers looked toward the rocky escarpment back of which lay the big dam under construction.

The wrinkled, leathery face told no tales. "Still blasting away on his dinged dam project. That fellow Merrick is either plumb fool or else we are. I got to find out which."

"I reckon he can't make water run uphill," the dark man commented.

"No, Don. But maybe he does n't have to do that. Maybe the Government engineers are wrong. I'll admit that don't look reasonable to me. They put it down in black and white—three of 'em, one after another—that Elk Creek Cañon is higher at the far end than this dam site of his. They dropped the scheme because it was n't feasible. Probably Merrick's one of these squirts that know it all. Still—" The sentence died out, but the man's thoughts raced on.

Black desisted from chewing tobacco to hum a fragment of a song he had cherished twenty-five years.

> "Every daisy in the dell
> Knows my story, knows it well,"

he murmured tunelessly.

"If he should be right, by jiminy by jinks—" Prowers was talking to himself. He let the conditional clause stand alone. Slowly the palm of his hand rasped back and forth over a rough, unshaven chin.

"Did they catch this tramp that shot up Clint?" asked Black.

"Not yet. Daniels is patrolling the railroad. If the fellow has n't made his getaway on the night freight, they'll likely get him. He's got to stick to the railway."

"Why has he?" the rider inquired. He was watching a moving object among the rocks below.

"So's to skip the country. He ain't acquainted here—knows nothing about these hills. If he was n't taken by some rancher and turned over to Daniels, he'd starve to death. Likely he's lying under cover somewheres along the creek."

"Likely he ain't," differed Black. "Likely he's ducked for the hills." His gaze was still on the boulder field below. From its case beside the saddle he drew a rifle.

"Why would he do that?"

"I dunno why, except that a fellow on the dodge can't always choose the road he's gonna travel. Any reward for this guy?"

"Ain't heard of any. Yore conscience joggin' you to light out and hunt for the man that shot up Clint, Don?" his employer probed derisively.

"I would n't have to hunt far, Jake," the herder replied, a note of triumph in the drawling voice. For once he had got the better of the boss in a verbal duel. "He's right down there among the rocks."

"Down where?"

The barrel of the rifle pointed to a group of large boulders which, in prehistoric days, perhaps, had broken from the ledge above and rolled down.

"Don't see any one," Jake said after the pale-blue eyes had watched the spot steadily for several moments.

"He's seen us, an' he's lying hid. You keep him covered while I go down and collect him."

Prowers gave this consideration and vetoed the suggestion. "No, you stay here, Don, and I'll go get him."

"If there's any reward—"

"Don't you worry about that. There ain't gonna be any reward."

The ranchman swung down from the saddle and descended from the bluff by way of a wooded gulch at the right. Ten minutes later, Black saw him emerge and begin to cross the rock slide toward the big boulders.

Presently Prowers stopped and shouted. "You fellow in the rocks, I wantta talk with you."

There came no answer.

He moved cautiously a little closer, rifle ready for action. "We got you, fellow. Better come outa there an' talk turkey. I

68

don't aim for to turn you over to the sheriff if you're anyways reasonable," he explained.

"Wotcha want with me?" a voice called from the rocks.

"Wantta have a pow-wow with you. Maybe you 'n' me can do business together. No can tell."

"Who are you?"

"Name's Jake Prowers. No friend of Clint Reed if that's what's eatin' you?"

After a delay of several seconds, a figure appeared and moved closer. The ranchman saw in the man's hand the gleam of an automatic revolver.

The fugitive stopped a few yards from Prowers and eyed him suspiciously. "Wotcha want to chew the rag about?" he asked.

Jake sat down on a rock with an air so casually careless that a tenderfoot might not have guessed that he was ready for instant action if need be.

"Fellow, sit down," he said. "We got all day before us. I don't reckon you got any engagements you have to keep immediate—not since you had that one at the Diamond Bar K ranch last night."

"I don't getcha."

"Sure you do. No use throwin' a sandy with me. I tell you, fellow, I'm playin' my own hand. Me, I don't like Reed any more'n you do. So, entrey noo, as the frog-eaters say, we'll take it for granted you were the uninvited guest at Reed's ranch a few hours since. Yore work was n't first-class, if you ask old Jake Prowers. You did n't burn but a small part of the wheat and you did n't get Clint anyways adequate."

"Meaning he was n't croaked?" Cig demanded out of the corner of his mouth.

"I'll say he wasn't by jiminy by jinks. But I don't know as that'll help you any when his boys catch you."

"They ain't gonna catch me," the New York crook boasted, his brain seething with suspicion of the dried-up little man in front of him.

Jake Prowers weighed this, a skeptical smile on his thin lips. "Interesting, but unreliable," he decided aloud, in regard to the other's prediction. "How do you aim to prevent it? The sheriff has got you cut off from the railroad. Food don't grow on bushes in these hills. You're done, unless—"

"You gotta 'nother guess coming," the thug retorted. "Forget that stuff. I ain't no hobo. Come to a show-down these country boobs 'll find me right there with a gun. I'm a good man to lay off."

The Westerner laughed, softly and derisively. "Fellow, you talk plumb foolish. This ain't New York. It's Colorado. That popgun of yours ain't worth a billy be damn. Why, I could pick you off right now an' never take a chance. Or my man could do it from the ledge up there. But say, for the sake of argument, we let you go. Say you ain't found by any posse or cowpuncher. What's the end of the trail you're following? It don't lead anywhere but round an' round in a circle. You got nothing to eat and no place to go for food. Maybe you can stick it out a week. Then you're done."

"I might get to a town and jump a freight."

"Not a chance. In a country like this news spreads in all directions. There ain't a man within fifty miles but has his eyes peeled for you. No, sir, you're in Dutch."

Cig felt his helplessness, in spite of the bluff he was putting up. This land of wide spaces, of a thousand hills and valleys, shook his confidence. In New York he would have known what to do, but here he was a child. The shrunken little man finished in brown leather was giving him straight facts and he knew it.

"Nothing to that. Say, old Jonah, do I look like I had a yellow streak?" the New York tough demanded.

"All right. Suits me if it does you." Jake rose and waved a hand airily into space. "Drift right along, my friend. I'll not keep you—not for a minute. But when you come to the end of yore trail, you'll remember that you had one good bet you would n't back because you're one of these wise guys that know it all."

The fugitive listened with sullen resentment. He did not want to trust this old man. His instinct told him that, if he did so, Prowers would be for the time at least his master. But he was driven by circumstances which gave him no choice.

"I ain't said I would n't listen to you, have I?" he growled.

Prowers sat down again on the rock. "If I help you, we've got to come to an understanding right now. It'll be a business deal. I hide you an' feed you. Some day I'll need you. When I do, you'll take orders like a lamb. If that ain't agreeable to you, why, all you got to do is start on yore travels now."

"Need me what for?" demanded Cig.

Into the mild, skim-milk eyes of the cattleman there flashed for an instant an expression of cold cruelty scarcely human.

As Prowers's thin lip smile met Cig, the tramp still felt the shock of that ruthless ferocity.

"How the jumpin' Jehosaphat do I know?" the old man said suavely, almost in a murmur. "For murder, massacre, or mayhem. Not yore business, my friend. All you've got to do is jump when I say so. Understand?"

Cig felt a cold sinking of the heart. He belonged to the dregs of humanity, but he knew that this mild old man was his master in villainy. It was as though he were smoking a cigarette with a keg of gunpowder scattered all around him. Jake Prowers was a center of danger almost Olympic in possibilities.

"I dunno about that," the crook snarled.

Again the wrinkled hand of the ranchman lifted in a gesture that included all space. "The world's before you," he said ironically. "The peace of the hills go with you while you hunt for a nice lonesome gulch as a coffin."

"What do I get out of it if we do business? Or do youse figure on workin' me for a sucker?"

Jake had won, and he knew it. "Now you're talkin' sense, my friend. You'll find me no tightwad. I pay for what I get, and I pay big." An ominous flash of warning was in his eyes as he leaned forward and spoke slowly and softly. "But if you throw me down—if there's a finger crook about you that ain't on the level with me—better say yore prayers backward and forward. No man ever double-crossed Jake Prowers an' got away with it. It ain't being done in this neck of the woods."

Hardy villain though he was, Cig felt a shiver go down his spine. He was superstitious, as all criminals are. He had the feeling that some one was walking on his grave, that this wrinkled old devil had been appointed by fate to put a period to his evil ways and days.

He shook off the wave of foreboding and slouched forward, slipping the automatic into his coat pocket. "I'll play square, boss, if you do. See me through an' I'll go the limit for you. It's a bargain."

Jake shook hands on it.

"Done, by jiminy by jinks," he said in his high weak voice.

Cig was puzzled and a little annoyed. How had he ever been fooled into thinking that this inoffensive little specimen was dangerous? It was written on him that he would not hurt a fly.

CHAPTER XV

THE HOMESTEADER SERVES NOTICE

In later years the man who had called himself Tug Jones looked back on the days and nights that followed as a period of unmitigated dejection and horror. The craving for the drug was with him continually. If he had had a supply on hand, he would have yielded a hundred times to the temptation to use it. But he had burned the bridges behind him. There was no way to get the stuff without going in person to a town of some size.

This meant not only a definite surrender of the will, but a promise of relief that could not be fulfilled inside of twenty-four hours at the earliest. Just now this stretch of time was a period of torment as endless as a year.

Somehow he stuck it out, though he spent much of his time in an inferno of feverish desire. He tried to kill the appetite with work. Merrick, moving to and fro with a keen eye on the men, observed that the foreman was sloughing his work and letting it fall on Jones. At the end of the week, Merrick discharged him and raised the former tramp to his place as foreman. Jones accepted the promotion without thanks. He knew he had earned it, but he did not care whether he received it or not.

He grew worn and haggard. Dark shadows emphasized the hollows of the tortured eyes. So irritable was his temper that at a word it flashed to explosion. By disposition he was not one to pass on to subordinates the acerbity that was a residue of the storm that was shaking him. A sense of justice had always been strong in him. Fifty times a day he clamped his teeth to keep back the biting phrase. In general he succeeded, but malingerers found him a hard taskmaster.

They appealed to Merrick and got small comfort from him. The new cement foreman was getting the work done both rapidly and well. That was all the chief engineer asked of him. The details could be arranged by Jones as he pleased.

The nights were the worst. During the day he had the work to occupy his mind, but when darkness fell over the hills its shadows crept over his soul. He could not sleep. Sometimes he borrowed technical books from Merrick and tried to bury himself in study. More often he tramped till physical exhaustion drove him back to his cot to stare up sleeplessly at the canvas roof of his tent.

Suffering wears itself out at last. There came a time when the edge of the craving grew less keen, when its attack was less frequent. In the pure, untempered air of the hills the cement gang foreman came to sounder health. His appetite increased with his physical stamina. One day it struck him with a little shock of surprise that he had not had one of his racking headaches for two weeks. He began to sleep better, though there were still nights when he had to tramp the hills in self-defense.

Inevitably during those days the foreman found himself studying the project upon which Merrick had staked his reputation. As an engineer he took off his hat to the efficiency with which his chief got results. Merrick was a driver, but he was more than that. He had the fighting spirit that lifts from defeat to victory. Good engineers had said it was not feasible to water the Flat Tops by means of ditches carrying water from the drainage area above. Justin Merrick had not accepted their verdict. He had made his own surveys and meant to demonstrate that they were wrong.

He knew that a certain group of cattlemen, under the leadership of old Jake Prowers, were watching him sullenly. They believed, from the surveys made by Government engineers, that the grade made it impossible to bring water from the dam through Elk Creek Cañon to the mesa below. Yet Merrick knew, too, that they were uneasy. It was on the cards that the Reclamation Service experts might be wrong in their surveys. If Prowers discovered that they were, Justin felt sure he would move to ruthless and dynamic action.

The big dam was practically finished. Merrick kept a night guard over it and the tools. Sometimes, after supper, he strolled down to look it over and think out under the quiet stars the problems of supplies or canal construction. It was on such a night visit that he came face to face with the new concrete work foreman.

The superintendent of construction had been watching Tug

Jones. He had found out that the man was one who would accept responsibility and could be trusted to get efficient results without supervision. Twice he had taken him from the work he had in charge and given him engineering difficulties to solve. Each time the man from Massachusetts Tech had eliminated the tangle in the clearest and simplest way.

Merrick was not given to asking advice of his subordinates, no matter how capable they might be. Tonight he simply made an announcement of a detail in his plans that involved the foreman.

"About time we began work on Elk Creek Cañon, Jones," he said. "I'm going to put you in charge and run the ditch line through right away. We may have trouble there. That fellow Prowers had one of his men, a rider named Don Black, file a homestead claim right in the cañon. It won't stick. He knows that, but he wants some ground to fight us. Look out for him."

"Yes," agreed the foreman.

The habit of mind of the Massachusetts Tech man was to be thorough. He studied the surveys very closely and went over the ground carefully from the dam site to the cañon entrance. The conclusion was forced upon him that Merrick had made a mistake. The grade through the hills to Elk Creek Cañon would not do. He could put his finger on the very spot that made it impossible.

It was hard for him to believe that Merrick had made a blunder so vital to the success of the enterprise. He checked up his figures a second time and made a re-survey of that part of the line. There was no possible doubt about it. Since water will not run uphill by gravity, it could not flow from the dam to the upper entrance of the cañon.

He reported to his chief what he had discovered.

Merrick took this facer with no least hint of dismay. So far as his strong, square-cut visage gave any expression, it was one of impatience.

"Suppose you leave that to me, Jones," he said curtly. "I know what I'm doing. What I'm asking of you is to determine the best path for the ditch along the side of the cañon. That's all."

"But if you can't get the water to the cañon—"

"That's my business. You 're not responsible for that."

There remained nothing more to be said. Jones carried away with him the knowledge that his chief had flatly declined to

74

give weight to his findings. He could either resign or he could do as he was told.

The younger man was puzzled. Was it possible that Merrick, after all, was a pig-headed four-flusher? That he could be a pretentious incompetent fed up with a sense of infallibility?

To see him on the work was a refutal of this view. He was an egoist through and through. To look at the salient jaw, into the cool, flinty eyes, was to recognize the man's self-sufficiency. He was dominant and masterful. But it was hard to believe that his shrewd, direct, untiring energy masked any incapacity. He did not seem to have the quality of mind that is content to fool itself.

Tug knew that his chief had a much wider experience in engineering than he. This project must have been studied by him from every angle, all difficulties considered, all technical problems solved. Yet the fact stood in the way like a Rock of Gibraltar that water flows downhill and not up.

He shrugged his shoulders and stepped out from under. Merrick had told him with cool finality that it was none of his business. That was true. He had done his full duty when he reported the matter to the chief. He turned his attention to running the ditch line through the gorge.

To save time he moved his outfit to Elk Creek. A chuck wagon, mule teams, scrapers, and necessary supplies followed the little group of surveyors. Within a week the sound of blasting echoed from wall to wall of the ravine.

Two men rode up the defile to the engineer's camp one sunny morning. Jones, in flannel shirt, corduroys, and high laced boots, directed operations as the workmen set out on the day's work.

One of the visitors to the camp was a long, black-bearded, fierce-eyed man in blue overalls. The other was a mild little fellow in years well past middle age.

The dark man introduced himself rudely. "What the blue blazes you doing here? This is my homestead. You trying to jump my claim?"

The engineer met this brusque attack suavely. During the past weeks, as he had slowly fought his way back toward self-respect, the defiance and the bitter irony had disappeared from his manner. He was recovering the poise that characterizes the really able man of affairs when he is subjected to annoyance and worry.

"You are Mr. Donald Black?" he asked.

"I'm him. An' I'm here to say that no man—I don't care if he is backed by a big corporation—can jump my property an' get away with it."

"I don't think we have any intention of prejudicing your rights, Mr. Black," the engineer answered. "Of course, I'm only an employee. Mr. Merrick is the man you ought to see. You'll find him up at the dam."

"I'm servin' notice on you right here an' now to get off my land. I'm givin' you till night to get yore whole outfit outa here. I ain't a going to see anybody. Understand? You've got me in one word short an' sweet—git."

The dried-up little man beside Black let out a cracked cackle of laughter. "Seems like that should ought to be plain enough," he murmured.

Tug looked at the wrinkled cattleman. He guessed that this was Jake Prowers, of whose sinister reputation rumors had reached him. But it was to Black he spoke.

"Don't you think, perhaps, you had better see a lawyer? There's always a legal way to straighten out difficulties that—"

"Lawyer!" exploded Black with an oath. "Listen, fellow! I don't aim for to see no lawyer. You'd like fine to tie this up in the courts while you went right on building yore end gates an' runnin' yore ditches on my land. No, sir. Cattle was here first, an' we don't aim to let you chase us off. See?"

"I expect the law will have to decide that, Mr. Black. But that's merely an opinion of mine. I'm here to run a ditch through this cañon—an employee hired at so much a week. Unless I get orders to stop work, the ditch will be dug." Jones spoke evenly, without raising his voice, but there was a ring of finality in his tone.

"You crow damn loud," Black retorted angrily. "Think I don' know who you are—a good-for-nothin' tramp liable to go to the pen for burnin' up wheat an' bush-whackin' Clint Reed? You're all swelled up, ain't you? Forget it, fellow. I'm givin' you orders to clear out. If you don't, some of you're liable to be sorry. This here is a man's country."

Tug looked straight at the rawboned, dark man. "Meaning?" he asked pointedly.

Prowers answered. He knew that enough had been said. More would be surplusage and might carry the danger of a come-back in case men should be killed.

"You'd be sorry to beat a pore man outa his claim, would n't

76

you?" he said, tee-heeing with virulent laughter. "Come on, Don. Might as well be pushin' on our reins."

Over his shoulder the homesteader flung a last word that might be taken as a threat, a warning, or a prophecy. "Till tonight, Mr. Hobo."

CHAPTER XVI

THE STAMPEDE

JONES sent a messenger to his chief with word of Don Black's threat, and Merrick at once rode to Elk Creek to consult with the man he had put in charge.

"Do they mean to attack you? Is that what you gathered from what he said?" asked the chief engineer of his assistant.

"Don't know. Prowers smoothed over what Black said. I judge he did n't want to go on record as having made any threats. But the last thing the big fellow yelled at me was that we had till to-night to get out."

"Good of him to give you warning. What do you suggest, Jones?"

"Give me half a dozen rifles and I'll hold the fort," the younger man replied, eyes gleaming. "Double the gang and let me rush the work."

Merrick shook his head. "No, this is n't a little private war we're having. Think I'll just let you sit tight and see what happens. Prowers is n't likely to go far to start with."

"Suits me, but don't blame me if they drive us out. I'm rather looking for a bunch of armed cowboys to descend upon us."

"In which case you'll enter a formal protest and retire in good order without resistance. The law's with us. I filed our maps and plans with the Land Office before Black homesteaded. He obviously took up this quarter section only to hamper us."

"Will it delay you much?"

Justin Merrick smiled, a rather peculiar smile that suggested

77

a knowledge of facts not on the surface. "I don't think so, but there's no reason why Prowers should n't."

"Rather tame surrender, would n't it be? If you're within your rights, why not stand our ground and fight them off?"

"For the moral effect, you mean?"

"Yes. Is n't it a sign of weakness for us to hoist the white flag after the first brush?"

"That's a point of view. We're playing for position. Let Prowers break the law and get in wrong. If we're armed and looking for trouble, we don't come into court with clean hands ourselves. I'd rather let him show his plan of campaign. Even though we should be driven out, we can come back whenever we want to. He can't keep his men here and hold the gulch."

"No. At least he won't."

The man who had fought in Flanders was not satisfied. The irrigation company was in the right. Prowers and the group of men with him were obstructionists, trying to hold back the progress of the country for their own selfish ends. They were outside the law, though they were using it as a cover. The policy to be expected of Merrick would have been bolder, less opportunistic. Why had the chief marched his men up the hill, like the King of France in the rhyme, only to march them down again? This did not seem to go well with his salient, fighting jaw.

Since it was his business to obey orders and not to ask for reasons, Tug said no more. He understood that Merrick was holding back something from him, and he had no desire whatever to force a confidence.

Merrick rode back to the dam and left his subordinate in charge of the camp. Throughout the day work went on uninterrupted. At dusk the surveyors and ditch-diggers returned to the draw where the tents had been set. At this point of the gorge the wall fell back and a slope led to the rim above.

At the summit of this rise the engineer posted a sentry with orders to fire a revolver in case of an attack. Two other guards were set, one at each mouth of the cañon. At the expiration of four hours, these were relieved by relays. At midnight, and again in the chill pre-dawn hours, Jones himself made a round of the posts to see that all was well.

He had scarcely lain down after the second tour when the crack of a revolver sounded. Tug leaped to his feet and was drawing on a boot before the echoes had died away.

As he ducked out from the tent flap, revolver in hand, a

78

glance showed him scantily clad men spilling from their sleeping quarters.

"What is it? Where are they?" some one yelled.

A light breeze was stirring. On it was borne a faint rumble as of thunder. It persisted—seemed to be rolling nearer. The sound deepened to a steady roar. Tug's startled glance swept the cañon sword cleft. Could there have been a cloudburst in the hills? The creek bed was still dry. His eyes swung round to the saddle ridge of the draw above him.

A living tidal wave was pouring across the rim and down the draw. Hundreds of backs tossed up and down like the swell of a troubled sea. Though he had never seen one before, the engineer knew that the camp was in the path of a cattle stampede.

He shouted a warning and raced for the higher ground at the edge of the draw. The men scattered to escape from the path of that charging avalanche. They were in a panic of fear. If any were caught beneath the impact of those scores of galloping hoofs, they would be crushed to death instantly. Startled oaths and staccato shouts rang out. An anguished yell of terror lifted itself shrilly. A running man had stumbled and gone down.

The thud of the hoofs died away. The stampede had swept down into the dry bed of the stream and swung to the right. It left behind it a devastated camp. Tents had been torn down and ripped to pieces. Cots were smashed to kindling. From the overturned chuck wagon scattered food lay trampled into the ground by sharp feet. The surveying instruments were broken beyond repair.

A huddled mass lay motionless in the track of the avalanche. Tug knelt beside it and looked into the battered outline of what a few moments earlier had been a man's face quick with life. No second glance was necessary to see that the spirit had passed out of the crushed body. The engineer recognized him by the clothes. His name was Coyle. He had been a harmless old fellow of many quips and jests, one full of the milk of human kindness. He, too, had fought against his weakness, a fondness for liquor that had all his life kept him down. Now, in a moment, his smiles and his battles were both ended.

Jones straightened the twisted body and the sprawling limbs before he covered the face with a handkerchief. He rose and looked grimly round at the group of appalled men whose blanched faces made a gray semicircle in the faint light of coming dawn. They were a rough-and-ready lot. Most of them had seen the lives of fellow workmen snuffed out suddenly. But this had come like a bolt from heaven. Each of them knew that it might have been he lying there; that if the boss had not set a watch, the stampede would have destroyed many of them. The shock of it still chilled the heart.

"They've murdered poor Coyle," the engineer said, and his voice was a solemn accusation.

"How's that?" asked one, startled.

"These cattle did n't gather up there by themselves. They were rounded up and stampeded over the crest."

"Jake Prowers!" exclaimed a mule-skinner.

"We'll name no names yet, boys, not till we've put it up to Mr. Merrick." The camp boss glanced up the hill. The sound of some one running had reached his ears. "Here comes Jensen. We'll hear what he has to say."

Jensen confirmed the charge of the engineer. He had heard voices, shots, the crack of whips, and then the thundering rush of cattle. He had fired once and fled for the safety of the rocks. The stampede had stormed past and down the slope. But he had seen and heard no more of the men who had been exciting the wild hill cattle to a panic of terror. They had disappeared in the darkness.

The engineer made arrangements for carrying the body of Coyle to the dam and sent a messenger to notify Merrick of what had taken place. This done, he climbed to the saddle of the draw with the intention of investigating the lay of the land where the stampede had started. He knew that, if he were only expert enough to read it, the testimony written there would convict those who had done this crime.

At work of this sort he was a child. He was from the East, and he knew nothing of reading sign. Stamped in mud, with outlines clear-cut and sharp, he would have known, of course, a pony's tracks from those of a steer. But unfortunately the marks imprinted on the short brittle grass were faint and fragmentary. They told no story to Jones.

He quartered over the ground carefully, giving his whole mind to the open page which Nature had spread before him and covered with her handwriting. Concentration was not enough. It was written in a language of which he had not learned the vocabulary. Reluctantly he gave up the attempt. Sheriff Daniels was a Westerner, an old cattleman, skilled at cutting sign. This was a problem for him to solve if he could.

It was afternoon when the sheriff arrived. He had made one discovery before reaching the camp. A cow had broken a leg in the stampede and lay helpless in the bed of Elk Creek. The brand on it was the Diamond Bar K.

"Fine business," he commented dryly. "Clint's enemies try to bust up the irrigation proposition he's interested in by stampedin' his own cattle down the draw here. Maybe we can find out the *hombres* that rounded up a bunch of his stock yesterday. That'd help some."

If the sheriff discovered anything from his examination of the lane over which the stampede had swept, he did not confide in either Jones or Merrick. Like many men who have lived much in the open, he had a capacity for reticence. He made his observations unhurriedly and rode away without returning to the camp.

Merrick gave his assistant orders to break camp and return to the dam. A force was still to continue at work in the cañon, but the men would be taken up and brought back each day.

CHAPTER XVII

HIS PICTURE IN THE PAPER

SUMMER had burned to autumn. The first frosts had crisped the foliage of the quaking asps and the cottonwoods to a golden glory in tune with the halcyon Indian summer. Faint threats of coming winter could be read in an atmosphere grown more pale and sharp, in coloring less rich and warm.

Betty could count the time in months now since she had sent her salvaged tramp into the hills to help her lover wrestle with the problems of the Sweetwater Dam project. It was still a joy to her that she had been intuitively right about him. He was making good. He had brains and ability and the power of initiative which marks the strong man from the subordinate. Justin admitted this generously, giving her credit for a keener insight than his own.

But that was not the best of it. She knew now, through Merrick, what the vice was that had dragged him down: and from the same source she learned that he had so far fought his campaign out to victory. Not since the day after her father had been shot had she seen the young man, but she wished she could send him a message of good cheer and faith.

She thought of him a good deal. She was thinking of him this morning as she cleaned the pantry shelves and substituted new papers for the old. Justin had been down the evening before and had told her of the threat Prowers had made through Don Black in case the young engineer did not evacuate the cañon. It was in her character to look for good rather than ill in men, but she had a conviction that the cackling little cattleman was a sink of iniquity. He would do evil without ruth. There was, she felt, something demoniac, unhuman about him.

How far would he go to begin with? She did not know, but she was glad Justin had given orders to retire from Elk Creek in case of attack. His reasons she appreciated and approved. He was no hothead, but a cool, hard-hitting, determined fighter. In the end he would win, no matter what difficulties were thrown in his way. She could not think of Justin in any way except as a success. He was the kind of man who succeeds in whatever he undertakes.

The telephone rang. Her father, at Wild Horse, was on the line.

"There's been trouble at the cañon," he explained. "I've been talkin' with Daniels. Merrick has sent for him. A man was killed—some one working on the job. Have n't heard any particulars yet. I'll let you know if I do."

"Killed—on purpose, you mean?"

"Yes."

"You did n't hear who?"

"Daniels does n't know."

Betty returned to her work very much disturbed in mind. There was no reason for assuming that the man who had been killed was her redeemed vagrant, but she could not get this possibility out of her mind. He would be in the forefront of danger if there was any. She knew him well enough for that.

She tried to get Merrick on the telephone, but the word that came down to her from the dam was that he had ridden to Elk Creek. Did the assistant superintendent know when he would be back? No, he did not.

Tremulously Betty asked another question. "Have you heard, Mr. Atchison, who the man is that was killed?"

"His name's Coyle—a man sent out to us by an employment agency in Denver."

Betty leaned against the wall a moment after she had hung up the receiver. She was greatly relieved, and in the reaction from the strain under which she had been holding herself tautly felt oddly weak.

"Don't be a goose!" she told herself with stinging candor. "What does it matter to you who it was?"

But she knew it mattered a great deal. Nobody had ever stimulated her imagination as this tramp had. Her liking for Justin was of quite another sort. It had not in it the quality that set pulses pounding. She would have denied to herself indignantly that she did not love him. If not, why was she engaged to him? But her affection was a well-ordered and not a disturbing force. This was as it should be, according to her young philosophy. She gave herself with energy and enthusiasm to the many activities of life. The time had not yet come when love was for her a racing current sweeping to its goal so powerfully that there could be no dalliance by the way.

Betty moved the dishes from the last shelf. As she started to gather the soiled newspaper folded across the plank, her glance fell upon the picture of a soldier in uniform. The eyes that looked into hers were those of the man who had called himself Tug Jones.

Her breath caught as she read. The caption beneath the photograph was, "Captain Thurston K. Hollister, awarded the Distinguished Service Cross for Gallantry in France." The story below mentioned the fact that the man who had been given this recognition had disappeared and could not be found.

The girl's blood sang. She had known from that first day he was of good blood, but she had not been sure that his record was worthy of him. He had not only fought in France; he had covered himself with glory. It was almost too good to be true.

She was on the porch to meet her father before he had swung down from the saddle. He told her details of the affair at Elk Creek as far as he had heard them.

Betty had cut the Hollister story out of the paper. She handed it to her father, all but the picture folded under.

"Who is this, Daddy?"

Reed glanced at it and answered promptly. "Looks like that young fellow Jones."

Triumphantly she nodded. "That's who it is. Read what it says about him."

The cattleman read. "Hmp!" he grunted. "An' I called him a slacker."

"It does n't matter now what you called him, Dad. But I'm awf'ly glad he was n't one."

"Some li'l' stunt that—breakin' up a German machine-gun nest and sittin' tight for two days under fire till the boys reached him." Clint smiled sardonically, the memory of the tongue-lashing he had given this man still vividly with him. "I reckon I can be more kinds of a durn fool in an hour than 'most anybody you know, Bess."

"I'm so glad he's making good with Justin. I just knew he was a splendid fellow."

"I'm so dawg-goned hot-headed. Can't wait an' give myself time to cool off," he grumbled.

"He told Justin about it. The doctors gave him a lot of morphine or something when he was wounded and he got in the habit of using it to relieve the pain. Before he knew it he could n't stop."

"You'd think I'd learn a lick or two of sense, an' me 'most fifty."

"He has n't touched the stuff since he went up to the dam. Justin says it must have been horrible for him. Some nights he kept walking till morning."

"What else was it I called him besides a slacker—after I'd beat him up till he could n't stand, an' him a sick man at that?"

Betty laughed at the way each of them, absorbed in a personal point of view, was carrying on a one-sided conversation.

"Are you going up to Elk Creek to-day, Dad? If you are, I wish you'd let me go along."

"I was thinkin' about it. Like to go, would you? All right. We might drive and take Ruthie."

"That'd be fine. Let's go."

Betty flew into the house to get ready.

CHAPTER XVIII

A HOT TRAIL

SHERIFF DANIELS rode across the hogback above Elk Creek to a small ranch recently taken up by a homesteader, much to the annoyance of Jake Prowers. He found the man in a shed that served temporarily as a barn.

Here a cow was proudly licking a very wobbly calf.

" 'Lo, Sheriff. How're things comin' with you? Fine an' dandy?"

"No complaint, Howard. Had an increase in yore herd, looks like."

"Yessir, though it did n't look much thataway 'bout three o'clock this mo'ning a.m."

"Come near losing her?"

"Bet I did. Both of 'em. But you never can tell, as the old sayin' is. I stayed with it, an' everything's all right now."

"I come across the hogback to have a chin with Black. Know whether he's home?" the officer asked.

"No, sir, I don't. He passed down the road whilst I was up with old bossie here right early."

The sheriff complimented his humor by repeating it. "At three o'clock this mo'ning a.m.?"

"Yessir. I figured he must be going somewheres to be settin' off at that time o' day."

"Alone, was he?"

"Why, no, I reckon there was some one with him."

Daniels threw a leg across a feed-rack, drew out a knife from his pocket, and began to sharpen it on the leather of his boot. "Dark as all git out, was n't it? How'd you know it was Don?"

The homesteader grinned. "Every daisy in the dell knows his story too darned well," he parodied.

"Singin' 'Sweet Marie,' was he?"

85

"Yep. Say, what kind of a mash would you feed her? She's right feverish yet, I should n't wonder."

The sheriff gave advice out of his experience before he came back ten minutes later to a subject that interested him more.

"Don was out rounding-up cattle yesterday, was n't he? Seems some one told me so."

"Likely enough. He was away from the shack all day. Was n't home by dark. I seen a light up there somewheres about nine-thirty."

The officer rode up to the cabin Black was using. The door was hospitably unlatched, but nobody was at home. Daniels walked in and looked aound. It was both dirty and untidy, but it told no tales of what its occupant had been doing in the past twenty-four hours.

Daniels remounted, skirted the edge of the Government reserve, and descended a draw which led into a small gorge almost concealed by a grove of young quaking asps. This received its name from box elders growing up the sides. If Black and his friends had rounded-up a bunch of cattle during the day, and wanted to keep them unobserved until they could be stampeded into Elk Creek Cañon, there was no handier spot to hold them than in this little gulch. The sheriff had ridden these hills too many years as a cattleman not to know the country like a familiar book. In his youth, while riding as a puncher for Prowers, he and a companion had been caught in a blizzard and reached Box Elder Cañon in time to save themselves by building a fire. Since then he had been here many times.

A one-room log cabin clung to the slope at the edge of the quaking asps. It had been built by a hermit prospector thirty years before, and had many times in the intervening years been the refuge of belated punchers.

The officer walked in through the sagging door. On the floor was a roll of soiled blankets. Greasy dishes and remnants of food were on the home-made table. Three persons had eaten here as late as this morning. He could tell that by the live coals among the charred ends of wood in the fireplace. Also, the lard left in the frying-pan had not yet hardened.

Daniels made deductions. Of the three, one had spent the night here to keep an eye on the cattle, assuming that his guess about the herd was a correct one. The other two had ridden up to Black's cabin and slept there, returning in the early morning for the drive to Elk Creek.

From the cabin the sheriff walked down into the bottom of

the gulch. There was plenty of evidence to show that a large number of cattle had been here very recently. He followed the trail they made out of the cañon to the mesa and saw that it headed toward Elk Creek. He could not be quite sure, but he believed that three horsemen rode after them. The character of the ground made certainty impossible. The tracks were all faint and blurred. Daniels followed them for two or three miles to the rim of the draw down which the frightened herd had been stampeded.

The sheriff rode across the hills to the Circle J P ranch. He found Jake Prowers and Don Black greasing a wagon.

Black looked up as the officer came around the corner of the house and thrust his hand beneath the belt of his trousers. Prowers said something to him in a low voice and the hand came out empty.

Daniels rode up and looked down at them. He gave a little nod of greeting.

"How do, Jake—Don? I dropped over to talk with you about that business in Elk Creek Cañon," he said.

"What about it?" asked Black suspiciously.

"I'd like to hear all you know about it."

Prowers answered promptly and smoothly. "I don't know a thing about it, if you're meanin' me, except what I've heard over the 'phone. The story is, some cattle stampeded an' a fellow got in their way—"

"Yes, I know the story, Jake," the sheriff interrupted quietly. "I'm askin' you what you can tell me about that stampede."

"Me! Why pick on me?" the wrinkled little man piped. "Did n't I tell you I did n't know a thing about it?"

"How about you, Don?" asked Daniels.

"Don don' know a thing—"

"Talk for himself, can't he, Jake?" the sheriff wanted to know.

"Don't get on the prod, Frank," advised the owner of the Circle J P. Voice and manner were still mild and harmless.

"No," agreed Daniels, smiling. "How about it, Don?"

Black met his steady gaze sulkily. "Did n't know there was a stampede till Jake told me so after he'd been at the 'phone."

"I expect you'll have a chance to prove that, Don. I got to arrest you."

"What for?" demanded the dark man.

"For causing the death of that fellow in the cañon this mo'ning by stampeding cattle down the draw."

"Any evidence, Frank?" This from Prowers, on whose face a thin lip smile rested.

"Some. Don made threats yesterday. He spent the day rounding-up cattle and drove 'em into Box Elder Cañon for the night. About nine in the evening he reached home an' ate supper there, him and another fellow. They took the road back to the cañon before daybreak this mo'ning—not later than three o'clock. A friend of theirs stayed in the old Thorwaldson cabin to watch the stock. They ate breakfast with him."

A flicker of fire burned in the skim-milk eyes. "My, Frank, you know a lot. Anything more?"

"Some things I don't know, I only guess, Jake. I know Don an' his friends had ham and cornbread and coffee for breakfast, but I don't know yet who his two friends are."

"Only guess that, eh?"

"That's right, Jake."

"You'll know that soon," jeered Prowers. "Any one with an imagination active as yore's won't let a li'l' thing like facts stand in his way."

"I'll have to take Don down to Wild Horse with me," Daniels replied impassively.

"That's yore business," the old cattleman said. "You're makin' a mistake. Don spent the night with me, if you want to know."

"Sure you did n't spend it with him?"

"You arrestin' me, too, Frank?"

"No."

"Only guessin' at me?"

"I'm not doing my guessin' out loud—not all of it."

Prowers's splenetic laugh cackled. "You'd ought to get one o' these brass stars from a detective agency, by jiminy by jinks. A fellow that can mind-read Don here an' tell what he had for breakfast is a sure-enough sleuth and no ornery sheriff."

The old cattleman's irony did not disturb Daniels. "I know what he had for breakfast because I saw the fry-pan an' the dishes."

"Better go slap a saddle on yore horse, Don," jeered Prowers. "Frank's arrestin' you because you had ham an' cornbread an' coffee for breakfast."

"You know why I'm arrestin' him. He'll have plenty of chances to show he's not guilty if he ain't," the sheriff answered, not unamiably.

The owner of the Circle J P spoke to Black. "Saddle old

Baldy for me. I'll ride down to Wild Horse with you. Reckon I'll have to go on yore bond. No use us gettin' annoyed. Election ain't so fur away now. Frank has got to make a showing. We had n't ought to grudge him some grandstandin'."

Daniels smiled. "That's the way to look at it, Jake."

CHAPTER XIX

CAPTAIN THURSTON K. HOLLISTER

RUTH squealed with delight and clapped her hands when Betty told her of the approaching drive to Elk Creek.

"Oh, goody, goody! An' we'll take Prince 'n' Baby Fifi 'n' Rover. They'll enjoy the ride too."

With a smile that took the sting out of her refusal, Betty vetoed this wholesale transportation of puppies. "There is n't room, dear."

The child's face registered disappointment. "I could take 'em on my lap," she proposed.

Betty reflected a moment, then decided briskly. "We'll take one to-day, and the others next time."

"Umpha!" Ruth nodded approbation vigorously, all animation again. "I'll 'splain it to 'em so's they won't have their feelin's hurted."

The blue eyes of the little girl inspected judicially the small creatures whose tilted heads and wagging tails appealed to her. To decide which one to take was a matter of grave consideration. Their mistress wanted to do exact justice. She changed her mind several times, but voted at last for Baby Fifi.

"She's the teentiest, 'n' o' course the baby must go," she told the other two.

They accepted without protest the verdict of the super-goddess who was mistress of their destinies. Apparently they took the occasion as seriously as she did.

" 'N' the delicatest," she went on. "But if you're good, 'n' bee-have, 'n' everyfing, Mamma'll bring you somefing awful nice. So you be the goodest children."

Thus it chanced that Baby Fifi, a clean blue ribbon tied round her neck in honor of the event, looked out from the tonneau of the car upon a panorama of blue sky and bluer mountain and sunbathed foothill moving past in a glory of splendor satisfying to both eye and soul.

They drove to the lower mouth of the cañon. A man with pick and shovel was clearing rocks and débris away from what was evidently to be the line of the ditch. Reed guessed that he was really posted at this point as a sentinel to guard against another possible attack.

The boss of the gang, the man said, was doing some surveying from the top of the wall above the rim of the gorge. A steep and rough road led to the upper mesa.

"Don't know as you can make it with your car," the man with the pick added. "It's a mighty stiff grade when you get past the dugway, 'most all a team can do to get up."

"We'll go far as we can," Reed answered.

He had to go into low long before they reached the dugway. Just beyond it was a stretch of road so precipitous that the car balked. The cowman became convinced that the machine could go no farther.

"Have to walk the rest of the way," he said.

Betty looked at her little sister dubiously. "It'll be a hard climb for those little legs, and she's too heavy to carry far. We'd better leave her in the car."

"Maybe we had," assented her father, and added, in a low voice: "If she'll stay alone."

"Oh, Ruthie does n't mind that. Do you, dearest, a big girl like you? You'll have Baby Fifi, and we'll not be gone half an hour."

Ruth accepted her sister's judgment without demur. She would rather play with Baby Fifi than tire herself climbing the long hill.

"Stay right in the car, dear. Daddy and Betty won't be long," the young woman said, waving a hand as she started.

Betty breasted the slope with the light, free step of a mountaineer. Though slender, she was far from frail. Tested muscles moved with perfect coördination beneath the smooth satiny skin.

At sight of her an eye leveled behind a surveyor's transit became instantly alive. The man caught his breath and watched eagerly. In her grace was something fawnlike, a suggestion of sylvan innocence and naïveté. Was it the quality of which this was an expression that distinguished her from a score of other nice girls he knew? Did she still retain from the childhood of the race a primal simplicity the others had lost by reason of their environment? What was it Wordsworth had written?—

". . . trailing clouds of glory do we come
From God, who is our home."

The glory still haloed her dusky head. It glowed in her warm eyes and sparkled in her smile.

He strode through the kinnikinnick to meet them.

As they approached, Betty was conscious of a sharp stab of joy. This clean-cut, light-footed man was not the shuffling, slouchy tramp she had first met two months earlier. The skin had taken on the bronzed hue of health. The eyes were no longer dull and heavy, but quick with life. The unpleasant, bitter expression had gone from the good-looking face.

Betty knew what had transformed him. He had found again the self-reliance of which he had been robbed. There burned in him once more a bright light of manhood strong and unwavering.

He shook hands with Clint Reed so frankly that she knew he cherished no grudge. There flashed into her mind the hesitant prophecy she had once made, that he might look back on that first day on the Diamond Bar K as a red-letter one. It had come true. Then he had reached the turning of the ways and had been led into the long hard uphill climb toward self-respect.

"Glad to see you," he said as his fingers met firmly those of the girl. "You've come to see how Mr. Merrick is getting along with the project, I suppose."

"We heard about the trouble here and came to find out the facts first-hand," Reed answered.

The engineer told what he knew. One of his assistants standing near was drawn into the conversation. The cattleman asked him questions. Betty and the man who called himself Tug Jones found themselves momentarily alone.

"Fortunate I was here when you came," the young man said. "Another man is taking charge. Mr. Merrick is putting me somewhere else. I don't know where, but I report for duty at once."

Betty took from her handbag a clipping from a newspaper.

91

She had written the date of publication on the headlines. It was about nine months before that time.

She handed the slip of paper to him.

"Did you ever hear of Captain Thurston K. Hollister?" the girl asked, on a note of tremulousness.

He looked during what seemed a long silence at the picture of the officer in uniform and the caption beneath it.

"Where did you get this?" he asked at last.

"I found it covering our pantry shelf, where it had been ever since spring."

"And you've brought it to me because you think I'm Hollister?"

"Are n't you?"

"Yes."

"I'm glad," she said.

"I don't know quite what you mean. Why are you glad?"

"From that first day I knew you were—somebody. Can't I be glad to learn I was right?"

He read the clipping, and as his eyes moved down the column there came over his face a touch of the sardonic bitterness she knew of old.

"I deserve a cross, don't I?"

"Two of them!" she cried impetuously.

He looked into her ardent, generous eyes. "Oh, half a dozen," he mocked.

But she noticed the mordant flash was gone. What she did not know was that her faith had exorcised it.

"Two," the girl insisted, an underlying flush of color in the dark cheeks. "One for this." She touched the paper he was holding.

"And the other?" he asked, not yet caught up with her leaping thought.

A qualm of fear shook her courage. Ought she to speak of it? Was she one of those who "rush in"? It was his personal business, and he had a right to resent any mention of it by her. But the desire was strong in her to say just a word and then close the subject for always.

"For that braver thing you've been doing every day since I saw you last," she said in a low voice.

He, too, flushed beneath the tan of the cheeks. Their eyes held fast an instant.

When he spoke, it was to say with studied lightness, "You and your father did n't walk up, did you?"

Betty was relieved. It is an embarrassing thing to talk with a man about those hidden things of his life that are important to him. She felt almost as though she had escaped from some peril.

"No, the car's on the road halfway up the hill. We could n't make it. Ruth's waiting for us there," she answered, hurrying to follow the lead he had given. "She has her favorite little puppy in the car with her. We thought the climb up might be a little too much for her."

Hollister walked back with them to the car. He talked with her father about the outrage that had resulted in the death of poor Coyle. Betty walked beside the men, saying nothing. She was acutely conscious of the presence of the sunburnt young fellow beside her. His rags had given place to a serviceable khaki that modeled itself to the clean lines of his figure. He walked firmly and lightly, with character. It was observable that he had shaved not many hours since. There was a faint line of golden hair along the cheekbone at the place where the stroke of the razor had terminated. He was not wearing a hat. The girl liked the way his copper-red hair crisped in short curls over his forehead.

"Jake Prowers, that's who," her father was saying. "He'll maybe hide behind Black. That's the way the old wolf does business."

"He does n't look like a wolf." This from Hollister. "No. More like a sheep. But don't let that fool you. He's the most dangerous man in this county. Jake pulled this off to serve notice that it was n't safe to work here in the cañon. Might have been a dozen men killed. A lot he cares for that. You'll find his tracks are covered, too. He won't show at all, an' there won't be evidence enough to convict Black or anybody else."

Betty heard with her surface mind what they were saying, but the undercurrent of it was considering something else. Was Hollister offended at her? Had he meant to rebuff her for presumption? There had been a certain rigor in his inscrutable face when he had turned the conversation. Already she was castigating herself for officiousness. Did he think her bold, unmaidenly? Well, he had a right to think it. Whatever had possessed her to say what she had? She had meant well, of course, but that can be said of half the fools of the world in their folly.

Baby Fifi came prancing up the road to meet them with ineffective puppy barks of welcome.

Betty picked up the small dog and questioned it. "Did Ruth

93

send you to meet us? And did you both have a good time while we were away?"

The child was not in the car. Betty smiled at her father. Both of them knew the ways of Mistress Ruth. Presently she would pounce on them from behind that rock just above the road with piping shrieks of glee.

"Where can she be, Dad?" Betty asked, in a voice intended to carry.

"I wonder. You don't suppose—"

Clint did not finish his sentence. His gaze had fastened on a cigarette stub lying on the running-board of the car. It had not been there when they left. He was sure of that.

"Some one's been here," he said quickly.

Betty caught the note of tenseness in his voice. Her eyes followed his to the bit of cigarette. She was not frightened. There was nothing to be afraid of. Nobody in these hills would hurt Ruth. None the less, her heart action quickened.

"Ruth!" she called.

There came no answer.

Clint called, sharply, imperatively. "Come out, Ruth! No nonsense!"

The child did not appear. Hollister clambered up and looked back of the big rock. She was not there. They searched the hillside, shouting as they did so.

Ruth was not to be found. The echo of their alarmed voices was the only answer.

CHAPTER XX

A CLASH

FROM behind the cover of a huge boulder on the steep hillside a man watched a car labor up the grade and give up. He trained field-glasses on the occupants. From his throat there came a sound like the snarl of a wild animal. He had recognized the driver and the girl in the tonneau.

94

Out of a hip pocket he drew an automatic revolver. His teeth bared like the fangs of a wolf. Not once did his eyes lift from the driver and the young woman with him until they disappeared round a bend in the road above.

He rose and stretched his cramped limbs, then moved cautiously down the hill slope to the car. A child was in the back seat playing with a puppy.

"Mamma's gotta go to town an' buy Baby Fifi some shoes wif silver buckles 'n' a new blue dress 'n' free pair of stockings. 'N' while she's gone, you better bee-have or Mamma 'll have to spank you good when she gets back," the little girl advised.

At the sound of footsteps she looked up.

The gay make-believe fled her face. Surrounded by love though she had always been, some instinct told her that this man represented for her the opposite of it. She felt a sudden imperative desire to call to her father.

"Wot's yer name?" the man asked.

"Ruth Reed."

"That Clint Reed yer dad?"

She told him he was.

The man's teeth showed like fangs. "Wot luck! We're pals, him an' me. I'll take yer along with old Cig."

"I don' wantta go. I want my daddy," Ruth announced promptly.

His grin widened. It was an evil thing to see.

"He'll want you, too, a while before he gets yer," he jeered.

He opened the door of the tonneau and stood on the running-board. "Come here, kid," he ordered.

Ruth shrank back to the farther side of the car. "You go 'way. I'll call my daddy."

He caught her by the frock and dragged her forward. "Cut out that stuff, missie. When Cig says to step lively, why, you get a hop on yer. See?"

She began to scream. He clapped a dirty hand over the child's mouth and turned to climb the mountainside with her in his arms.

Ruth kicked fiercely, impelled by terror. His right arm tightened on the struggling legs. The tramp climbed fast. He had to get over the summit before Reed came back or he would be in trouble.

At an altitude of a mile and a half the breath comes short when a strain is put on the lungs and heart. Cig panted as he

95

struggled up the rock-strewn slope. The weight in his arms dragged him down. More than once he slipped on the dry grass and just recovered himself without stumbling. Before he reached the divide, he was hot and exhausted.

But he dared not stop to rest. Once, near the crest, he turned for an instant to make sure he had not been seen. His eyes swept the road anxiously. Nobody was in sight.

Ruth twisted her mouth free and began to shriek. He clamped his hand over her lips again with an oath. It was all he could do to stagger with her over the rocky brow.

Here, for the moment, he was safe. With the sleeve of his coat he wiped the perspiration out of his eyes and from his face.

A saddled horse was tied to a stunted pine not far away. He dragged the child to it, mounted, and hauled her up in front of him. A moment, and the hoofs of the cowpony rang out as they struck the stony rubble.

Cig had never been on a horse till recently. It could not be claimed that he really knew how to ride now. But he could stick on if the animal was gentle. The ways of the West were not his ways. He could not walk out a mile from the cabin where he was staying and not get lost, unless he followed familiar trails. For he was up in the high lands of the Rockies, in a district broken with ravines of twisted pines and jutting rock out-croppings. Each hill and draw and gorge looked to him just like its neighbor.

Cig rode into a small cañon the entrance of which was well concealed by a growth of young quaking asps. Through these he pushed to a cabin on the edge of the grove.

He dropped the child to the ground and swung down.

"You take me back to my daddy," she sobbed.

"Nix on that stuff. Old Cig's gonna keep yer right here with him. I'll learn Clint Reed how safe it is to beat me up like his men done."

"I wantta go to my daddy. You take me to my daddy," the child wailed.

The hobo picked up a switch lying on the ground. "Youse stop whinin'. Hear me? I'll not have it!" he snarled.

His manner was so threatening that the sobs stuck in her throat. She shivered with dread, while she tried to fight back the expression of it.

"I—I want my sister Betty an' my daddy," she whimpered.

"Cut it out!" he ordered from a corner of his mouth.

Ruth flung herself to the ground and gave way to a passionate outbreak of grief and terror. The violence of her emotion shook the small body of the little girl.

Cig took a step toward her, switch in hand. He stopped. A sound had reached him. Something was moving in the quaking asps.

Two men emerged along the winding trail. They were on horseback. The one riding in front was Jake Prowers, the other Don Black.

The tramp waved a hand at them. "Woilcome to our city," he called, grinning toward them. "An' look who's here."

Prowers pulled up. "What the jumpin' Jehosaphat!" he exclaimed.

"I got lonesome, so I brought back comp'ny for myself," explained Cig. It was plain that he was proud of himself.

"Where'd you get her?" asked Black.

"Down above Elk Creek?"

"Was she lost?"

"Lost!" the tramp snickered. "Not so you could notice it none. She was sittin' in a car waitin' for Clint Reed an' that high-heeled goil of his to come back."

"But—what's she doing here?" inquired Black, still in the dark.

"Why, I brought her."

"What for?"

Cig sneered contempt. "Ain't you got any brains under that big lid you wear? I brought her because she's Clint Reed's kid, an' I ain't squared my account with him. See?"

Any one watching closely would have seen a change in Black's eyes. Something hard and steely passed into them. "What you aimin' to do with her?" he asked quietly.

"Ain't made up my mind. Mebbe I never will give her back. Mebbe I'll stick that bird Reed for a ransom. No can tell."

"So?" Black swung from the saddle and lounged forward in the bandy-legged, high-heeled fashion of the range rider. "I'll do a li'l' guessin' my own self. Mebbe I'll take her right back to Clint p.d.q."

The eyes of the crook narrowed. "Say, where d' youse get that stuff, fellow? When was youse elected king o' Prooshia?"

"What kind of an outfit do you figure this is?" the range rider asked. "Think we're makin' war on kids, do you? Well, we're not."

"Who asked youse to butt in on my business?" Cig

97

crouched, snarling, a menace and a threat. "That ain't supposed to be safe for black-headed guys, I'll tell the world."

"Not yore business any more'n mine. We're in this together. I'll tell you right now you can't pull a play like that an' get away with it."

"Can't I?" The New Yorker's lip curled in a sneer. "Says *you*."

"Says *I*." Black's steady gaze did not waver a thousandth part of an inch.

Cig spoke to Prowers, jerking the thumb of his left hand toward the cowpuncher. "What's eatin' this black bird? He claims to be sore at this Reed guy, same as we are. He ain't above stampedin' cattle onto sleepin' men and croakin' 'em. Mebbe he's yellow an' gettin' ready to rap to the bulls. Mebbe—"

The quid of tobacco stood out in Black's cheek like a marble. His jaws had stopped moving. He, too, addressed the old cattleman.

"Call off this wolf of yore's, Jake, onless you want him sent to Kingdom Come. Nobody can tell me I'm yellow without a come-back," he said in a low, even voice.

Prowers had been watching them both, curious, vigilant, small intent eyes sweeping from one to the other as the quarrel progressed. Now he spoke, curtly, first to the homesteader, then to the crook.

"Don't pull yore picket pin, Don. That'll be enough, Cig. I don't need any demonstration."

Black did not for an instant relax his rigid wariness. "Tha's what I'm waitin' to find out, Jake. He said I was yellow an' gettin' ready to squeal."

"Back water, you," the ranchman ordered Cig.

Cig hesitated, still defiant. "I ain't lookin' for no trouble—"

"So, of course, you'll tell Don there's nothin' to what you said, that you was a li'l' het up under the collar."

"—but I ain't duckin' it either. I'm willing to eat what I said, but he can't dictate about the kid. See?"

The cattleman's light eyes stabbed bleakly at the man. "You ain't playin' a lone hand, Cig. Don's right about it. We're all in this. An' another thing. Don't you forget for a minute that you'll do as I say, you an' Don both."

Black looked at his employer with a kind of fierce resentment. He had followed this man a good many years, not to his own good. There had been times when he had been close to a break with him, but Prowers held for him a sinister attraction.

He never had liked him, yet could not escape his influence.

"What about the kid? I'm standin' pat on that, Jake," he said sullenly.

The old cattleman reflected. By nature he had in him a vein secretive and malignant. The thought of striking at Clint Reed through his little girl was not repellent to him. But he had lived fifty years in the West and knew its standards. The thing that Cig had done, unless it were promptly repudiated by him, would make Paradise Valley and the adjoining mountains buzz like a hornets' nest. His allies would fall away from him instantly.

"You'll take the kid back home to Clint, Don," Prowers said. "You'll tell him we sent her back soon as we found she had been taken. An' that's all you'll tell him. No mention of Cig here. Understand?"

Black's jaws began to move again regularly and evenly. "Suits me," he agreed. "When do I go?"

"Why, the sooner the quicker."

The instinct of a child as to grown-ups is not always sound, but Ruth knew which of these three was her friend. She had run to Black and caught him by the coat, screening herself behind him. His hand rested on the soft flaxen hair gently. Don was a bad *hombre,* a hard, tough citizen. But something tugged at his heart now. He knew that if it had been necessary bullets would have stabbed the air to save the little girl who had put herself under his protection.

"Don't forget, Don. Turn her over to Clint with my compliments. An' you brought her home soon as we found her. No explanations. Let him take it or leave it."

Black nodded. "I getcha. It'll be thataway."

After he had swung to the saddle he lifted the child to the back of the horse. She was still sobbing.

"Don'cha, honey," he soothed. "I'm takin' you right home to yore paw. That bad man ain't 'a' gonna hurt you none."

He rode out of the cañon and across the hills. Nobody knew this country better than Black. All his life he had ridden it. Following the path of least resistance, he deflected many times from the airline that led to the Diamond Bar K; but none could have traveled a shorter distance to reach it.

Within the hour he was jogging down into Paradise Valley.

A cloud of dust in the distance caught his eye. It was moving swiftly along a road toward him.

"Some folks in a powerful hurry," he murmured aloud, and guessed at once the reason for their haste.

His fingers closed for an instant on the butt of a revolver to make sure there would be no hitch in the draw in case of need.

As the riders drew near, he held up the palm of his hand to stop them. He counted eight. Clint Reed and Lon Forbes were in the lead. Betty was among the others.

"I reckon I got here what you want, Clint," Black said evenly.

He lowered Ruth from the saddle and she ran to her father. Clint swung down and caught her into his arms with a sound in his throat that was like a dry sob. He murmured broken endearments while he fondled her.

"Oh, daddy, my daddy!" Ruth wailed.

Betty swung from the saddle and ran to them. Clint passed the child to her. They clung together, Betty crooning little love words of happiness. "Ruthie—Ruthie—darling—precious!"

Between hugs and kisses Ruth explained. "A bad man tooked me 'way 'way off on a horse 'n' we rode 'n' we rode. 'Nen anuvver man comed 'n' said he'd bring me home, 'n' he did bring me, the nice man did."

Reed strode across the road to the man who had brought back his child. "I'll hear your story, Black," he said sternly.

"I don't reckon I've got any story to tell, Clint—none in particular. She was lost. I found her an' brought her back. Ain't that enough?"

"No. Where did you find her? Who took her?"

"Nothin' doing on that witness-stand stuff," the other answered. "Jake Prowers an' me was lookin' for strays up on Elk Creek when we found her. Jake told me to tell you here she was with his compliments. That's all I know."

"You and Jake found her?"

"Yessir. Did n't I tell you that twict?"

"Was she alone?"

"There was a guy with her, but I did n't know him. He lit out."

"What kind of lookin' fellow?"

"Why, I did n't see him right close." The quid of tobacco stuck out in the homesteader's cheek. He watched Reed closely, jaws motionless.

"You're not a good liar, Black. You know a lot more than you're telling," the owner of the Diamond Bar K accused.

100

"I'm gonna have it out of you, man, if I have to tear it from your throat."

Black's figure stiffened. "Try any funny business with me, an' I'll show you where to head in at, Clint," he said quietly.

"Why don't you ask the kid?" Forbes said in an aside to his employer. "Black did n't steal her. A blind man could see that."

"He knows who did."

"Sure, an' he's hell-bent not to tell. You won't get it outa him. I know Don."

"It's some of Jake Prowers's work."

"I don't think it, Clint." The foreman turned to Ruth. "Who was it took you outa the automobile, honey?"

"A man. He was gonna whip me wiv a great big stick, like he said Daddy did him."

"What? Whip you, like—" Lon stopped to wrestle with and overthrow a thought. "Why, dog-gone my hide, it's that tramp Daniels has been lookin' for."

Clint fired questions at Black like shots out of a machine gun. "Was he a small man? Lean? Town clothes? Talk outa the corner of his mouth? A rat-faced fellow? Fingers cigarette-stained?"

Black shook his head. "You've sure enough got me there, Clint. I only seen him at a distance, but seemed like he was a big husky guy. Yes, I'm 'most sure he was. Big as the side of a barn."

"Did he seem big to you, Ruthie?" Lon asked gently.

"Umpha!" She nodded her head vigorously. "He was a nawful man, 'n' he said he'd whip me like Daddy did him."

"Talk like this, honey?" Lon drew down a corner of his mouth and spoke out of it. " 'De king o' Prooshia on de job.' "

Her curls danced violently up and down with acquiescence.

The foreman turned to Reed. "He's sure enough the same bird. Where's he been keepin' himself at, you reckon?"

"Jake Prowers could tell us that," his employer replied grimly.

This suggested another question to Forbes. "Listen, honey Ruth. This here bad man—did him an' Black here act kinda like they was friends?"

"They had a fuss," she said.

"What about?" her father asked.

" 'Bout me. The bad man said I was n't comin' home to Daddy, 'n' he said I was too. They had a nawful fuss."

101

"The bad man an' Black here?"

She nodded. " 'N' he tooked me on his horse 'n' broughted me."

Forbes drew aside his friend and spoke low. "Looks like he's got it on you, Clint. Here's about the size of it, the way I figure it. This scalawag Cig's hidin' out in the hills. Jake Prowers is likely lookin' after him. Well, he steals Ruth, an' Don here bumps into him whilst he's makin' his getaway. They have a rumpus, an' Don brings her home. He acted pretty near like a white man, seems to me. 'Course, he ain't gonna give away this tramp if he's one of Prowers's push. That would n't be hardly reasonable to expect."

"No, I reckon not," admitted Reed.

"You got no kick at Black. Had n't been for him I'll bet Ruth would n't 'a' been here a-tall. Point is, that with him there Jake and this Cig could n't put over any shenanigan."

The owner of the Diamond Bar K stepped across to the homesteader. "Take it all back, Don. I'm mightily obliged to you for bringing my li'l' girl home. If I ever get a chance—"

Black interrupted. "Oh, that's all right. What do you take me for, anyhow? I ain't any Apache. Why would n't I bring a kid home when I find her lost? You birds make me tired."

He nodded brusquely, wheeled his horse, and rode away.

CHAPTER XXI

IRREFUTABLE LOGIC

MERRICK sat at a table in the log cabin that served him as field headquarters. A cheap lamp pinned down one corner of the map in front of him, a jar of tobacco the opposite one. Tug Hollister looked over his shoulder. He was here to get instructions for his new assignment.

Piñon knots cracked cheerfully in the fireplace, emphasizing the comfort within the cabin as compared with the weather outside. It was raining heavily and had been for forty-eight hours.

"Here's where the engineers of the Reclamation Service ran their lines," Merrick said, following with the point of a pencil a crooked course from Sweetwater Dam to the upper mouth of Elk Creek Cañon. "They made a mistake, probably because they were short of time. It was clear that the water from the dam had to get down to the Flat Tops by way of Elk Creek if at all. As soon as they learned that the upper entrance to the cañon is higher than the site of the dam by eighty feet they admitted the project would not do. All the reports are based on that. Water won't flow uphill. Therefore no feasible connecting canal could be built."

Hollister walked round and took the chair at the other side of the table. "Irrefutable logic," he said.

"Absolutely. But I was n't sure of the facts upon which it was based."

"You mean you were n't sure the canal had to run to the upper mouth of the cañon."

The chief of construction looked at his assistant quickly. This young fellow had more than once surprised Merrick by the clearness of his deductions.

"Exactly that. So I proceeded to find out for myself."

"And you learned that you could carry it over the hills and down the draw where Prowers stampeded the cattle."

"How do you know that?" demanded Merrick.

"More irrefutable logic." Hollister tilted back his chair and smiled. "There's only one break in the walls of the cañon in the whole five miles. That's at the draw near the lower mouth. Since the ditch must get into the foothills from the gorge and can't reach them any other way, and since it can't enter the cañon at the upper end on account of the law of gravity, I'm driven to the alternative—and that's the draw."

"You use your brains," admitted the older man dryly. "Of course, you're right. We're going down the draw."

"Then the survey you had me make of the upper part of the cañon was camouflage."

"Yes." A smile of grim amusement broke the lines of his firm mouth. "Black's homestead claim does n't reach as far down as the draw. Prowers thought it would be enough to close the upper mouth of the gorge to us. So we don't touch his land at all—don't come within miles of it in point of fact.

103

To make sure Prowers won't jump in later, I've had a dummy file on the draw."

Hollister looked at his chief with admiration. The man had all the qualities that make for success—technical skill, audacity, confidence in himself, steadiness, force, restrained imagination, and a certain capacity for indomitable perseverance. He would go a long way, in spite of the fact that he was not quite the ideal leader, or perhaps because of the lack of the fire that inspires subordinates. For he was not one to let a generous enthusiasm sweep him from the moorings of common sense.

"You've made the canal survey to the draw?" the younger man asked.

"Yes. A hogback below Jake's Fork bars the way."

"You're going round it?"

"Can't. Through it. You're to begin running the tunnel tomorrow."

They discussed plans, details, equipment necessary to attack the hogback.

Hollister moved camp next day in a pelting rain and set up his tents on the soggy hillside close to the ridge. For a week the rain kept up almost steadily. The whole country was sloshing with moisture. During a visit to the main camp for a consultation with Merrick, he went down to the dam and observed that a heavy flow of water was pouring into the reservoir. With an ordinary winter's snowfall in the mountains, Sweetwater would be full to the brim long before the spring freshets had ended.

Day by day the drills bored deeper into the hogback and the tunnel grew longer. By means of a chance rider of the hills, word reached Prowers of it. He and Don Black, who was out on bond signed by Jake, rode over to see what this new development meant.

"What do you fellows think you're doing?" asked the cattleman in his high, crackling voice.

"Mining," answered Hollister.

"What for? What's the idea?"

"We're driving a tunnel."

"I got eyes, young fellow. What for?"

"Mr. Merrick did n't tell me what he wanted it for. He told me to get busy. Mine not to reason why, Mr. Prowers."

"Smart, ain't you, by jiminy by jinks?"

A foreman came up and propounded a difficulty to Hollister. That young man walked briskly away to look the matter over and did not return. The two riders hung around for a time, then disappeared over the brow of a hill.

"The old man's got something to think about," the foreman said to Hollister, chuckling.

"Yes, and his thinking will bring him straight to one conclusion; that we're not going to run through Black's homestead claim. When he figures out where we *are* going, he'll start something."

"I don't quite see what he can do."

"Nor I, but we did n't foresee what he would do last time. He killed poor Coyle, and he did n't leave enough evidence to prove in a law court that he did it."

"He'd ought to be behind the bars right now—him an' that Black too," the foreman said bitterly.

"But they're not—and they won't be. That's his reputation, to do all sorts of deviltry and get away with it. That's why men won't cross him, why they're so afraid of him. He's got no scruples and he's as cunning as the devil."

"I've heard he's a tough nut, too. He don't look it, with them skim-milk eyes of his and that little squeaky voice."

"No. Size him up beside Merrick, say, and he does n't look effective," admitted Hollister. "But he's one of these quiet sure killers, according to the stories they tell. Not a fighting man, unless he's got his back to the wall. You've heard of dry-gulching. It means shooting an enemy from ambush when he does n't know you're within fifty miles. That's Prowers's style. He gives me a creepy feeling."

"Here, too. You know that fool cackling laugh of his. Well, the other day when he was pulling off the ha-ha I got a look from him that jolted me. Lord, it dried my blood up. I'd hate to meet him in one o' them dry gulches if he had any reason for wantin' me outa the way."

"Yes." Hollister came back to business. "Believe I'd increase the size of the shots, Tom. We're in pretty hard rock right now."

They were running the tunnel at the narrowest point of the hogback, which rose at a sharp angle. The snows began before it was more than half finished. Not willing to risk being cut off from supplies, Hollister had enough staples hauled in to last him till he would be through. What needs might come up unexpectedly could be met by packers coming in over the drifts from the dam.

Still Prowers had not shown his hand. Hollister began to

think him less dangerous than he had supposed. The big bore grew longer every day. In a few weeks it would be finished. Surely the cattleman would not wait to strike until after the job was done.

CHAPTER XXII

A STERN CHASE

THE clean bracing air of the Rockies, together with hard work and plenty of it, had poured new life into the blood of Tug Hollister. The ashen, pasty look had been replaced on his face by a coat of healthy brown. The fierce, driving headaches had gone, but there were still hours when the craving for the drug possessed him and sent him tramping through the night to fight the depression that swept in waves through his heart.

Winter settled over the hills. The wind roared along the slope of the divide and drove before it great scudding clouds heavily laden with moisture. Storms fought and screamed around the peaks. Snow fell day after day. It packed in the gulches and drifted into the draws. The landscape became a vast snowfield across which the bitter winds drove and flung themselves at the flapping tents.

There came, too, nights of wonderful stillness broken only by the crackling of branches in the cold, nights when the stars were out in myriads and the white valley was a vast open-air cathedral built and decorated by the Master Hand.

On such a night Hollister turned in and slept till the small hours. He woke, to find himself restless and irritable, the craving for the drug strong on him. His chance of further sleep was gone.

Without lighting a lantern, he pulled on his heavy wool socks, his o.d. breeches, and his fourteen-inch Chippewa pattern boots. His groping fingers found a leather vest with corduroy sleeves. Outside, he fastened on his skis.

During the night the weather had changed. It had come on

to snow. The flakes were large and few, but experience told the engineer that soon they would be coming thick enough. He put on a slicker before he started on his tramp.

Uncertain which way to go, he stood for a moment outside the flap of the tent. The rim of the saucer-shaped valley lay straight ahead. Beyond were the great white snow wastes, stretching mile on mile, isolating the little camp more effectually than a quarantine. He decided to climb out of the draw and push across the hilltops.

To his ears came a faint slithering sound. He listened, heard it again. The crunching of a ski on crusted snow! Who could be out at this time of night? Why? For what purpose?

It was probably one of the men, he reflected. But none of them would be on skis to move over the beaten paths around the camp. Some sixth sense warned of danger in the vicinity. He crept around the tent in the direction from which the sound had come. His glance took in the other tents, scarcely visible against the background of white in the dim light of pre-dawn. Everything there was still and silent.

Again there came to him the hiss of a ski. A hundred yards distant was the mouth of the tunnel. A moving figure stood out, black against the pale background. Some one who had obviously just emerged from the tunnel was shuffling away through the snow.

Hollister did not shout an order to halt. Instinctively he knew that something was wrong, and already he was bending to his stride. Before he had taken half a dozen steps the head of the other man swung round hurriedly. Instantly the unknown quickened his pace.

Before they had traveled a hundred yards, Hollister knew he was more expert in the use of the runners than the fugitive. Barring accidents he would catch him.

The pursued man made for the rim of the valley. From time to time he turned without stopping to see whether he was losing ground. The distance between the two was lessening. Hollister knew it. Evidently the other knew it, too, for he tried desperately to increase his pace.

The hundred yards had become seventy-five, fifty, twenty-five. They were out of the valley now, swinging toward the left where a patch of timber lay back of a clump of quaking asps. A pile of boulders were huddled beneath a rock-rim a stone's throw to the right.

The snow was falling more heavily now. It was plain that

the fugitive was hoping to reach the timber and escape in the thickening storm. To prevent this, Hollister worked farther to the left. He came up quickly with the other and passed him fifteen yards or less away.

A gun cracked. Hollister's long stride did not slacken. He was keeping well away because he had known the other would be armed. The engineer had made a serious mistake in not stopping to get his revolver.

Again the revolver sounded. The bullet flew harmlessly past. Tug had circled ahead of his prey and cut him off from the grove of quaking asps. He was relying on a piece of audacity to protect him from the armed man. The stranger would assume that he, too, was armed.

Evidently this was the man's reasoning. He swung to the right, making for the refuge of the rocks. Presently he glanced back to see if he was followed and how closely. The end of the ski must have caught under a rock beneath the snow, for the man was flung forward to his face. The binder of a ski had broken. He rose quickly, caught up the long snowshoe, and ran forward at a gait between a hobble and a shuffle.

Tug did not pursue directly. He had no desire to stop any of the bullets left in the chambers of the revolver. Instead of taking the trail made for him, he broke a new one that led to the summit of the rock-rim above the boulder bed. There was a chance that in doing this he might lose his man, but it was a chance that had to be taken. His guess was that the refugee would find a hiding-place in the rocks and would stay there long enough, at any rate, to mend the broken strings of the ski.

From the rock-rim Hollister looked down upon the boulder bed through the thick snow. He made out a crouched figure below. Satisfied that his victim was not still traveling, he examined the terrain to work out a plan of campaign. A heavy snow comb yawned above the rock-rim. This might very well serve his purpose. Using one of his skis as a lever, he loosened the heavy pack of snow. It moved at first slowly, but went at last with a rush. There was a roar as it plunged over the bluff and tore a way down to the rocks below. The slide gathered momentum as it went.

Hollister peered down. The crouched figure was gone, had been buried in the giant billow of white.

The engineer refastened his ski, took a few swinging strokes forward, and came to a smooth incline. Down this he coasted rapidly.

The buried man was just struggling out of the white mass when a hand closed on his coat collar. It dragged him from the pack and held him firmly down. Not till Tug made sure that the revolver was missing did he let the man rise.

"Wot'ell 's eatin' youse?" the rescued man growled, snarling at him.

Tug Hollister stood face to face with the tramp he knew by the name of Cig. Recognition was simultaneous.

"What were you doing at my camp?"

"Aw, go chase yoreself. I ain't been near your camp."

"All right, if that's your story. We'll go back there now. The sheriff wants you."

The evil face of the crook worked. Out of the corner of his twisted mouth he spoke venomously. "Say, if I had my gun I'd croak youse."

"But you have n't it. Get busy. Dig out your skis."

"Nothin' doing. Dig 'em yourself if youse want 'em."

Hollister knew of only one argument that would be effective with this product of New York's underworld. He used it, filled with disgust because circumstances forced his hand. When Cig could endure no longer, he gave way sullenly.

"'Nuff. But some day I'll get you right for this. I aimed to bump you off, anyhow. Now I soitainly will. I ain't forgot you rapped on me to that guy Reed."

"I've told you once I did n't, and you would n't believe me. We'll let it go at that. Now get those skis."

The snowshoes were rescued and the broken one mended. Hollister watched his prisoner every minute of the time. He did not intend to run the risk of being hit in the head by a bit of broken rock.

The two moved down into the valley, Cig breaking trail. He made excuses that he was dead tired and could n't go another step. They did not serve him well. His captor would not let the crook get in his rear for a single second. He knew that, if the fellow got a chance, he would murder him without the least hesitation.

In a blinding snowstorm the two men reached camp. Twice Cig had tried to bolt and twice had been caught and punished. This was a degrading business, but the engineer had no choice. It was necessary to bring the man in because he had been up to some deviltry, and Hollister could not let him go without first finding out what it was.

He took him into his own tent and put him through a searching quiz. The result of it was precisely nothing. Cig jeered at him defiantly. If he could prove anything against him, let him go to it. That was the substance of the New Yorker's answers.

"All right. I'll turn you over to Clint Reed. He's got something to say to you for stealing his little girl. From the way he talked, I judge you're in for a bad time of it."

Cig protested. He had n't stolen the girl. How did they know he had? Who said so? What would he do a crazy thing like that for? To all of which Hollister said calmly that he would have to explain that to Reed. If he could satisfy the cattleman, it would be all right with him. Reed could pass him on to Sheriff Daniels without further delay.

"You're a heluva pardner, ain't youse?" sneered the crook with an ugly lift of his upper lip. "T'row me down foist chance youse get."

"I'm not your partner. We hit different trails the day we left the Diamond Bar K ranch. You need n't play baby on me. That won't buy you anything."

"Gonna turn me over to Reed, then, are youse?"

"I've no time to bother with you. He'll know how to handle the case. Better that way, I reckon."

Cig said nothing. For half an hour there was silence in the tent. Holister knew that his threat was sinking in, that the kidnapper was uneasily examining the situation to find the best way out.

Daylight came, and with it signs of activity around the camp. Smoke poured out of the stovepipe projecting from the chuck tent. Men's voices sounded. At last the beating of an iron on the triangle summoned them to breakfast.

"We'll eat before we start," Hollister said.

"Don' want nothin' to eat," growled the prisoner.

"Different here. I do. You'll come along, anyhow."

The men at breakfast looked with surprise at the guest of the boss when he appeared. Hollister explained what he was doing there.

"I want to go into the tunnel and have a look around before any of you do any work," he added. "This fellow was up to some mischief, and I want to find out what it was."

Cig's palate went dry. He knew better than they did in what

110

a predicament he had put himself. If he let the thing go through as originally intended, these men would never let him reach a sheriff. If he confessed—what would they do to him?

He ate mechanically and yet voraciously, for the exercise of the night had left him hungry. But every moment his mind was sifting the facts of the case for an out.

Hollister rose to leave. "Take care of this fellow till I get back, Tom. I don't know what he was up to, but if anything happens to me, rush him right down to Daniels."

"We will—in a pig's eye," the foreman answered bluntly. "If anything happens to you, we'll give this bird his, muy pronto."

The engineer was lifting the flap of the tent when Cig spoke huskily from a parched throat. "I'll go along wid youse."

"All right." Not the least change of expression in his face showed that Hollister knew he had won, knew he had broken down the fellow's stiff and sullen resistance.

Cig shuffled beside Tug to the tunnel. The months had made a difference in the bearing of the ex-service man. When the New Yorker had met him first, Hollister's mental attitude found expression in the way he walked. He was a tramp, in clothes, in spirit, in habit of life, and in the way he carried his body. The shoulders drooped, the feet dragged, the expression of the face was cynical. Since then there had been relit in him the spark of self-respect. He was a new man.

He stepped aside, to let Cig pass first into the tunnel. At the entrance he lit two candles and handed one to his prisoner.

"What did you want to come for?" he asked. "Have you something to show me? Or something to tell me?"

Cig moved forward. He spoke over his shoulder, protecting the candle with one hand. "Just a bit of a lark. Thought I'd throw a scare into yore men."

"How?"

The former convict continued through the tunnel to the face of the rock wall. He set his candle down on a niche of jutting sandstone. With his fingers he scraped away some sand from the ragged wall.

"What's that?" Hollister's voice was sharp. He held out his hand. "Let's have it."

From beneath the sand Cig had taken a stick of dynamite. He dug up five others.

The object of putting them there was plain enough. If a workman had struck any one of them with a pick, there would have been an explosion, and the sand beds round the rocks were precisely the places into which the pick points would have gone. The thing had been a deliberate attempt at cold-blooded wholesale murder.

"Sure you have them all?" Hollister asked.

"Yep. Had only six." He added, with a whine: "Did n't aim to hurt any o' the boys, but only to scare 'em some."

The engineer made no comment. He drove his prisoner before him back into the light. Tom met him at the entrance to the tunnel. The foreman examined the sticks of dynamite, listened to what Hollister had to say, and jerked his head toward Cig.

"The boys'll fix him right so's he'll never pull another trick like this," he told his chief.

"No," opposed Hollister. "Nothing of that sort, Tom. I'm going to take him down to the sheriff. We'll send him over the road."

"Like blazes we will!" the foreman burst out. "If you had n't happened to see him this morning, three or four of us might be dead by now. Hanging's too good for this guy."

"Yes," agreed Tug. "But we're not going to put ourselves in the wrong because he is. The law will deal with him."

"The boys ain't liable to feel that way," Tom said significantly.

"They won't know anything about it till we've gone. You'll tell them then." His hand fell on the foreman's shoulder with a grip that was almost affectionate. "We can't have a lynching here, Tom. We'd be the ones in bad then."

Tom had to feel his way through a few moments of sulkiness to acceptance of this point of view. "All right. You're the doctor. Hustle this fellow outa camp an' I'll wait till you're gone. Sure he's picked up every stick of this stuff?"

Cig was quite sure about that. He spoke humbly and with all the braggadocio gone from his manner. He had been thoroughly frightened and did not yet feel wholly out of the woods. Not till he was behind the bars would he feel quite safe again.

CHAPTER XXIII

OUT OF THE BLIZZARD

Tom called a warning to Hollister as the engineer and his prisoner struck out into the blinding storm. "Careful you don't get lost. Looks like she's gettin' her back up for a reg'lar snifter."

The snow was still falling thickly, but it had behind it now a driving wind that slapped it in the faces of the men at a slanting angle. Presently under the lee of a hill they got their backs to the storm, but this did not greatly improve conditions, for the whip of the wind caught up the surface drifts and whirled them at the travelers.

Hollister had buckled on a belt with a revolver and had taken the precaution to rope his prisoner to him with ten feet of slack between. They ploughed through the new snow that had fallen above the crust, making slow progress even with the wind to help.

From the shelter of the gulch they came into the full force of the howling hurricane. It caught them as they crossed a mesa leading to a cañon. Hollister realized that the snow was thinning, but the wind was rising and the temperature falling. He did not like that. Even to his lack of experience there was the feel of a blizzard in the air. Moreover, before they were halfway across the mesa he had a sense of having lost his direction.

Cig dropped back, whining. This was an adventure wholly out of his line. He was game enough in his way, but bucking blizzards was not one of the things he had known in his city-cramped experience.

"We gotta go back. It'll get us sure if we don't," he pleaded.

Tug would have turned back gladly enough if he had known which way to go, but in the swirl of white that enveloped them he did not know east from west. The thing to do, he judged, was to strike as straight a line as possible. This ought to take

113

them off the mesa to the shelter of some draw or wooded ravine.

"It'll be better when we get where the wind can't slam across the open at us," he said.

For the moment at least the former convict was innocuous. He was wholly preoccupied with the battle against the storm. Tug took the lead and broke trail.

The whirling snow stung his face like burning sand. His skis clogged with the weight of the drifts. Each dragging step gave him the sense of lifting a leaden ball chained to his feet.

Cig went down, whimpering. "I'm all in!" he shrieked through the noise of the screaming blasts.

"Forget it, man!" Hollister dragged him to his feet. "If you quit now you're done for. Keep coming. We'll get off this mesa soon. It can't be far now."

He was none too confident himself. Stories came to his mind of men who had wandered round and round in a circle till the blizzard had taken toll of their vitality and claimed them for its own.

The prisoner sank down again and had to be dragged out of the drift into which he had fallen. Five or six times the taut rope stopped Tug's progress. Somehow he cheered and bullied the worn-out man to the edge of the mesa, down a sharp slope, and into the wind-break of a young grove of pines.

Into the snow Cig dropped helplessly. The hinges of his knees would n't hold him any longer. His expression reminded Hollister of the frightened face of a child.

"I'm goin' west," he said.

"Not this trip," the engineer told him. "Buck up and we'll make it fine. Don't know this country, do you? We're at the mouth of a gulch."

Cig looked around. In front of him was a twisted pine that looked like an umbrella blown inside out. He recognized it.

"This gulch leads into another. There's a cabin in it," he said. "A heluva long ways from here."

"Then we'd better get started," Tug suggested. "The cabin won't come to us."

He gave the Bowery tough a hand to help him to his feet. Cig pulled himself up.

"Never get there in the world," he complained. "Tell you I'm done."

He staggered into the drifts after his leader. The bitter wind and cold searched through their clothing to freeze the life out

114

of them. At the end of a long slow two hundred yards, the weaker man quit.

Hollister came back to him. He lay huddled on the newly broken trail.

"Get up!" ordered Tug.

"Nothin' doing. I'm through. Go on an' leave me if youse want to, you big stiff."

It was the man's last flare of defiance. He collapsed into himself, helpless as a boxer counted out in the roped ring. Hollister tugged at him, cuffed him, scolded, and encouraged. None of these seemed even to reach his consciousness. He lay inert, even the will to live beaten out of him.

In that moment, while Hollister stood there considering, buffeted by the howling wind and the sting of the pelting sleet, he saw at his feet a brother whose life must be saved and not an outlaw and potential murderer. He could not leave Cig, even to save himself.

Tug's teeth fastened to one end of a mitten. He dragged it from his hand. Half-frozen fingers searched in his pocket for a knife and found it. They could not open the blade, and he did this, too, with his teeth. Then, dropping to one knee awkwardly, he sawed at the thongs which fastened the other's skis. They were coated with ice, but he managed to sever them.

He picked up the supine body and ploughed forward up the gulch. The hope he nursed was a cold and forlorn one. He did not know the cañon or how far it was to the gulch in which the cabin was. By mistake he might go wandering up a draw which led nowhere. Or he might drop in his tracks from sheer exhaustion.

But he was a fighter. It was not in him to give up. He had to stagger on, to crawl forward, to drag his burden after him when he could not carry it. His teeth were set fast, clinched with the primal instinct to go through with it as long as he could edge an inch toward his goal.

A gulch opened out of the cañon. Into it he turned, head down against a wind that hit him like a wall. The air, thick with sifted ice, intensely cold, sapped the warmth and vitality of his body. His numbed legs doubled under the weight of him as though hinged. He was down and up again and down, but the call of life still drove him. Automatically he clung to his helpless load as though it were a part of himself.

Out of the furious gray flurry a cabin detached itself. He weaved a crooked path toward it, reached the wall, crept along

115

the logs to a door. Against this he plunged forward, reaching for the latch blindly.

The door gave, and he pitched to the floor.

He lay there, conscious, but with scarcely energy enough of mind or body to register impressions. A fire roared up the chimney. He knew that. Some one rose with an exclamation of amazement at his intrusion. There was a hiatus of time. His companion of the adventure, still tied to him, lay on the floor. A man was stooping over Cig, busy with the removal of his ice-coated garments.

The man cut the rope. Hollister crawled closer to the fire. He unfastened the slicker and flung it aside. If he had not lost his knife, he would have cut the thongs of the skis. Instead, he thrust his feet close to the red glow to thaw out the ice-knots that had gathered.

He was exhausted from the fight through the deep drifts, but he was not physically in a bad way. A few hours' sleep would be all he needed to set him right.

"Take a nip of this," a squeaky voice advised.

Hollister turned his head quickly. He looked into the leathery face and skim-milk eyes of Jake Prowers. It would be hard to say which of them was the more startled.

"By jiminy by jinks, if it ain't the smart-aleck hobo engineer," the cattleman announced to himself.

"Is he alive?" asked Tug, nodding toward the man on the floor.

"Be all right in a li'l' while. His eyes flickered when I gave him a drink. How'd you come here, anyhow?"

"Got lost in the storm. He played out. Had to drag him." Tug rubbed his hands together to restore circulation.

"Mean you got lost an' just happened in here?"

"Yes."

"Hmp! Better be born lucky than with brains, I'll say. What were you doin' out in the blizzard? Where you headed for?"

"I was taking him to Wild Horse—to the sheriff."

A mask dropped over the eyes of the little cattleman. "What for? What's he been doin'?"

"He's wanted for shooting Mr. Reed and firing his wheatfield."

"You been appointed deputy sheriff since you took to playin' good?"

"And for other things," the engineer added, as though Prowers's sneer had not been uttered.

116

"Meanin' which?"

"Kidnapping Reed's little girl."

"No proof of that a-tall. Anything more?"

The eyes of the two met and grew chill. Hollister knew that the rancher was feeling out the ground. He wanted to find out what had taken place to-day.

"What more could there be?" Tug asked quietly.

Neither relaxed the rigor of his gaze. In the light-blue orbs of the older was an expression cold and cruel, almost unhuman, indefinably menacing.

"Claims I was tryin' to blow up his mine." The voice came from behind Prowers. It was faint and querulous. "Say, I'm froze up inside. Gimme a drink, Jake."

Prowers passed the bottle over. He continued to look at the uninvited guest who knew too much. "How come you to get that notion about him blowin' up yore tunnel?" he asked.

"Caught him at it. Dragged him back and made him show where he had put the sticks of powder," Hollister answered grimly. "You interested in this, Mr. Prowers?"

"Some. Why not? Got to be neighborly, have n't I?" The high voice had fallen to a soft purr. It came to Hollister, with a cold swift patter of mice feet down his spine, that he was in deadly danger. Nobody knew he was here, except these two men. Cig had only to give it out that they had become separated in the blizzard. They could, unless he was able to protect himself, murder him and dispose of the body in entire safety. If reports were true, Prowers was an adept at that kind of sinister business. Tug had, of course, a revolver, but he knew that the cattleman could beat him to the draw whenever he chose. The old man was a famous shot. He would take his time. He would make sure before he struck. The blow would fall when his victim's wariness relaxed, at the moment when he was least expecting it.

Tug knew that neither of these two in the room with him had any regard for the sanctity of human life. There are such people, a few among many millions, essentially feral, untouched by any sense of common kinship in the human race. Prowers would be moved by one consideration only. Would it pay to obliterate him? The greatest factor in the strength of the cattleman's position was that men regarded him with fear and awe. The disappearance of Hollister would stir up whisperings and suspicions. Others would read the obvious lesson. Daunted, they would sidestep the old man rather than oppose him. Yet no proof could be found to establish definitely a crime, or at any rate to connect him with it.

The issue of the Sweetwater Dam project meant more to Prowers than dollars and cents. His power and influence in the neighborhood were at stake, and it was for these that he lived. If the irrigation project should be successful, it would bring about a change in the character of the country. Settlers would pour in, farm the Flat Tops, and gobble up the remnants of the open range. To the new phase of cattle-raising that must develop, he was unalterably opposed. He had no intention, if he could prevent it, of seeing Paradise Valley dominated by other men and other ways. The development of the land would make Clint Reed bulk larger in the county; it would inevitably push Jake into the background and make of him a minor figure.

To prevent this, Prowers would stick at nothing. Hollister was only a subordinate, but his death would serve excellently to point a sinister moral. If more important persons did not take warning, they, too, might vanish from the paths of the living.

"You're neighborly enough, even if you visited us by deputy this morning," Hollister answered, level gaze fixed on the cattleman.

"Did I visit you by deputy?" Jake asked, gently ironical.

"Did n't you? One with six sticks of dynamite to help us on the job."

"News to me. How about it, Cig? What's yore smart-aleck friend drivin' at?"

Cig had crept forward to the fire and lay crouched on the hearth. His twitching face registered the torture of a circulation beginning to normalize itself again in frozen hands and feet.

"Said he'd turn me over to that guy Reed. Took advantage of me while I was played out to beat me up," snarled the city tough. He finished with a string of vile epithets.

The splenetic laughter of the cattleman cackled out. "So you're aimin' to take Cig here down to Daniels with that cock-an'-bull story you cooked up. Is that the play?"

"Yes, I'm going to take him down—now or later."

This appeared to amuse the little man. His cracked laughter sounded again. "Now or later, by jiminy by jinks. My hobo friend, if you'd lived in this country long as I have, you would n't gamble heavy on that 'later.' If you'd read yore Bible prop-

118

er, you'd know that man's days are as grass, which withers up considerable an' sudden. Things happen in this world of woe right onexpected."

Tug did not dodge this covert threat. He dragged it into the open. "What could happen to me now we're safe out of the storm, Mr. Prowers?"

The skim-milk eyes did not change expression, but there seemed to lie back of them the jeer of mockery. "Why, 'most anything. We eat canned tomatoes for supper, say—an' you get lead poisonin'. I've known real healthy-lookin' folks fall asleep an' never wake up."

"Yes. That's true," Hollister agreed, an odd sinking in the pit of his stomach. "And I've seen murderers who could have passed a first-class life insurance examination quit living very suddenly. The other day I read a piece about a scoundrel in Mexico who had killed two or three people. He rather had the habit. When he shot another in the back, his neighbors rode to his ranch one night and hanged him to his own wagon tongue."

"I always did say Mexico was no place for a white man to live," the old fellow piped amiably. "Well, I expect you boys are hungry, buckin' this blizzard. What say to some dinner?"

"Good enough. No canned tomatoes, though, if you please."

Once more Hollister and Prowers measured eyes before the cattleman grinned evilly.

"Glad you mentioned it. I was aimin' to have tomatoes," he said.

CHAPTER XXIV

"COME ON, YOU DAMN BUSHWHACKER"

THE fury of the storm rattled the window panes. Down the chimney came the shrill whistle of the gale. The light of day broke dimly through the heavy clouds that swept above the gulch from peak to peak.

Two of the men sitting at dinner in the cabin watched each other intently if covertly. The third, dog-tired, nodded over the food he rushed voraciously to his mouth.

"Gonna pound my ear," Cig announced as soon as he had finished eating.

He threw himself on a bunk and inside of five minutes was snoring.

Tug, too, wanted to sleep. The desire of it grew on him with the passing hours. Overtaxed nature demanded a chance to recuperate. Instead, the young man drank strong coffee.

Jake Prowers's shrill little voice asked mildly, with the hint of a cackle in it, if he was not tired.

"In the middle of the day?" answered Tug, stifling a yawn.

"Glad you ain't. You 'n' me 'll be comp'ny for each other. Storm's peterin' out, looks like."

"Yes," agreed the guest.

It was. Except for occasional gusts, the wind had died away. Tug considered the possibility of leaving before night fell. But if he left, where could he go in the gathering darkness? Would Prowers let him walk safely away? Or would a declaration of his intention to go bring an immediate showdown? Even so, better fight the thing out now, while he was awake and Cig asleep, than wait until he slipped into drowsiness that would give the little spider-man his chance to strike and kill.

Tug had no longer any doubt of his host's intention. Under a thin disguise he saw the horrible purpose riding every word and look. It would be soon now. Why not choose his own time and try to get the break of the draw?

He could not do it. Neither will nor muscles would respond to the logical conviction of his mind that he was entitled to any advantage he could get. To whip out his gun and fire might be fair. He had no trouble in deciding that it was. But if luck were with him—if he came out alive from the duel—how could he explain why he had shot down without warning the man who was sheltering him from the blizzard? For that matter, how could he justify it to himself in the years to come? A moral certainty was not enough. He must wait until he *knew*, until the old killer made that lightning move which would give him just the vantage-ground Tug was denying himself.

All that Tug could do was watch him, every nerve keyed and muscle tensed, or bring the struggle to immediate issue. He came, suddenly, clearly, to the end of doubt.

"Time I was going," he said, and his voice rang clear.

"Going where?" Prowers's hand stopped caressing his unshaven chin and fell, almost too casually, to his side.

They glared at each other, tense, crouched, eyes narrowed and unwinking. Duels are fought and lost in that preliminary battle of locked eyes which precedes the short, sharp stabbings of the cartridge explosions. Soul searches soul for the temper of the foe's courage.

Neither gaze wavered. Each found the other stark, indomitable. The odds were heavily in favor of the old cattleman. He was a practiced gunman. Quicker than the eye could follow would come the upsweep of his arm. He could fire from the hip without taking aim. Nobody in the county could empty a revolver faster than he. But the younger man had one advantage. He had disarranged Prowers's plans by taking the initiative, by forcing the killer's hand. This was unexpected. It disturbed Jake the least in the world. His opponents usually dodged a crisis that would lead to conflict.

A cold blast beat into the house. In the open doorway stood a man, the range rider Black. Both men stared at him silently. Each knew that his coming had changed the conditions of the equation.

Under the blue cheek of the newcomer a quid of tobacco stood out. It was impossible to tell from his impassive face how much or how little of the situation he guessed.

"Ran outa smokin'," he said. "Thought I'd drap over an' have you loan me the makin's."

He had closed the door. Now he shuffled forward to the fire and with a charred stick knocked the snow from his webs.

"A sure enough rip-snorter, if any one asks you," he continued mildly by way of comment on the weather. "Don't know as I recall any storm wuss while it lasted. I seen longer ones, unless this 'un 's jest gatherin' second wind."

Tug drew a deep breath of relief and eased down. Red tragedy had been hovering in the gathering shadows of the room. It was there no longer. The blessed homely commonplace of life had entered with the lank homesteader and his need of "the makin's."

"Not fur from my place," Black went on, ignoring the silence. But I'll be dawg-goned if it was n't 'most all I could do to break through the drifts. If I'd 'a' known it was so bad I'm blamed if I would n't 'a' stayed right by my own fireside an' read that book my sister give me twenty-odd

121

years ago. Its a right good book, I been told, an' I been waitin' till I broke my laig to read it. Funny about that, too. The only time I ever hurt my laig an' got stove up proper was 'way down on Wild Cat Creek. The doc kep' me flat on a bunk three weeks, an' that book 'David Coppermine' a whole day away from me up in the hills."

"David Copperfield," suggested Tug.

"Tha's right, too. But it sure fooled me when I looked into it onct. It ain't got a thing to do with the Butte mines or the Arizona ones neither. Say, Jake, what about that tobacco? Can you lend me the loan of a sack?"

Prowers pointed to a shelf above the table. He was annoyed at Black. It was like his shiftlessness not to keep enough tobacco on hand. Of all the hours in the year, why should he butt in at precisely this one? He was confoundedly in the way. The cattleman knew that he could not go on with this thing now. Don was not thoroughgoing enough. He would do a good many things outside the law, but they had to conform to his own peculiar code. He had joined in the cattle stampede only after being persuaded that nobody would be hurt by it. Since then Jake had not felt that he was dependable. The homesteader was suffering from an attack of conscience.

Cig had wakened when the rush of cold air from the open door had swept across the room. He sat up now, yawning and stretching himself awake.

"What a Gawd-forsaken country!" he jeered. "Me for de bright lights of li'l' ol' New York. If Cig ever lands in de Grand Central, he'll stick right on de island, b'lieve me. I wisht I was at Mike's Place right dis minute. A skoit hangs out dere who's stuck on yours truly. Some dame, I'll tell de world." And he launched into a disreputable reminiscence.

Nobody echoed his laughter. Hollister was disgusted. Black did not like the tramp. The brain of Prowers was already spinning a cobweb of plots.

Cig looked round. What was the matter with these boobs, anyhow? Did n't they know a good story when they heard one?

"Say, wot'ell is dis—a Salvation Army dump before de music opens up?" he asked, with an insulting lift of the upper lip.

Tug strapped on his skis, always with an eye on Prowers. Which reminded Cig. A triumphant venom surged up in him.

"Gonna take me down to de cop, are youse?" he sneered.

122

"Say, will youse ring for a taxi, Jake? I gotta go to jail wid dis bird."

In two sentences Prowers gave his version of the story to Black. Tug corrected him instantly.

"He came to blow us up in the tunnel. When I took him back, he dug six sticks of dynamite out of the dirt in the rock wall."

Black spat into the fire. His face reflected disgust, but he said nothing. What was there to say, except that his soul was sick of the evil into which he was being dragged by the man he accepted as leader?

Tug put on his slicker.

"Where you going?" asked Black.

"To the camp."

" 'S a long way. Better stay at my shack to-night."

"Much obliged. I will."

They went out together. Tug was careful to walk with Black between him and the cabin as long as it was in sight.

The wind had died completely, so that the air was no longer a white smother. Travel was easy, for the cold had crusted the top of the snow. They worked their way out of the gulch, crossed an edge of the forest reserve, and passed the cabin of the homesteader Howard. Not far from this, Black turned into his own place.

The range rider kicked off his webs and replenished the fire. While he made supper, Hollister sat on the floor before the glowing piñon knots and dried his skis. When they were thoroughly dry, he waxed them well, rubbing in the wax with a cork.

"Come an' get it," Black called presently.

They sat down to a meal of ham, potatoes, biscuits, plenty of gravy, and coffee. Tug did himself well. He had worked hard enough in the drifts to justify a man-size hunger.

Their talk rambled in the casual fashion of hap-hazard conversation. It touched on Jake Prowers and Cig, rather sketchily, for Black did not care to discuss the men with whom he was still allied, no matter what his private opinion of them might be. It included the tunnel and the chances of success of the Sweetwater Dam project, this last a matter upon which they differed. Don had spent his life in the saddle. He stuck doggedly to the contention that, since water will not run uphill, the whole enterprise was "dawg-goned foolishness."

123

Hollister gave up, shrugging his shoulders. "All right with me. A man convinced against his will, you know. Trouble with you is that you don't want the Flat Tops irrigated, so you won't let yourself believe they can be."

"The Government engineers said they couldn't be watered, did n't they? Well, their say-so goes with me all right."

"They were wrong, but you need n't believe it till you see water in the ditches on Flat Top."

"I won't."

Tug rose from the table and expanded his lungs in a deep, luxurious yawn. "Think I'll turn in and sleep round the clock if you don't mind. I can hardly keep my eyes open."

Black waved his hand at the nearest bunk. "Go to it."

While he was taking off his boots, the engineer came to a matter he wanted to get off his mind. "Expect you know the hole I was in when you showed up this afternoon. I'll say I never was more glad to see anybody in my life."

"What d' you mean?" asked Black, blank wall eyes full on his guest.

"I mean that Prowers was watching for a chance to kill me. I'd called for a showdown a moment before you opened the door."

The range rider lied, loyally. "Nothin' to that a-tall. What would Jake want to do that for? Would it get him anything if he did? You sure fooled yoreself if that's what you were thinking."

"Did I?" The eyes of the younger man were on Black, hard, keen, and intent. "Well, that's exactly what I was thinking. And still am. Subject number two on which we'll have to agree to disagree."

"Jake's no bad man runnin' around gunnin' men for to see 'em kick. You been readin' too much Billy the Kid stuff, I should n't wonder."

Tug dropped the second boot on the floor and rose to take off his coat.

There came the sound of a shot, the crash of breaking glass. Hollister swayed drunkenly on his feet, groped for the back of a chair, half turned, and slid to the floor beside the bunk.

Usually Black's movements were slow. Now no panther could have leaped for the lamp more swiftly. He blew out the light, crept along the log wall to the window, reached out a hand cautiously, and drew a curtain across the pane through which a bullet had just come. Then, crouching, he ran across the room and took a rifle from the deer's horns upon which it rested.

"Come on, you damn bushwhacker. I'm ready for you," he muttered.

CHAPTER XXV

A DIFFERENCE OF OPINION

BETTY was whipping mayonnaise in the kitchen when a voice hailed the Diamond Bar K ranch in general.

"Hello the house!"

Through the window she saw a rider on a horse, and a moment later her brain localized him as a neighborhood boy who had recently joined the forest rangers. She went to the door, sleeves still rolled back to the elbows of the firm satiny arms.

"Hoo-hoo!" she called, flinging a small hand wildly above her head in greeting. "Hoo-hoo, Billy boy!"

He turned, caught sight of her, and at once began to smile. It was noticeable that when Betty laughed, as she frequently did for no good reason at all except a general state of well-being, others were likely to join in her happiness.

"Oh, there you are," he said, and at once descended.

"Umpha! Here I am, but I won't be long. I'm making salad dressing. Come in to the kitchen if you like. I'll give you a cookie. Just out o' the oven."

"Listens good to Billy," he said, and stayed not on the order of his coming.

She found him a plate of cookies and a stool. "Sit there. And tell me what's new in the hills. Did you pass the dam as you came down? And what d' you know about the tunnel?"

The ranger stopped a cookie halfway to his mouth. "Say, that fellow—the one drivin' the tunnel—he's been shot."

"What!"

"Last night—at Don Black's cabin."

125

A cold hand laid itself on her heart and stopped its beating. "You mean—on purpose?"

He nodded. "Shot through the window at dark."

"Mr. Hollister—that who you mean?"

"Yep. That's what he calls himself now. Jones it was at first."

"Is he—hurt badly?"

"I'll say so. In the side—internal injuries. Outa his head when I was there this mo'ning."

"What does the doctor say?"

"He ain't seen him yet. On the way up now. I 'phoned down from Meagher's ranch. He'd ought to pass here soon."

"But why did n't they get the doctor sooner? What were they thinking about?" she cried.

"Nobody with him but Don Black. He could n't leave him alone, he claims. Lucky I dropped in when I did."

Impulsively Betty made up her mind. "I'm going to him. You'll have to take me, Billy."

"You!" exclaimed the ranger. "What's the big idea, Betty?"

"Dad's gone to Denver to the stock show. I'm going to look after him. That's what Dad would want if he were here. Some one's got to nurse him. What other woman can go in on snowshoes and do it?"

"Does he have to have a woman nurse? Can't Mr. Merrick send a man up there to look after him?"

"Don't argue, Billy boy," she told him. "You see how it is. They don't even get a doctor to him for fifteen or sixteen hours. By this time he may be—" She stopped and bit her lip to check a sudden swell of emotion that choked up her throat.

Bridget came into the kitchen. Betty's announcement was both a decision and an appeal. "Mr. Hollister's been hurt—shot—up in the hills. I'm going up to Justin to make him take me to him."

"Is he hur-rt bad?" asked the buxom housekeeper.

"Yes. I don't know. Billy thinks so. If I hurry I can get there before night."

Bridget hesitated. "I was thinkin' it might be better for me to go, dearie. You know how folks talk."

"Oh, talk!" Betty was explosively impatient. She always was when anybody interfered with one of her enthusiasms. "Of course, if you could go. But you'd never get in through the snow. And what could they say—except that I went to save a man's life if I could?"

126

"Mr. Merrick might not like it."

"Of course he'd like it." The girl was nobly indignant for her fiancé. "Why would n't he like it? It's just what he'd want me to do." Under the brown bloom of her cheeks was the peach glow of excitement.

Bridget had traveled some distance on the journey of life, and she had her own opinion about that. Merrick, if she guessed him at all correctly, was a possessive man. He could appreciate Betty's valiant eagerness when it went out to him, but he would be likely to resent her generous giving of herself to another. He did not belong to the type of lover that recognizes the right of a sweetheart or a wife to express herself in her own way. She was pledged to him. Her vocation and avocation in life were to be his wife.

But Bridget was wise in her generation. She knew that Betty was of the temperament that had to learn from experience. She asked how they would travel to the dam.

"On horseback—if we can get through. The road's not broken yet probably after yesterday's storm. We'll start right away. I can't get Justin on the 'phone. The wire must be down."

The ranger saddled for her and they took the road. Betty carried with her a small emergency kit of medical supplies.

Travel back and forth had broken the road in the valley. It was not until the riders struck the hill trail that they had to buck drifts. It was slow, wearing work, and, by the time they came in sight of the dam, Betty's watch told her that it was two o'clock.

Merrick saw them coming down the long white slope and wondered what travelers had business urgent enough to bring them through heavy drifts to the isolated camp. As soon as he recognized Betty, he went to meet her. Billy rode on down to the tents. He knew when he was not needed.

Rich color glowed in her cheeks, excitement sparkled in her eyes.

"What in the world are you doing here?" Merrick asked.

She was the least bit dashed by his manner. It suggested censure, implied that her adventure—whatever the cause of it —was a bit of headstrong folly. Did he think it was a girl's place to stay at home in weather like this? Did he think that she was unmaidenly, had bucked miles of snowdrifts because she could not stay away from him?

"Have you heard about Mr. Hollister? He's been hurt—shot."

"Shot?"

"Last night. At Black's cabin."

"Who shot him?"

"I don't know. He's pretty bad, Billy says."

"Doctor seen him yet?"

"He's on the way now. I want you to take me to him, Justin."

"Take *you?* What for?"

"To nurse him."

He smiled, the superior smile of one prepared to argue away the foolish fancies of a girl.

"Is your father home yet?"

"No. He'll be back to-morrow. Why?"

"Because, dear girl, you can't go farther. In the first place, it's not necessary. I'll do all that can be done for Hollister. The trip from here won't be a picnic."

"I've brought my skis. I can get in all right," she protested eagerly.

"I grant that. But there's no need for you to go. You'd far better not. It's not quite—" He stopped in mid-sentence, with an expressive lift of the shoulders.

"Not quite proper. I did n't expect *you* to say that, Justin," she reproached. "After what he did for us."

"He did only what any self-respecting man would do."

Her smile coaxed him. "Well, I want to do only what any self-respecting woman would do. Surely it'll be all right if you go along."

How could he tell her that he knew no other unmarried woman of her age, outside of professional nurses, who would consider such a thing for the sake of a comparative stranger? How could he make her see that Black's cabin was no place for a young girl to stay? He was exasperated at her persistence. It offended his *amour propre*. Why all this discussion about one of his employees who had been a tramp only a few months since?

Merrick shook his head. His lips smiled, but there was no smile in his eyes. "You're a very impulsive and very generous young woman. But if you were a little older you would see—"

She broke impatiently into his argument. "Don't you see how I feel, Justin? I've got to do what I can for him. We're not in a city where we can ring up for a trained nurse. I'm the only available woman that can get in to him. Why did I take my Red Cross training if I'm not to help those who are sick?"

"Can't you trust me to look out for him?"

"Of course I can. That's not the point. There's so much in nursing. Any doctor will tell you so. Maybe he needs expert care. I really can nurse. I've done it all my life."

"You don't expect to nurse everybody in the county that falls sick, do you? Don't you see, dear girl, that Black's shack is no place for you?"

"Why is n't it? I'm a ranchman's daughter. It does n't shock or offend me to see things that might distress a city girl." She cast about in her mind for another way to put it. "I remember my mother leaving us once for days to look after a homesteader who had been hurt 'way up on Rabbit Ear Creek. Why, that's what all the women on the frontier did."

"The frontier days are past," he said. "And that's beside the point, anyhow. I'll have him well looked after. You need n't worry about that."

"But I would," she urged. "I'd worry a lot. I want to go myself, Justin—to make sure it's all right and that everything's being done for him that can be. You think it's just foolishness in me, but it is n't."

She put her hand shyly on his sleeve. The gesture was an appeal for understanding of the impulse that was urgent in her. If he could only sympathize with it and acknowledge its obligation.

"I think it's neither necessary nor wise. It's my duty, not yours, to have him nursed properly. I'll not shirk it." He spoke with the finality of a dominant man who has made up his mind.

Betty felt thrown back on herself. She was disappointed in him and her feelings were hurt. Why must he be so obtuse, so correct and formal? Why could n't he see that she *had* to go? After all, a decision as to what course she would follow lay with her and not with him. He had no right to assume otherwise. She was determined to go, anyhow, but she would not quarrel with him.

"When are you going up to Black's?" she asked.

"At once."

"Do take me, please."

He shook his head. "It is n't best, dear girl."

In her heart flamed smokily rebellious fires. "Then I'll go with Billy."

129

He interpreted the words as a challenge. Their eyes met in a long, steady look. Each measured the strength of the other. It was the first time they had come into open conflict.

"I would n't do that, Betty," he said quietly.

"You don't know how I feel about it. You won't understand." Her voice shook with emotion. "I've *got* to go."

Merrick knew that he could prevent the ranger from guiding Betty to the gulch where the wounded man was, but it was possible to pay too great a price for victory. He yielded, grudgingly.

"I'll take you. After you've seen Hollister, you can give us directions for nursing him. I should think the doctor ought to know, but, if you have n't confidence in him, you can see to it yourself."

Betty found no pleasure now in her desire to help. Justin's opposition had taken all the joy out of it. Nor did his surrender give her any gratification. He had not yielded because he appreciated the validity of her purpose, but because he had chosen to avoid an open breach. She felt a thousand miles away from him in spirit.

"Thank you," she said formally, choking down a lump in her throat.

CHAPTER XXVI

BLACK IS SURPRISED

It is not in youth to be long cast down for the troubles of a stranger, even one who has very greatly engaged the sympathy. In spite of Betty's anxiety about the wounded man, her resilient spirits had sent her eagerly upon this adventure.

She would see Justin. He would approve her plans with enthusiasm. Together they would ski across the white waters, they two alone in a vast world of mysterious stillness. The thin clear air of the high Rockies would carry their resonant voices like the chimes of bells. Silences would be significant, laughter the symbol of happy comradeship. For the first time they would come glowing through difficulties, perhaps dangers, conquered side by side. And at the end of the journey waited for them service, that which gave their joyous enterprise the value of an obligation.

And it was not at all like that—not a bit as she had daydreamed it on the ride to Sweetwater Dam. The joy was struck dead in her heart. Miserably she realized that Justin could not understand. The ardent fire that burned in her soul seemed only mushy sentiment to him, on a par with the hysteria that made silly women send flowers to brutal murderers they did not know.

The bars were up between them. The hard look in his eyes meant anger. There would be no expression of it in temper. He was too self-contained for that. None the less it was anger. The reflection of it gleamed out from under her own dark lashes. She told herself she hated the narrowness in him that made him hold so rigidly to the well-ordered, the conventional thing. Why could n't he see that there was an imperative on her to *live?* Well, she would show him. Probably he thought that in every clash of will she ought to yield. He could learn his lesson just as well now as later.

She held her head high, but there was a leaden weight in her bosom that made her want to sob.

Often she had been proud of his tremendous driving power, the force that made of him a sixty-horse-power man. She resented it fiercely to-day. He was traveling just a little too fast for her, so that she could hardly keep up with him. But she would have fallen in her tracks rather than ask him to go slower.

Once the slither of his runners stopped. "Am I going too fast?" he asked coldly.

"Not at all," she answered stubbornly.

He struck out again. They were climbing a long slope that ended in a fringe of timber. At the top he waited, watching her as she labored up heavily. The look he gave her when she reached him said, "I told you so."

Before them lay a valley, beyond which was another crest of pines.

"How far now?" Betty asked, panting from the climb.

"Just beyond that ridge."

"That all?" she said indifferently. "Thought it was a long way."

131

"We'll coast into the valley," he replied curtly.

She watched him gliding into the dip of the slope. He was not an expert on runners as her father was, but he had learned the trick of the thing pretty well. It was in line with his thoroughness not to be a novice long at anything he set out to master.

Betty shot down after him, gathering impetus as she went. She was watching the path ahead, and it was not till she was close upon him that she saw Merrick had fallen. She swerved to the left, flinging out her arms to prevent herself from going down. Unsteadily she teetered for a moment, but righted herself with an effort and kept going till she reached the bottom.

Merrick was on his feet when she turned.

"Anything wrong?" she called.

"One of my skis broken."

She went back to him. "How did it happen?"

"Dipped into a rock under the snow." His voice was sullen. Like many men who do well whatever they undertake, he resented any mishap due to lack of his own skill. His sense of superiority would have been satisfied if the accident had befallen her instead of him.

Betty did not smile, but, nevertheless, she was maliciously pleased. It would bring him down a peg, anyhow.

"What'll you do?" she asked.

"I suppose I can hobble along somehow. Perhaps I'd better take your skis and hurry on. I could borrow a pair at the cabin and come back for you. Yes, I think that would be better."

She shook her head. "No, I'll go on and send Mr. Black with a pair. I'd rather not wait here in the cold. I'll not be long. You can keep moving."

This did not suit Merrick at all. He did not want to be regarded as an incompetent who had bogged down in the snow. It hurt his pride that Betty should go on and send back help to him, especially when they felt criss-cross toward each other.

"I'd rather you did n't," he said. "You don't know who is at the cabin. That tramp Cig may be there—or Prowers. They're dangerous, both of them. Yesterday they tried to blow up the men working on the tunnel."

"You can lend me your revolver, then, if you like. But I'm not afraid. Mr. Black would n't let them hurt me even if they wanted to."

"It's not very cold. I'd be back in a little while. And, as you say, you could keep moving."

"No, I'm going on," she answered, and her quiet voice told him she had made up her mind.

He unbuckled his belt and handed it to her. "You'll be safer with that .38," he said. What he thought is not of record.

"Thanks." Betty's little smile, with its hint of sarcasm, suggested that there was not the least need of the revolver; if she wore it, the only reason was to humor his vanity and let him feel that he was protecting her.

She crossed the valley and climbed the ridge. From the farther side of it she looked down upon a log cabin of two rooms, a small stable, and a corral. They nestled in a draw at her feet, so close that a man could have thrown a stone almost to the fence. The hillside was rough with stones. With Justin's mishap in mind, she felt her way down carefully.

Smoke poured out of the chimney and polluted the pure light air. No need of seeing the fire inside to know that the wood was resinous fir.

Betty knocked on the door.

It opened. Black stood on the threshold looking down at her in ludicrous amazement. She had taken off her coat and was carrying it. Against a background of white she bloomed vivid as a poinsettia in her old-rose sweater and jaunty tam. The cold crisp air had whipped the scarlet into her lips, the pink into her cheeks.

"What in—Mexico!" he exclaimed.

"How's Mr. Hollister?"

"A mighty sick man. Howcome you here, miss?"

The sound of a querulous voice came from within. "Tell you I don't want the stuff. How many times I got to say it?"

"I've come to nurse him. Billy brought us word. Father wasn't home—nor Lon. So Mr. Merrick brought me."

"Merrick," he repeated.

"He's over the hill, a ways back. Broke a ski. He'd like you to take him a pair. I'll look after Mr. Hollister."

As she followed the lank range rider into the cabin, she pulled off her gauntlets. Her cold fingers fumbled with the ski ties.

"Lemme do that," Black said, and dropped on a knee to help.

"I guess you can do it quicker." She looked at the patient and let her voice fall as she asked a question. "Is he delirious?"

"Crazy as a hydryphoby skunk." He repeated what he had said before. "A mighty sick man, looks like."

133

Betty looked into the hot, fevered face of the man tossing on the bed. From her medicine kit she took a thermometer. His fever was high. She prepared medicine and coaxed him to swallow it.

"Where is he wounded?" she asked.

"In the side."

"Did you wash out the wound and bind it up?"

"Yes'm. I've took care of fellows shot up before."

"Bleed much?"

"Right smart. Did you hear when Doc Rayburn was comin'?"

"He's on the way." She found cold water and bathed the burning face.

"Wisht he'd hustle along," the range rider said uneasily.

"He won't be long." With a flare of anger she turned on Black. "Who shot him?"

"I dunno. He was shot through the window whilst he was ondressin' for bed. We come together from the old Thorwaldson cabin a while before."

"Did that Cig do it?"

"Might have, at that." Black was putting on his webs. "Reckon I'll drift back an' pick up yore friend Merrick."

"Yes," she said absently. "It was that tramp Cig or Jake Prowers, one."

"Yore guess is as good as mine," he said, buttoning to the neck a leather coat.

"Can't we have more light in here? It's dark. If you'd draw back that window curtain—"

"Then Mr. Bushwhacker would get a chanct for another shot," he said dryly. "No, I reckon we'll leave the curtain where it's at."

Her big startled eyes held fascinated to his. "You don't think they'd shoot him again now."

"Mebbeso. My notion is better not give 'em a show to get at him. You keep the door closed. I'll not be long. I see you got a gun."

There was something significant in the way he said it. Her heart began to beat fast.

"You don't think—?"

"No, I don't. If I did, I'd stay right here. Not a chanct in a hundred. How far back's yore friend?"

"Less than a mile."

"Well, he's likely been movin' right along. When I reach

134

the ridge, I'll give him the high sign an' leave the skis stickin' up in the snow there."

"Yes." And, as he was leaving, "Don't be long," she begged.

"Don't you be scared, miss. Them sidewinders don't come out in the open an' do their wolf-killin'. An' I won't be gone but a li'l' while. If anything worries you, bang away with that .38 an' I'll come a-runnin'.'"

He closed the door after him. From behind the curtain she watched him begin the ascent. Then she went back to her patient and bathed his hot hands. Betty echoed the wish of the range rider that the doctor would come. What could be keeping him? From the Diamond Bar K ranch to Wild Horse was only a few miles. He must have started before she did. It would not be long now.

In spite of a two days' growth of beard, the young fellow on the bed looked very boyish. She gently brushed back the curls matted on the damp forehead. He was rambling again in desultory speech.

"A cup o' cold water—cold lemonade. Happy days, she says. No trouble friendship won't lighten, she says, with that game smile lighting up her face. Little thoroughbred."

A warm wave of exultant emotion beat through her blood. It reached her face in a glow of delicate beauty that transformed her.

"You dear boy!" she cried softly, and her eyes were shining stars of tender light.

CHAPTER XXVII

THE MAN WITH THE BLEACHED BLUE EYES

THERE was not much she could do for him except bathe again his face and hands. He asked for a drink, and Betty propped him up with her arm while she held the tin cup to his lips. Exhausted by the effort, he sank back to the pillow and panted. All the supple strength of his splendid youth had been drained from him. The muscles were lax, the movements of the body feeble.

Sunken eyes stared at her without recognition. "Sure I'll take your hand, and say 'Thank you' too. You're the *best* little scout, the best ever."

She took the offered hand and pressed it gently. "Yes, but now you must rest. You've been sick."

"A Boche got me." His wandering subconscious thoughts flowed into other memories. "Zero hour, boys. Over the top and give 'em hell." Then, without any apparent break from one theme to another, his thick voice fell to a cunning whisper. "There's a joint on South Clark Street where I can get it."

Into his disjointed mutterings her name came at times, spoken always with a respect that was almost reverence. And perhaps a moment later his voice would ring out clear and crisp in directions to the men working under him. Subjects merged into each other inconsequently—long-forgotten episodes of school days, college larks, murmured endearments to the mother who had died many years since. Listening to him, Betty knew that she was hearing revelations of a soul masculine but essentially clean.

A sound startled her, the click of the latch. She turned her head swiftly as the door opened. Fear drenched her heart. The man on the threshold was Prowers. He had come out of a strong white light and at first could see nothing in the dark cabin.

Betty watched him as he stood there, his bleached blue eyes blinking while they adjusted themselves to another focus.

"What do you want?" she asked sharply, the accent of alarm in her voice.

"A woman, by jiminy by jinks!" The surprise in his squeaky voice was pronounced. He moved forward to the bed. "Clint Reed's girl. Where you come from? How'd you get here?"

She had drawn back to the wall at the head of the bed in order to keep a space between them. Her heart was racing furiously. His cold eyes, with the knife-edge stab in them, held hers fast.

"I came in over the snow to nurse him."

"Alone?"

"No. Mr. Merrick's with me."

"Where?"

"At the top of the hill. He broke a ski."

"Where's Don?"

136

"Gone to meet him. They'll be here in a minute."

A cunning, impish grin broke the lines of the man's leathery face. He remembered that he had come prepared to be surprised to hear of Hollister's wound.

"Nurse who?" he asked suavely.

"Mr. Hollister, the engineer driving the tunnel."

"Sick, is he?" He scarcely took the trouble to veil his rancorous malice. It rode him, voice, manner, and mocking eye. His mouth was a thin straight line, horribly cruel.

"Some one shot him—last night—through the window." She knew now that he had done it or had had it done. The sense of outrage, of horror at his unhuman callousness, drove the fear out of her bosom. Her eyes accused him, though her tongue made no charge.

"Shot him, by jiminy by jinks! Why, Daniels had ought to put the fellow in the calaboose. Who did it?"

"I don't know. Do you?" she flashed back.

His evil grin derided her. "How would I know, my dear?"

He drew up a chair and sat down. The girl did not move. Rigid and watchful, she did not let her eye waver from him for an instant.

He nodded toward the delirious man. "Will he make it?"

"I don't know."

"Doc seen him yet?"

"No."

"Glad I came. I can help nurse him." He cut short a high cackle of laughter to ask a question. "What's yore gun for, dearie? You would n't throw it on poor Jake Prowers, would you?"

He was as deadly as dynamite, she thought, more treacherous than a rattlesnake. She wanted to cry out her horror at him. To see him sitting there, humped up like a spider, not three feet from the man he had tried to murder, filled her with repulsion. There was more in her feeling than that; a growing paralysis of terror lest he might reach out and in a flash complete the homicide he had attempted.

She tried to reason this away. He dared not do it, with her here as a witness, with two men drawing closer every minute. Don Black had told her that he wouldn't strike in the open, and the range rider had known him more years than she had lived. But the doubt remained. She did not know what he would do. Since she did not live in the same world as he, it was not possible for her to follow his thought processes.

137

Then, with no previous intimation that his delirium had dropped from him, the wounded man startled Betty by asking a rational question.

"Did you come to see how good a job you'd done?" he said quietly to Prowers.

The cowman shook his head, still with the Satanic grin. "No job of mine, son. I'm thorough."

"Your orders, but maybe not your hand," Hollister insisted feebly.

Betty moved into his line of vision, and to his startled brain the motion of her was like sweet unearthly music. He looked silently at her for a long moment.

"Am I still out of my head?" he asked. "It's not really you, is it?"

"Yes," she said, very gently. "You must n't talk."

"In Black's cabin, are n't we?"

"Yes."

"Shot through the window, Black told me. Remember, if I don't get well, it was this man or Cig that did it."

"I'll remember," she promised. "But you're going to get well. Don't talk, please."

"Just one thing. What are you doing here?"

"I came to look after you. Now that's all—please."

He said no more, in words. But the eyes of sick men are like those of children. They tell the truth. From them is stripped the veil woven by time and the complexities of life.

Sounds of voices on the hillside drifted to the cabin. Betty's heart leaped joyfully. Friends were at hand. It was too late for Prowers to do any harm even if it was in his mind.

The voices approached the cabin. The girl recognized that of Merrick, strong and dominant and just a little heavy. She heard Black's drawling answer, without being able to distinguish the words.

The door opened. Four men came into the room. The two who brought up the rear were Dr. Rayburn and Lon Forbes.

"Oh, Lon!" Betty cried, and went to him with a rush. "I'm awf'ly glad you came."

She clung to him, trembling, a sob in her throat.

The rawboned foreman patted her shoulder with a touch of embarrassment. "There—there, honey, 's all right. Why did n't you wait for old Lon instead o' hoppin' away like you done?"

Prowers tilted back his chair on two legs and chirped up

with satiric comment. "We got quite a nice party present. Any late arrivals not yet heard from?"

Both Lon and Justin Merrick were taken aback. In the darkness they had not yet recognized the little man.

The foreman spoke dryly. "Might 'a' known it. Trouble and Jake Prowers hunt in couples. Always did."

"I could get a right good testimonial from Mr. Lon Forbes," the cowman said, with his high cackle of splenetic laughter. "Good old Lon, downright an' four-square, always a booster for me."

Betty whispered. "He's an awful man, Lon. I'm scared of him. I did n't know any minute what he was going to do. Oh, I *am* glad you came."

"Same here," Lon replied. "Don't you be scared, Betty. He can't do a thing—not a thing."

Merrick had been taking off his skis. He came up to Betty now. "Did he annoy you—say anything or—?"

"No, Justin." A shiver ran down her spine. "He just looked and grinned. I wanted to scream. He shot Mr. Hollister. I know he did. Or had it done by that Cig."

"Yes. I don't doubt that."

The doctor, disencumbered of impedimenta of snowshoes and wraps, fussed forward to the bedside. "Well, let's see— let's see what's wrong here."

He examined the wound, effervesced protests and questions, and prepared for business with the bustling air that characterized him.

"Outa the room now—all but Miss Reed and one o' you men. Lon, you'll do."

"I'll stay," announced Merrick with decision.

"All right. All right. I want some clean rags, Black. You got plenty of hot water, I see. Clear out, boys."

"You don't need a good nurse, Doc?" Prowers asked, not without satiric malice. He was playing with fire, and he knew it. Everybody in the room suspected him of this crime. He felt a perverted enjoyment in their hostility.

Black chose this moment to make his declaration of independence. "I'd light a shuck outa here if I was you, Jake, an' I would n't come back, seems to me."

The cold, bleached eyes of the cowman narrowed. "You're givin' me that advice *as a friend,* are you, Don?" he asked.

The range rider's jaw stopped moving. In his cheek the tobacco quid stuck out. His face, habitually set to the leathery

139

imperturbability of his calling, froze now to an expressionless mask.

"I'm sure givin' you that advice," he said evenly.

"I don't hear so awful good, Don. As a friend, did you say?" The little man cupped an ear with one hand in ironic mockery.

Black's gaze was hard as gun-metal. "I said I'd hit the trail for home if I was you, Jake, an' I'd stay there for a spell with kinda low visibility like they said in the war."

"I getcha Don." Prowers shot a blast of cold lightning from under his scant brows. "I can take a hint without waitin' for a church to fall on me. Rats an' a sinkin' ship, eh? You got a notion these fellows are liable to win out on me, an' you want to quit while the quittin' is good. I been wonderin' for quite a while if you was n't yellow."

"Don't do that wonderin' out loud, Jake," the other warned quietly. "If you do, you'll sure enough find out."

The little man laughed scornfully, met in turn defiantly the eyes of Betty, Merrick, and Forbes, turned on his heel, and sauntered out.

CHAPTER XXVIII

BETTY HAS HER OWN WAY

DON BLACK had not himself built the cabin where he lived. While he was still a boy jingling his first spurs, two young Englishmen had hewn its logs out of the untouched forest on the western slope of Pegleg Pass. They were remittance men, exiled from their country for the peace of mind of their families. In the casual fashion of their class they had drifted to the Rockies to hunt for big game and, less industriously, for elusive fortune. Long since they had returned to the estates which Britishers of this type seem always to be inheriting from convenient relatives.

By the simple process of moving in, Black had become owner of the cabin. He hung his pinched-in cowboy hat in a peg in the wall and thereby took possession. His title was perfectly good in the eyes of the range riders who dropped in occasionally and made themselves at home. Whether Don was or was not on the place, they were welcome to what they found. The only obligation on them was to cut a fresh supply of firewood in place of that they used.

One room was enough for Black's needs. The other served as a place in which to store old saddles, mountain-lion pelts, worn-out boots, blankets, unused furniture, and a hundred odds and ends. With the help of the owner, Lon Forbes set to work housecleaning. Useless litter went flying out of doors. A vigorous broom in the hands of Lon raised clouds of dust. In the fireplace old papers and boxes blazed cheerfully. A Navajo rug, resurrected from the bottom of a hingeless trunk, covered the floor in front of a walnut bed imported by one of the Englishmen from Denver.

It took hours to make the transformation, but the foreman was quite pleased with himself when he ushered Betty into the bedroom he had prepared for her.

She clapped her hands softly. "My, Lon! What a fine wife some Suffragette's lost in you. Maybe it is n't too late yet. You can keep house while she—"

"Help! Help!" expostulated Forbes.

"Oh, if you've got your eye on one of these little flapper girls, of course, there's no use my saying a word," she teased. "I know how stubborn you are when you get 'sot.' "

She was in a mood of happy reaction from the fears that had oppressed her all day. Dr. Rayburn had told her—with some reservations, to be sure—that, barring unexpected complications, Hollister ought to get well. It would take time and nursing and good food, but all of these the patient would get.

"You're right I've got my eye on one of them li'l' flapper girls—this very minute," he rapped back promptly. "An' she's a sure-enough warnin' to a fellow to play his hand out alone unless he wants to be bossed somethin' scandalous."

"It would do you good to be bossed," she told him, eyes dancing. "The refining influence of a young woman—say about forty-five or maybe fifty—"

"You're pickin' her for me, are you?" he snorted.

"She'll do the picking when the time comes. I suppose you'll have to give up smoking—and you'll have to shave every day —and probably be a deacon in the church at Wild Horse—"

"Yes, I will not. All I got to do is look at Clint an' see how a half-grown kid has got a check rein on him. That scares me a plenty." He shook his head in mock despair, but his eyes gave him away. "Gallivantin' into the hills, through 'steen million tons of snow, to nurse a scalawag who—"

"He's no scalawag, Lon Forbes."

"Like to know why he ain't. Nothin' but a hobo when you first met up with him."

"Now, Lon, you know very well you told me you thought he was a man from the ground up. Those were the very words you used."

"Well, a hobo may be a man," he defended. "Anyways, that don't mean you'd ought to bust up yore happy home to hike over the hills for him."

"Justin's been talking to you," she charged.

"Maybeso, an' maybe not. That ain't the point. While Clint's away, it's up to me to run the Diamond Bar K."

"With Justin's help," she cut in.

Betty thought, though she did not express it in words, that Lon would have his hands full if he intended to take charge of her activities as a part of the ranch. She knew that this would never have occurred to him as included in his duties if it had not been suggested by Merrick.

"I'm not askin' any one's help. I reckon I'm as grown-up as I'll ever be. Anyways, Clint put me in charge, figurin' I was man-size an' competent. Question is, Would yore father want you up here?"

Betty decided to carry the war indignantly into the territory of the enemy. "Of course, he would. After knowing Dad all these years I should think you'd be ashamed to doubt him. Dad pays his debts. He's a good friend. This boy—this young fellow Hollister—tried to do us a good turn after we had behaved pretty bad to him. You know Dad has been looking for a chance to help him. Well, it's come. What are we going to do about it? Go through—or quit on the job?"

"Go through. I ain't proposin' anything else. But you don't have to stay here. I can look after him, an' Merrick'll see you home."

"What do you know about nursing?" she scoffed. "Or cooking? You know what the doctor said. He's got to have nice things to eat after he gets a little better. And good nursing. Dr. Rayburn told you—I heard him say it—that he was glad I'd come because Mr. Hollister needs a woman's nursing."

142

Lon scratched his head to help him think. It was sometimes a laborious process. He knew cattle and crops, but chaperoning a young woman was untried territory.

"Times has changed, Betty," he explained. "You kinda growed up helter-skelter an' run wild. But you're a young lady now, an' you can't be too careful. You gotta think about what folks'll say."

"Fiddlesticks! What'll they say? What can they say if you stay up here with me? It'll be only a day or two till Dad gets home. It's just that you've been getting notions from Justin. He's a city man and does n't know our ways. But you've always lived here, Lon. I'm surprised at you."

"O' course there ain't any real harm in yore stayin," he conceded hesitantly. "I'll be here to look after you an' see Prowers don't trouble you. An' it won't be long."

"I'm staying because I really can help, Lon. Justin thinks it's only foolishness, but you know it is n't. In Denver, where he lives, there are plenty of trained nurses, but it's different here. If Bridget could get in, I would n't say a word about staying. But she can't. If I went away and left this poor boy, you'd never respect me again."

"I would, too. But there. You're gonna stay. I see that."

"Yes, I am." She caught the lapels of the big foreman's coat and coaxed him with the smile that always had proved effective with him. "And you know I'm right. Don't you, Lon?"

"Nothin' of the kind," he blustered. "An' you need n't try to come it over me. I know you too blamed well, miss. You're bound an' determined to have yore own way—always were since you were a li'l' trick knee-high to a duck. Trouble is, you've been spoiled."

"Yes," she admitted, "and you did it."

"No such a thing. I always did tell Clint he'd find out some day what'd come of lettin' you boss the whole works." To save his face he finished with a peremptory order. "Don's fixin' up some supper. Soon as you've had yours, why, you'll go right straight to bed. Doc an' me are aimin' to look after Hollister to-night."

"Yes, Lon," Betty replied meekly. She had got what she wanted, and she was willing to propitiate him by a demure obedience calculated to remove the sting of her victory.

Don opened the door and announced that supper was ready.

Betty saw Merrick's eye flash a question at Forbes as they came into the larger room. She went directly to him. Betty was a woman; therefore complex. But she usually expressed herself simply.

"It's all settled, Justin. Lon is going to stay with me."

He made no answer in words, but his salient jaw set grimly. Like many masterful men, he did not relish defeat.

They drank coffee from tin cups and ate bacon, tomatoes, and beans served in tin plates. Don's biscuits were appetizing, and four or five pans of them disappeared before his guests were fed.

Betty lived up to the promise she had made Lon. She whispered with Dr. Rayburn for a minute, then said "Good-night" to the company generally, and vanished into her bedroom.

The day had been a full one. To come in over the snow had taxed the strength of her muscles. She was tired, and, as she sat before the glowing coals taking the pins out of her hair, she yawned luxuriously.

Just now her mind was on Merrick. The vague disappointment in their relationship had crystallized today into definite dissatisfaction. To use one of her father's expressions, Justin and she had not come out of the same pasture. They thought in different languages.

That he had not sympathized with the urge in her to spend herself in service for the wounded man was important beyond the immediate question. And, even if he did not agree with her, he should have understood her obligation to do as she thought best. It involved their whole future. The trouble was that he did not recognize her right to follow the guidance of her own judgment. She must defer to him, must accept his decision as final.

Betty knew she could not do that. In essence she was a twentieth-century woman.

CHAPTER XXIX

A CHILD OF IMPULSE

BETTY went to sleep critical of Justin. She woke, in the dawn of a new day streaming through the window, to censure of her own conduct. Willful though the girl was, she had a capacity for generosity that saved her from selfishness.

It was just as Lon said, her thoughts ran. She had to boss everybody and everything, always had to have her own way without regard to others. No wonder Justin did not like it. If she had tried hard enough, she could have made him see that this adventure was a duty laid on her, one she could not escape and retain her self-respect. Instead, she had managed so badly that she had thrown him quite out of sympathy with her point of view.

A child of impulse, she decided swiftly as she dressed to have a little talk with him and say she was sorry. With this resolve came peace. Everything would be all right now between them.

Hollister smiled when she came to his bedside and asked him how he was. His face reassured her. It was very pale, but it held the look of one who means to get well. Dr. Rayburn backed its promise.

"He's doing fine. Fever gone down a lot. Nursing's the thing now, Miss Betty. You can do more for him than I can."

"Are you going back to town to-day?" she asked.

"Got to. No two ways about that. Be back day after to-morrow probably. Keep giving him the tablets. Every two hours. And a teaspoon of the liquid three times a day."

They had drawn away from the bedside and by mutual consent passed out of the door into the sunshine. The crisp morning air was delightful. A million glints of light sparkled from the snow.

"He's really better, is n't he?" she asked eagerly, and her voice throbbed with young life.

"Better, yes. But—sometimes a man seems definitely to be on the mend and then he relapses without any apparent cause. It's too soon to say he's getting better. All I can say is that, if no unfavorable complications set in, he ought to improve."

"Ought you to leave him?"

He threw up his hands in an energy of exasperation. "If you had half as much to do as I have, young lady—"

"I know, but if he's really still in danger—"

"Danger!" fumed the doctor. "Do you think Mrs. Pillsbury can wait for him to get out of danger?"

"I did n't know—"

"Babies are born when they're born," he sputtered. "I've got to leave for town right after breakfast."

Justin came round the corner of the house. Betty almost ran to give him her hand. Her eyes were shining wells of friendliness.

"I want to see you after breakfast," she whispered.

He nodded, non-committally.

Black called from inside, "Yore coffee's b'ilin', folks."

He gave them flapjacks and syrup.

"I love flapjacks," Betty told him.

Their host said nothing, but he was pleased.

Lon came in late and drew up a chair beside Betty. "How's everything this glad mo'ning?" he asked.

"Fine as the wheat." She added as an aside, "And the bossy little flapper is n't half so bossy as she sometimes lets on."

His grin met her smile. They understood each other very well and were still friends. Betty pushed into the back of her mind a fugitive wish that Justin could know and appreciate her as well as good old Lon did.

After breakfast Betty and Merrick took a short walk.

"Scrumptious day," she commented. Then, as though it were a continuation of the same thought: "I'm sorry, Justin."

"You mean—?"

"I'm kinda horrid sometimes. I flare out and say 'I will' or 'I won't' like a spoiled kid. That's no way to do." She smiled at him, a little whimsically, a little apologetically. "It keeps me busy eating humble pie."

He accepted her apology graciously. "Shall we forget it, Bess? It's a new day. We'll turn a page of the ledger and begin again."

146

Rather timidly, she went on: "I had to come. It's not that. But if I had n't been so tempery, I could have made you understand."

He stiffened at once. "I think I understood—perfectly."

"No, Justin. That's just it. You did n't, or you would n't have stood in my way. You're fair-minded, and when you see I was doing what I had to do—what it was my duty to do—"

"I can't agree with you about that, Betty. I'm older than you are. I think I know more of the world. It's not your duty—the duty of any unmarried girl for that matter, unless she is a trained professional nurse—to put herself in the position you have."

In spite of her good resolutions Betty began to feel her temper slip. "What position have I put myself in?" she asked quietly.

"I'm an old-fashioned man," he answered. "I believe that a young woman must be so circumspect that nobody can find any ground to talk about her."

"A girl is n't a china doll. She can't be put away in moth balls, Justin. Every girl is talked about some time or other by somebody if she's alive. It's of no importance what gossips say."

"It's of the greatest importance that a girl give no chance for idle gossip about her," he demurred.

Betty's irritation expressed itself in the voice, a trifle sharp. "How do you think I can run the Quarter Circle D E without been criticized? I'm there with the men hours and days at a time, and no other woman on the place except old Mandy, who is deaf as a post and can't see six feet from her nose. If any evil-minded person wants to talk—why, I'll just have to let him talk."

"On the contrary, I think you ought to have a foreman run the place for you except for some general supervision. It's not a girl's business."

"Isn't it? You never told me so before."

"You never asked me."

"For that matter, I'm not asking you now." Her manner was dangerously quiet. It suggested banked fires of anger. "But just the same I'm glad to have your opinion."

"I'm glad to give it. I've wanted to tell you what I think about it. Understand me. I admire your energy, your enthusiasm, your efficiency. I believe you are running the Quarter Circle D E better than a good many men could do it. That's not the question. Are n't you losing something you can't afford

147

to do without? I can't go into this in detail. Cattle raising—ranching—breeding Herefords—it's a splendid occupation for a man. But there's a side of it that's—well, I'd rather you'd turn it all over to Forbes."

"What do you want me to do—stay at home and knit?"

"You know what I want as soon as the Sweetwater project is finished."

Betty side-stepped the proposed excursion into sentiment. She was a downright young woman and wanted to know exactly where she stood.

"I did n't know you felt that way about the ranch, Justin. I thought you shared my view, that I was doing something worth while when I raised hundreds of cattle every year to help feed the world. If I had known you thought I was degrading myself—" She stopped, a tremolo of anger in her throat.

"I did n't say that, Betty."

"It's what you meant."

"No. No, it is n't. I meant only that—well, there's something very very precious that some girls have—that you have, Betty—something that's like the bloom of a peach. If you lose it—well, it's gone, that's all."

"And if I do anything that's worth while—if I pay my way in the world by giving value received—the peach bloom is rubbed off, is n't it?" she retorted scornfully.

"Are n't there different ways of giving service? We are in danger of forgetting the home, which is the normal place for a young girl."

"Is it? Thought you came from a city where thousands of girls go down to offices and stores every morning to earn a living."

They stood on a small hilltop and looked over a world blanketed in white which flashed back countless gleams of light to the heliographing sun, a world so virgin clean, so still and empty of life, that it carried Betty back to the birthday of the race. She was, miraculously, at the beginning of things again.

"You're not in a city fortunately," he answered. "There's no economic pressure on you to fight sordidly for a living."

Her eyes sparkled. "You're not consistent. When the city ways don't suit you, I'm to live like people in the country, but when you don't approve of ranch ways, then I'm to be like girls in Denver. I'm not to go into business, but I'm not to be neighborly as my mother was."

"You're distorting what I said, Betty."

"Am I? Did n't you say I was n't to help take care of a sick man because it was n't proper?"

"I said you were acting rather absurdly about this man Hollister," he replied tartly. "There's no call to turn the world upside down because he's wounded. You want a sense of proportion."

"I think that's what you need, Justin," she answered, a flush of anger burning her cheeks. "You've been horrid about it from the start without any reason."

She moved down the hill toward the cabin. Merrick walked beside her. His eyes were hard and his lips set close.

For the first time it dawned upon Betty that he was jealous of her interest in another man. He was possessive, wanted to absorb all her thoughts, intended to be the center of every activity she had. This did not please her. It alarmed the individual in her. Marriage, as she had dreamed it, was wonderful because it enhanced life. It was the union of two souls, releasing all the better forces of their natures. Through it would come freedom and not bondage. The joys of the senses would be shared and transmuted to spiritual power. They ought not to put chains on a man or a woman that would narrow the horizon.

An illusion had been shattered. Justin was not the man with whom she could walk hand in hand. She sighed, and drew the gauntlet from her left hand.

Merrick looked at the ring she had dropped into his hand, then straight at her with rigid gaze.

"Are you in love with this fellow Hollister? Is that what it means?" he asked harshly.

The color in her cheeks deepened. "That's—hateful of you, Justin," she said, her voice ragged with feeling.

"I've seen it for some time. You're infatuated with him."

She lifted her chin and looked at him with eyes that blazed anger. "Now I know I've done right in giving you back your ring. I'm not going to—to quarrel with you because you insult me. It's finished. That's enough."

A sob rose to her throat and choked her. She hurried on to escape him, the trail a blurred mist through her tears.

CHAPTER XXX

FATHOMS DEEP

THE days followed each other, clear, sparkling, crisp, with mornings in which Betty's lungs drew in a winey exhilaration of living, with evenings which shut the cabin on the slope of Pegleg Pass from a remote world of men and women engaged in a thousand activities.

Betty had time to think during the long winter nights after she had retired to her room. Some of her thoughts hurt. She was shocked at the termination of her engagement, at the manner of it. That was not the way it should have been done at all. She and Justin should have recognized frankly that their views of life could not be made to harmonize. They should have parted with esteem and friendship. Instead of which there had been a scene of which she was ashamed.

Her cheeks burned when she recalled his crass charge that she was infatuated with Hollister. Why had n't he been able to understand that she had signed a pact of friendship with the ex-service man? If he had done that, if he had been wise and generous and sympathetic instead of harsh and grudging, he would (so Betty persuaded herself) have won her heart completely. He had been given a great chance, and he had not been worthy of it.

Merrick had humiliated her, shattered for the time at least the gallant young egoism which made her the mistress of her world.

Her father came up as soon as he returned from Denver. She talked over with him the break with her fiancé. Clint supported her, with reservations that did not reach the surface.

"Never did like it," he said bluntly, referring to her engagement. "Merrick's a good man in his way, but not the one for you. I been figuring you'd see it. I'm glad this came up. His ideas about marriage are crusted. He'd put a wife in a cage

150

and treat her well. That would n't suit you, Bess. You've got to have room to try your wings."

She clung to him, crying a little. "You don't blame me, then, Dad?"

"Not a bit. You did right. If Merrick had been the proper man for you, he'd have understood you well enough to know you had to come here. Maybe it was n't wise to come. Maybe it was impulsive. I reckon most folks would agree with him about that. But he'd have known his Betty. He'd 'a' helped you, even though it was foolish. You would n't be happy with any man who could n't let you fly the coop once in a while."

"Was it foolish to come, Dad?" she asked.

He stroked her dark hair gently. "It's the foolishness we all love in you, honey—that way you have of giving till it hurts."

Betty had inherited her impulsiveness from him. He, too, could be generous without counting the cost. He rejoiced in the eagerness with which her spirit went out to offer the gift of herself. But he had to be both father and mother. Generosity might easily carry her too far.

"I do such crazy things," she murmured. "And I never know they're silly till afterward."

"This was n't silly," he reassured her. "I'd have figured out some other way if I'd been home. But I was n't. Rayburn says your cooking an' your nursing have helped young Hollister a lot. I'm glad you came, now it's over with. I reckon you've paid my debt in full, Bettykins."

"He's absurdly grateful," she said. "I have n't done much for him. You'd think I'd saved his life."

"Soon now we'll be able to get him back to the ranch and Bridget can take care of him. Ruth's wearyin' for you. I'll be more satisfied when we're there. I've got old Jake Prowers on my mind some. Never can tell what he'll be up to."

Hollister was grateful to Betty, whether absurdly so or not is a matter of definitions. His big eyes followed her about the room as she cooked custards with the eggs and milk brought from the Howard place just below. "Sweet Marie" did not entrance him when Black tunelessly sang it, but the snatches of song she hummed at her work filled the room with melody for him. She read "David Copperfield" aloud after he began to mend, and his gaze rested on her with the mute admiration sick men are likely to give charming nurses overflowing with good-will and vitality. Her laugh lifted like a lark's song. Even

151

her smile had the radiant quality of one who is hearing good news.

He noticed that she was no longer wearing Merrick's ring, and his thoughts dwelt on it a good deal. Was the engagement broken? He could not see that she was unhappy. Her presence filled the place with sunshine. It was a joy to lie there and know that she was near, even when she was in another room and he could not see her. There was something permeating about Betty Reed. She lit up men's souls as an arc-light does a dark street.

He hoped that she and Merrick had come to the parting of the ways. The engineer was the last man in the world to make her eager spirit happy. His strength never spent itself in rebellion. He followed convention and would look for the acceptance of it in her. But Betty was cast in another mould. What was important to him did not touch her at all, or if it did, seemed a worthless sham. She laughed at social usage when it became mere formalism. No doubt she would be a disturbing wife. Life with her would be exciting. That was not what Justin Merrick wanted.

The right man for her would be one who both loved and understood. He must be big enough to let her enthusiasms sweep over their lives and must even give them moral support while they lasted. Also, he must be a clean and stalwart outdoor man, not one who had been salvaged from the yellow swamp waters of vice. This last Hollister kept before him as a fundamental necessity. He laid hold of it to stamp down the passionate insurgent longings that filled him.

It was an obligation on him. He must not abuse her kindness by forgetting that he had been an outcast, had himself shut a door upon any future that included the fine purity of her youth. An effect of her simplicity was that he stood in constant danger of not remembering this. There was nothing of the Lady Bountiful about Betty. Her star-clear eyes, the song and sunlight of her being, offered friendship and *camaraderie* with no assumption of superior virtue. She saw no barrier between them. They came together on an equal footing as comrades. The girl's unconscious generosity enhanced her charm and made the struggle in his heart more difficult.

Those days while he lay there and gathered strength were red-letter ones in his life. Given the conditions, it was inevitable that he should come to care for the gracious spirit dwelling in a form that expressed so lovingly the mystery of maiden dreams. In every fiber of him he cherished her loveliness and pulsed to the enticement of her.

She gave the dull cabin atmosphere. A light burned inside her that was warm and bright and colorful. Black looked on her as he might a creature from another world. This slip of a girl had brought something new into the range rider's life, something fine and spiritual which evoked response from his long-dormant soul. He had till now missed the joy of being teased by a girl as innocent and as vivid as she.

Hollister was won the easier because her tenderness was for him. Black must hunt ptarmigan for broth, Clint Reed go foraging for milk and eggs. They submitted cheerfully to be bullied in the interest of the patient. His needs ruled the household, since he was an invalid. Betty pampered and petted and poked fun at him, all with a zeal that captivated his imagination.

In the evenings they talked, three of them in a semi-circle before the blazing logs, the fourth sitting up in the bed propped by pillows. The talk ranged far, from cattle to Château-Thierry. It brought to the sick man a new sense of the values of life. These people lived far from the swift currents of urban rush and haste, but he found in them something the world has lost, the serenity and poise that come from the former standards of judgment. The feverish glitter of post-war excitement, its unrest and dissatisfaction, had left them untouched. Betty and her father were somehow anchored to realities. They did not crave wealth. They had within themselves sources of entertainment. The simple things of life gave them pleasure. He realized that there must be millions of such people in the country, and that through them it would eventually be saved from the effects of its restlessness.

CHAPTER XXXI

BETTY MAKES A DISCOVERY

"To-morrow," Betty said, and did a little skip-step across the floor to put away the frying-pan she had been washing.

"You have dancing feet," Hollister told her.

"When I have a dancing heart."

To the man sitting before the fire she bloomed in that dark cabin like a poppy in the desert. She was a hundred miracles each hour to him. He saw the exquisite mystery of her personality express itself in all she was and did—in the faint crimson just now streaming through her cheeks beneath the warm and tawny skin, in the charmingly shy gesture with which she had accepted his compliment, in the low, vibrant voice that played so wonderfully on his heartstrings. Not often is a sweet and singing soul clothed so exquisitely in a body of grace so young and lissom and vital.

"And that's whenever there's an excuse for it," he said, smiling at her. "But why feature to-morrow? Is it your birthday?"

"We're going home to-morrow."

"Are you? I did n't know."

He fell silent, looking into the fire. It was not an unexpected announcement. These good days could not go on forever. She had done more for him than any other friend he had ever had. But, of course, life made its claims on her. She had to respond to them. It was a wholly undeserved happiness that she had stayed till he was out of danger and on the road to health. He wanted to tell her how he felt about it, but he would never be able to do that. Inside, he seemed to melt to a river of tears whenever he let himself dwell on her amazing goodness to one who had been dead when first she gave him her little hand and now was alive again.

"Umpha, to-morrow. I'm crazy to see Ruthie, and what the boys are doing on the ranch."

"I've been an awful nuisance," he admitted.

"Have n't you?" The little laugh that welled out of her was sweet and mocking. It enveloped him with her gracious and tender young womanhood.

He liked to think that her nursing had pulled him through just as earlier her faith had rekindled in him self-respect and courage. The facts might not quite justify this, but he did not intend to let brutal actualities murder a beautiful dream.

"But you can always point with pride, as the politicians say. I'm a credit to your nursing. Off your hands in ten days."

"You're not off my hands yet. You're going to the Diamond Bar K with us."

The blood drummed faster through his heart. He felt a stinging of the senses. Was there no end to the goodness of this astonishing and disturbing girl? Must she always be flinging out life lines to him?

"Good of you—awf'ly good of you." He looked at the fire, not at her. His voice was suspiciously low. "I might have known, knowing you. But I can't impose myself any longer. I'll be all right now at the camp."

"Do you think Dad and I will quit in the middle of a good job? No, sir. We're going to get credit for finishing it. Lon's breaking the road with a sled to-day. You're to go down in it. Dr. Rayburn says he has n't time to go up to the camp to look after your bandages. You'll have to put up with us for a while."

"I could go to the hotel at Wild Horse," he suggested.

"You've never eaten a meal there. I see that. It's impossible. No, it's all settled. You're coming to the ranch."

"Of course you know I can't . . . I can't . . . thank you." His voice shook. This annoyed him. He told himself savagely not to act like a baby.

"Oh, everybody works at the Diamond Bar K," she said lightly. "Ruthie can't go to school through the deep snow. You claim to be a college man. We'll find out whether you can teach the First Reader and two times two."

He tried to answer in the same spirit. "If you're going to call every bluff I make, I'll be more careful. Anyhow, I did n't study the First Reader at college. Don't think they teach it at Massachusetts Tech."

Later in the day he spoke to Reed on the subject. "I don't want to make a nuisance of myself. I can put up at the Wild Horse House till I'm strong enough to go back to camp."

Reed had come out of the old-time cattle days when there were always a plate and a bed at the ranch for whoever might want them. He still kept open house.

"Always room for one more, boy. Anyhow, if Betty's got it fixed up that way in her mind, you'd as well make up yours to do as she says. It'll be her say-so." The owner of the Diamond Bar K grinned at him confidentially, as one fellow victim of feminine tyranny to another.

Forbes arrived late in the afternoon and reported heavy roads. He had brought a four-horse team, and it had been all they could do to break through. They had dragged a sled with the body of a wagon on the wide runners.

"Deep drifts below the rim in the cut the other side o' Round Top. Be all right if the wind don't blow tonight," he said.

The wind blew, and was still whistling when it came time to start. But the sun was shining and the sky clear.

Betty was doubtful, on account of the patient.

"If we wrop him up good, he'll be all right," Lon said. The big foreman did not want to stay in the hills until the trail he had broken was filled up again with drifts.

"Yes," agreed Reed.

Tug and Betty were tucked in with warm blankets. Forbes took the reins and drove out of the draw, past the Howard place, and up the steep hill beyond. Betty had seen to it that her patient was wrapped to the nose in an old fur coat of her father. The whipping wind did not distress him.

From the summit they could see the great white wastes, stretching mile on mile. The snow was soft and heavy, and the wind had not drifted it a great deal since Lon had driven through the previous day. But the horses were pulling a load, and soon the sweat stood out on their bodies.

They reached and circled Round Top, passed a treacherous dugway, and moved into the deep drifts below the rim. Betty looked up once and a little shudder ran down her spine. The wind up on the bluff had a clean sweep. Over the edge yawned a great snow comb that might at any moment loosen and come down to bury them in an immense white mausoleum. It might, on the other hand, hang from the rim for months.

Lon cracked his whip close to the ear of the off leader. It might almost have been a signal. From far above came the sound of an answering crack. Reed looked up quickly. The snow comb slid forward, broke and came tearing down. It

156

gathered momentum in its plunge, roaring down like an express train.

The cowman flung Betty into the bed of the sled and crouched over her as a protection against the white cloud of death rushing at them.

The avalanche swept into the ravine with thunderous noise, a hundred tons of packed snow. The bulk of its weight struck in front of the horses, but the tail of the slide whipped a giant billow upon them and buried team and sled.

Betty fought and scrambled her way out of the snow. From it her father's head was emerging a few yards away.

"Hurt?" he asked.

"No. You?"

"Jarred up. That's all. Seen anything of Lon?"

The head and broad shoulders of the foreman pushed up. Lon shook snow out of his hair, eyes, and ears.

The others exchanged bulletins with him. He was, he said, as rampageous as a long-legged hill two-year-old.

"Mr. Hollister!" Betty quavered.

The engineer was nowhere to be seen. They called, and no answer came. Betty's heart dropped like a plummet. She turned upon her father anguished eyes. They begged him to do something. He noticed that her cheeks were blanched, the color had ebbed from her lips. His daughter's distress touched him nearly. He could not stand that stricken look.

"I'll find him," he promised.

Jammed between two trees, upside down, with one end sticking out of the snow, they found the wagon bed at the bottom of the ravine. Forbes spoke to Reed in a low voice, for his ears alone.

"Not a chance in fifty of findin' him in all this snow, an' if we do, he'll not be alive."

"Yes," agreed the ranchman. "If a fellow knew where to look. But no telling where the snow carried him."

"Might still be under the wagon bed, o' course."

"Might be."

A low groan reached them. They listened. It came again, from under the bed of the wagon apparently.

"He's alive," Clint called to Betty.

The drooping little figure crouched in the snow straightened as though an electric current had been shot through it. The girl waded toward them, eager, animate with vigor, pulsing with hope.

157

"Oh, Dad. Let's hurry. Let's get him out."

Reed rapped the wagon bed with his knuckles. "How about it, Hollister? Hurt much?"

"Knocked out," a weak voice answered. "Guess I'm all right now. Arm scraped a bit."

The handle of a shovel stuck out of the snow like a post. Lon worked it loose, tore the lower part free, and brought it to the bed. He began to dig. Reed joined him, using his leather gauntlets as spades. It took nearly half an hour to get Hollister out. He came up smiling.

"Cold berth down there," he said by way of comment.

"You're not really hurt, are you?" Betty said.

"Nothing to speak of. The edge of the sled scraped the skin from my arm. Feels a bit fiery. How about the horses?"

Lon and his employer were already at work on them. Three of the animals had pawed and kicked till they were back on their feet. The men helped them back to the road, after unhitching them from the sled. It was necessary to dig the fourth horse out of a deep drift into which it had been flung.

Betty sat beside Hollister in the wagon bed on a pile of salvaged blankets. She felt strangely weak and shaken. It was as though the strength had been drained out of her by the emotional stress through which she had passed. To be flung starkly against the chance, the probability, that Tug was dead had been a terrible experience. The shock had struck her instantly, vitally, with paralyzing force. She leaned against the side of the bed laxly, trying to escape from the harrowing intensity of her feeling. That she could suffer so acutely, so profoundly, was a revelation to her.

What was the meaning of it? Why had the strength and energy ebbed from her body as they do from one desperately wounded? It was disturbing and perplexing. She had not been that way when her father was shot. Could she find the answer to the last question in the way she had put it? Desperately wounded! Had she, until hope flowed back into her heart, been that?

"You're ill," she heard a concerned, far-away voice say. "It's been too much for you."

She fought against a wave of faintness before she answered. "I suppose so. It's—silly of me. But I'm all right now."

"It's no joke to be buried in an avalanche. Hello. Look there!"

Her gaze followed the direction in which he was pointing,

the edge of the bluff above. Two men were looking down from the place where the slide had started. It was too far to recognize them, but one carried a rifle. They stood there for a minute or two before they withdrew.

"Do you think—that they—?"

His grave eyes met hers. "I think they attempted murder, and, thank God! failed."

"Don't say anything to Dad—not now," she cautioned.

He nodded assent. "No."

Reed had looked at his watch just before the avalanche had come down on them. The time was then ten o'clock. It was past two before the outfit was patched up sufficiently to travel again.

Not till they were safely out of the hills and gliding into Paradise Valley did the cowman ask a question that had been in his mind for some time.

"Why do you reckon that slide came down at the very moment we were in the ravine?"

"I've been wonderin' about that my own se'f. O' course, it might just a-happened thataway." This from Forbes.

"It might, but it did n't."

"Meanin'?"

"There was an explosion just before the slide started. Some one dynamited the comb to send it off the bluff."

"Are you guessin', Clint? Or do you know it for a fact?"

"I'm guessing, but I pretty near know it."

Betty spoke up, quietly, unexpectedly. "So do Mr. Hollister and I."

The two ranchmen pivoted simultaneously toward her. They waited, only their eyes asking the girl what she meant.

"While you were digging, Mr. Hollister saw two men up there. He pointed them out to me."

"And why did n't you show 'em to me?" demanded her father.

"What would you have done if I had?" she countered.

"Done! Gone up an' found out who they were, though I could give a good guess right now."

"And do you think they would have let you come near? We could see that one of them had a rifle. Maybe both had. They did n't stay there long, but I was afraid every second that you'd look up and see them."

The foreman grunted appreciation of her sagacity. "Some head she's got, Clint. You'd sure have started after them birds, me like as not trailin' after you. An' you'd sure never have got to 'em."

The cowman made no comment on that. "He timed it mighty close. Saw us coming, of course, an' figured how long it would take us to reach where we did. Good guessing. An old fox, I'll say."

"Same here."

"He did n't miss smashing us twenty seconds," Hollister said. "As it was, that's no kind of snowstorm to be out in without an umbrella and overshoes."

Betty looked at him and smiled faintly. It was all very well to joke about it now, but they had missed being killed by a hair's breadth. It made her sick to think of that cackling little demon up there on the bluff plotting wholesale murder and almost succeeding in his plan. She lived over again with a bleak sinking of the heart that five minutes when she had not known whether Tug Hollister was dead or alive.

If he had been killed! She knew herself now. Justin's instinct of selfishness had been right, after all. His niggardliness resolved itself into self-protection. He had been fighting for his own. Even his jealousy stood justified. She had talked largely of friendship, had deceived herself into thinking that it was expression of herself she craved. That was true in a sense, but the more immediate blinding truth was that she loved Hollister. It had struck her like a bolt of lightning.

She felt as helpless as a drowning man who has ceased struggling.

CHAPTER XXXII

WITHOUT RHYME OR REASON

IT was an upsetting thing, this that had happened to Betty, as decided and far less explainable than a chemical reaction. It seemed to her as though life had suddenly begun to move at tremendous speed, without any warning to her whatever that

Fate intended to step on the accelerator. She was caught in the current of a stream of emotion sweeping down in flood. Though it gave her a great thrill, none the less it was devastating.

She wanted to escape, to be by herself behind a locked door, where she could sit down, find herself again, and take stock of the situation. To sit beside this stranger who had almost in the twinkling of an eye become of amazing import to her, to feel unavoidable contact of knee and elbow and shoulder, magnetic currents of attraction flowing, was almost more than she could bear.

Betty talked, a little, because silence became too significant. She felt a sense of danger, as though the personality, the individuality she had always cherished, were being dissolved in the gulf where she was sinking. But what she said, what Hollister replied, she could never afterward remember.

Ruth ran to meet them with excited little screams of greeting. "Hoo-hoo, Daddy! Hoo-hoo, Betty! Oh, goody, goody!"

Her sister was out of the sled and had the child in her arms almost before the horses had stopped. "You darling darling!" she cried.

Buxom Bridget came to the door, all smiles of welcome. "And is it your own self at last, Betty mavourneen? It's glad we are to see you this day."

Betty hugged her and murmured a request. "Better fix up the south bedroom for Mr. Hollister. He ought to rest at once. I'm kinda tired."

"Sure, an' I'll look after him. Don't you worry your head about that. The room's all ready."

The girl's desire to question herself had to be postponed. She had reckoned without Ruth, who clung to her side until the child's bedtime. Pleading fatigue, Betty retired immediately after her sister.

She slipped into a négligée, let her dark hair down so that it fell a rippling cascade over her shoulders, and looked into the glass of her dressing-table that reflected a serious, lovely face of troubled youth. A queer fancy moved in her that this girl who returned her gaze was a stranger whom she was meeting for the first time.

Did love play such tricks as this? Did it steal away self-confidence and leave one shy and gauche? She saw a pulse fluttering in the brown slender throat. That was odd too. Her nerves usually were steel-strong.

She combed her hair, braided it, and put on a crêpe-de-chine nightgown. After the light was out and she was between the sheets, her thoughts settled to more orderly sequence. She could always think better in the dark, and just now she did not want to be distracted by any physical evidences of the disorder into which she had been flung.

How could she ever have thought of marrying Justin? She had spent a good deal of time trying to decide calmly, without any agitation of the blood, whether she was in love with him. It was no longer necessary for her to puzzle over how a girl would know whether she cared for a man. She knew. It was something in nature, altogether outside of one's self, that took hold of one without rhyme or reason and played havoc with dispassionate tranquillity; a devouring flame clean and pure, containing within itself all the potentialities of tragedy—of life, of death, of laughter, love and tears.

And then, as is the way of healthy youth, in the midst of her puzzlement she was asleep—and with no lapse of time, as though a curtain had rolled up, she was opening her eyes to a new day.

If Tug had let himself count on long full hours with Betty in the pleasant living-room, of books and ideas to be discussed together, of casual words accented to meaning by tones of the voice and flashes of the eye, he was predestined to disappointment. In the hill cabin they had been alone together a good deal. She contrived to see that this never occurred now. Except at table or in the evening with Ruth and her father, he caught only glimpses of her as she moved about her work.

Her eyes did not avoid his, but they did not meet in the frank, direct way characteristic of her. She talked and laughed, joined in the give-and-take of care-free conversation. To put into words the difference was not easy. What he missed was the note of deep understanding that had been between them, born less of a common point of view than of a sympathy of feeling. Betty had definitely withdrawn into herself.

Had he offended her? He could not think how, but he set himself to find out. It took some contriving, for when one will and one will not a private meeting is not easily arranged.

He was in the big family room, lying on a lounge in the sunshine of the south window. Ruth had finished her lessons and was on the floor busy with a pair of scissors and a page of magazine cutouts. She babbled on, half to herself and half to him. They had become great friends, and for the time she was his inseparable, perhaps because he was the only one of the household not too busy to give her all the attention she craved. Her talk, frank with the egotism of childhood, was wholly of herself.

"I been awful bad to-day," she confided cheerfully, almost proudly. "Gettin' in Bridget's flour bin 'n' ev'ryfing to make a cake 'n' spillin' a crock o' milk on the floor."

"I'm sorry," he said.

"Oh, I been the baddest," she reflected aloud enjoyably. Then, unhampered by any theory of self-determination, she placed the blame placidly where it belonged. "When I said my prayers last night I asked God to make me good, but he did n't do it."

Tug did not probe deeper into this interesting point of view, for Betty came into the room with an armful of books and magazines.

"Thought from what you said at breakfast you're hungry for reading," she said. "So I brought you some. If you're like I am, you'll want to browse around a bit before you settle down. This Tarkington story is good—if you have n't read it. But maybe you like Conrad better."

Through the open door came a delicious odor of fresh baking from the kitchen. Out of the corner of his eye Tug took in Ruth. He sniffed the spicy aroma and audibly sounded his lips.

"My! Cookies!" he murmured.

Instantly Ruth responded to the suggestion. She scrambled to her feet and trotted out, intent on achieving cookies at once. Betty turned to follow, but her guest stopped her with a question.

"What's the Tarkington story about?"

"About a girl who's hanging on to the outskirts of society and making all kinds of pretenses—a pushing kind of a girl, who has to fib and scheme to get along. But he makes her so human you like her and feel sorry for her."

"Sounds interesting." He fired his broadside while he still held her eyes. "Miss Reed, why am I being punished?"

Into her cheeks the color flowed. "Punished?" she murmured, taken aback.

Betty had stopped by the table and half turned. He reached for the umbrella he used as a support and hobbled toward her. "Yes. What have I done?"

A turmoil of the blood began to boil in her. "The doctor said you were to keep off your feet," she evaded.

"Yes, and he said you were to entertain me—keep me interested."

"That was when you were too sick to read. And I'm busy now. Lots of work piled up while I was away."

"Then you're not offended about anything."

She had picked up a book from the table and was reading the title. Her eyes did not lift to his. "What could I be—offended about?" In spite of the best she could do, her voice was a little tremulous.

"I don't know. *Are* you?"

"No." The lashes fluttered up. She had to meet his gaze or confess that she was afraid to.

"You're different. You—"

He stopped, struck dumb. A wild hope flamed up in him. What was it the shy, soft eyes were telling him against her will? He stood on the threshold of knowledge, his heart drumming fast.

During that moment of realization they were lost in each other's eyes. The soul of each was drawn as by a magnet out of the body to that region beyond space where the spirits of lovers are fused.

Betty's hands lifted ever so slightly in a gesture of ultimate and passionate surrender to this force which had taken hold of her so completely.

Then, with no conscious volition on the part of either, they were in each other's arms, swept there by a rising tide of emotion that drowned thought.

CHAPTER XXXIII

THE BLUEBIRD ALIGHTS AND THEN TAKES WING

Tug pushed Betty from him. Out of a full tide of feeling he came to consciousness of what he was doing.

"I can't. I can't," he whispered hoarsely.

She understood only that something in his mind threatened

their happiness. Her eyes clung to his. She waited, breathless, still under the spell of their great moment.

"Can't what?" at last she murmured.

"Can't . . . marry you." He struggled for expression, visibly in anguish. "I'm . . . outside the pale."

"How—outside the pale?"

"I've made it impossible. We met too late."

"You're not—married?"

"No. I'm . . . I'm—" He stuck, and started again. "You know. My vice."

It took a moment to remember what it was. To her it was something done with ages ago in that premillennial past before they had found each other. She found no conceivable relationship between it and this miracle which had befallen them.

"But—I don't understand. You're not—"

She flashed a star-eyed, wordless question at him, born of a swift and panicky fear.

"No. I have n't touched it—not since I went into the hills. But—I might."

"What nonsense! Of course, you won't."

"How do I know?"

"It's too silly to think about. Why should you?"

"It's not a matter of reason. I tried to stop before, and I could n't."

"But you stopped this time."

"Yes. I have n't had the headaches. Suppose they began again. They're fierce—as though the top of my head were being sawed off. If they came back—what then? How do I know I would n't turn to the drug for relief?"

"They won't come back."

"But if they did?"

She gave him both her hands. There were gifts in her eyes —of faith, of splendid scorn for the vice he had trodden underfoot, of faith profound and sure. "If they do come back, dear, we'll fight them together."

He was touched, deeply. There was a smirr of mist obscuring his vision. Her high sweet courage took him by the throat. "That's like you. I could n't pay you a better compliment if I hunted the world over for one. But I can't let you in for the possibility of such a thing. I'd be a rotten cad to do it. I've got to buck it through alone. That's the price I've got to pay."

"The price for what?"

"For having been a weakling: for having yielded to it before."

"You never were a weakling," she protested indignantly. "You were n't responsible. It was nothing but an effect of your wounds. The doctors gave it to you because you had to have it. You used it to dull the horrible pain. When the pain stopped and you were cured, you quit taking it. That's all there is to it."

He smiled ruefully, though he was deadly in earnest. "You make it sound as simple as a proposition in geometry. But I'm afraid, dear, it is n't as easily disposed of as that. I started to take it for my headaches, but I kept on taking it regularly whether I needed it for the pain or not. I was a drug victim. No use dodging that. It's the truth."

"Well, say you were. You're not now. You never will be again. I'd—I'd stake my head on it."

"Yes. Because you are *you*. And your faith would help me —tremendously. But I know the horrible power of the thing. It's an obsession. When the craving was on me, it was there every second. I found myself looking for all sorts of plausible excuses to give way."

"It had n't any real power. You've proved that by breaking away from it."

"I've regained my health from the hills and from my work. That stopped the trouble with my head. But how do I know it has stopped permanently?"

Wise beyond her years, she smiled tenderly. "You mentioned faith a minute ago. It's true. We have to live by that. A thousand times a day we depend on it. We rely on the foundations of the house not to crumble and let it bury us. I never ride a horse without assuming that it won't kick me. We have to have the courage of our hopes, don't we?"

"For ourselves, yes. But we ought not to invite those we love into the house unless we're sure of the foundations."

"I'm sure enough. And, anyhow, that's a poor cold sort of philosophy. I want to be where *you* are." The slim, straight figure, the dusky, gallant little head, the eyes so luminous and quick, reproached with their eagerness his prudent caution. She offered him the greatest gift in the world, and he hung back with *ifs* and *buts*.

There was in him something that held at bay what he wanted more than anything else on earth. He could not brush aside

166

hesitations with her magnificent scorn. He had lost the right to do it. His generosity would be at her expense.

"If you knew, dear, how much I want you. If you knew! But I've got to think of you, to protect you from myself. Oh, Betty, why did n't I meet you two years ago?" His voice was poignant as a wail.

"You did n't. But you've met me now. If you really want me —well, here I am."

"Yes, you're there, the sweetest girl ever God made—and I'm here a thousand miles away from you."

"Not unless you think so, Tug," she answered softly, her dusky eyes inviting him. "You've made me love you. What are you going to do with me?"

"I'm going to see you get the squarest deal I can give you, no matter what it costs."

"Costs you or me?"

The sound in his throat was almost a groan. "Dear heart, I'm torn in two," he told her.

"Don't be, Tug." Her tender eyes and wistfully smiling lips were very close to him. "It's all right. I'm just as *sure.*"

He shook his head. "I've got to play the game," he said miserably.

Betty talked, pleaded, argued with him, but his point of view remained unchanged.

A reaction of irritation swept her. It was in part offended modesty. She had offered herself, repeatedly, and he would not have her. How did she know that he was giving the true reason? It might be only a tactful way of getting rid of her.

"Play it then," she replied curtly, and she walked out of the room without another look at him.

He was astounded, shocked. He had been to blame, of course, in ever letting his love leap out and surprise them. Probably he had not made clear to her the obligation that bound him not to let her tie up her life with his. He must see her at once and make her understand.

But this he could not do. A note dispatched by Ruth brought back the verbal message that she was busy. At supper Betty did not appear. The specious plea was that she had a headache. Nor was she at breakfast. From Bridget he gathered that she had gone to the Quarter Circle D E and would stay there several days.

"Lookin' after some fencing," the housekeeper explained. "That gir-rl's a wonder if iver there was one."

167

Tug agreed to that, but it was in his mind that the fencing would have had to wait if affairs had not come to a crisis between him and Betty. He had no intention of keeping her from her home. Over the telephone he made arrangements to stay at the Wild Horse House. Clint, perplexed and a little disturbed in mind, drove him to town.

Most of the way they covered in silence. Just before they reached the village, Reed came to what was in his mind.

"You an' Betty had any trouble, Hollister?"

The younger man considered this a moment. "No trouble; that is, not exactly trouble."

"She's high-headed," her father said, rather by way of explanation than apology. "But she's the salt of the earth. Don't you make any mistake about that."

"I would n't be likely to," his guest said quietly. "She's the finest girl I ever met."

The cowman looked quickly at him. "Did she go to the Quarter Circle D E because of anything that took place between you an' her?"

"I think so." He added a moment later an explanation: "I let her see how much I thought of her. It slipped out. I had n't meant to."

Reed was still puzzled. He knew his daughter liked the young fellow by his side. "Did that make her mad?" he asked.

"No. I found out she cared for me."

"You mean—?"

"Yes." The face of the engineer flushed. "It was a complete surprise to me. I had thought my feelings would n't matter because she would never find out about them. When she did— and told me that she—cared for me, I had to tell her where I stand."

"Just where do you stand?"

"I can't marry. You must know why."

Clint flicked the whip and the young team speeded. When he had steadied them to a more sedate pace, he spoke. "I reckon I do. But—you've given it up, have n't you?"

"Yes." He qualified the affirmative. "I'm not the first man who thought he'd given it up and had n't."

"Got doubts about it, have you?"

"No. I think I'm done with the cursed stuff. But how do I know?" Tug went into details as to the nature of the disease. He finished with a sentence that was almost a cry. "I'd rather see her dead than married to a victim of that habit."

168

"What did Betty say to that?"

"What I'd expect her to say. She would n't believe there was any danger. Would n't have it for a minute. You know how generous she is. Then, when I insisted on it, she seemed to think it was an excuse and walked out of the room. I have n't seen her since. She would n't let me have a chance."

"I don't see as there's much you could say—unless you're aimin' to renig." Reed's voice took on a trace of resentment. "Seems to me, young fellow, it was up to you not to let things get as far as they did between you an' Betty. That was n't hardly a square deal for her. You get her to tell you how she feels to you, an' then you turn her down. I don't like that a-tall."

Tug did not try to defend himself. "That's one way of looking at it. I ought never to have come to the house," he said with humility.

"I wish you had n't. But wishing don't get us anywhere. Point is, what are we going to do about it?"

"I don't see anything to do. I'd take the first train out if it would help any," Hollister replied despondently.

"Don't you go. I'll have a talk with her an' see how she feels first."

Hollister promised not to leave until he had heard from Reed.

CHAPTER XXXIV

BORN THAT WAY

It was impossible for Betty to escape the emotions that flooded her, but she was the last girl to sit down and accept defeat with folded hands. There was in her a certain vigor of the spirit that craved expression, that held her head up in the face of disaster.

At the Quarter Circle D E she was so briskly business-like that none of the men would have guessed that she was passing through a crisis. Except for moments of abstraction, she gave no evidence of the waves of emotion that inundated her while she was giving orders about the fencing of the northwest forty or the moving of the pigpens.

When she was alone, it was worse. Her longing for Hollister became acute. If she could see him, talk with him, his point of view would be changed. New arguments marshaled themselves in her mind. It was ridiculous to suppose that a man's past—one not of his own choosing, but forced on him—could determine his future so greatly as to make happiness impossible. She would not believe it. Every instinct of her virile young personality rebelled against the acceptance of such a law.

Tug's persistence in renouncing joy had wounded her vanity. But at bottom she did not doubt him. He had stood out because he thought it right, not because he did not love her. In spite of her distress of mind, she was not quite unhappy. A warm hope nestled in her bosom. She loved and was loved. The barrier between them would be torn down. Again they would be fused into that oneness which for a blessed ten minutes had absorbed them.

Her father drove over in the rattletrap car. Ostensibly he had come to discuss with her plans for fertilization and crops of the Quarter Circle D E for the coming season.

"I took Hollister to town this morning. He would n't stay any longer," Reed presently mentioned, as though casually.

"Oh! Why would n't he stay?" Betty was rather proud of the indifference she contrived to convey in her voice.

"Said he did n't want to keep you away from home."

"Was he keeping me away?" she asked.

"Seemed to think so. Was n't he?"

"I see you know all about it, Dad. What did he tell you?"

"I asked him point-blank what the trouble was between you and him. He told me."

A faint crimson streamed into her cheeks. "What did he say it was?"

"He's afraid. Not for himself, but for you."

"I think that's awf'ly silly of him."

"I'm not so sure about that, Betsykins. If there's any doubt whatever, he'd better wait till he's certain." He let his arm fall across her shoulders with a gentleness she knew to be a caress. "Have you found the man you want, dear? Sure about it?"

She smiled ruefully. "I'm sure enough, Dad. He's the one that seems in doubt." To this she added a reply to a sentence earlier in his period. "He did n't say anything to me about waiting. His 'No, thank you,' was quite definite, I thought."

Clint's wrath began to simmer. "If he's got a notion that he can take or leave you as he pleases—"

Betty put a hand on his arm. "Please, Dad. I don't mean what I said. It's not fair to him. He does n't think that at all."

"There's no man in the Rockies good enough for you—"

"Are you taking in enough territory?" she teased, her face bubbling to mirth. "I don't even know whether you're including Denver. Justin came from there, and he's too good for me."

"Who says he's too good?"

"Too perfect, then. I could n't live up to him. Never in the world." Her eyes fixed on something in the distance. She watched for a moment or two. "Talking about angels, Dad. There's the flutter of his engine fan."

Reed turned.

Merrick was killing the engine of his runabout. He came across to them, ruddy, strong, well-kept. Every stride expressed the self-reliant and complacent quality of his force.

The girl's heart beat faster. She had not seen him since that moment, more than two weeks ago, when they had parted in anger. Her resentment against him had long since died. He had not been to blame because they were incompatible in point of view and temperament. It was characteristic of her that she had written to ask him to forgive her if she had in any way done him a wrong. If she could, she wanted to keep him for a friend.

He shook hands with them. Reed asked about the work.

"We've finished the tunnel and are laying the line of the main canal between it and the draw where it runs into Elk Creek Cañon. Soon as the ground is thawed out, I'll have dirt flying on it," the engineer said.

"Lots of water in the dam?" asked the cowman.

"Full up. The mild weather this last week has raised it a lot. There's a great deal of snow in the hills. We'll have no difficulty about a sufficient supply."

"Good. You've got old Jake Prowers beat."

"Justin has done a big thing for this part of the country. That's more important than beating Mr. Prowers," Betty said.

"Yes," agreed Merrick impersonally. "By the way, the old fellow is still nursing his fancied injuries. He was hanging around the dam yesterday. I warned him off."

171

"Say anything?" asked Clint.

"Tittered the way he does and congratulated me on the good job I had done. He's a venomous old snake, but I don't see that he can do us any harm. There's nothing left to do now but the detail work of putting in the ditches."

They talked for a few minutes about the irrigation project. The engineer did not betray the least self-consciousness, but his mind, too, was running on the last time he had seen Betty and the break between them.

Reed was called away by one of the men to look at a sick horse.

Merrick's steady gaze at once challenged Betty. "I got your letter."

She was a good deal less composed than he. It disconcerted her to know that she was blushing. That was a silly way to do, she told herself. It annoyed her to give an exhibition of gaucherie.

"Yes," she murmured.

"I've come to the conclusion that we made a mistake," he said. "We rushed into a decision too hastily."

"Yes," Betty agreed.

"You're young. I had n't given enough consideration to that. Shall we forget our differences and be as we were, Betty?"

"You don't mean—be engaged?"

"That's exactly what I mean."

"Oh, Justin, I can't. I thought you meant we'd made a mistake in ever being engaged. We did. We're not suited to each other."

"I don't agree with you. Your letter convinced me that we are."

"I did n't mean it that way at all," she said unhappily. "We're not, Justin. Not a bit. I'm too—too kinda wild for you. You don't want a wife like me. If you knew, you would n't want me a bit."

"I'm the best judge of that," he answered, smiling a little.

"But you don't. I'd always be troubling you with my crazy ways."

"No. It's just that you're young," he insisted.

"It is n't. I'm born that way. I'll always be like that. Besides—" She stopped, searching for a way to put it gently. "Besides, I'd want a husband—if I ever marry at all—who needs me, who has to have me, who can't get along without me."

"I need you," he said.

172

"Oh no, you don't. Not really. You think you do, maybe, but not in the way I mean. You're strong—self-sufficient. Please, I don't mean it in an uncomplimentary way. But you *are* big, you know. A wife would have to fit into you—be just a—an important detail of your life. I could n't do that. I've got to be everything to a man—help him—talk over his difficulties with him—be just the biggest thing in the world to him. I could n't really *do* anything for you. You're complete. You don't need anything done for you. With or without me, you're going to be awf'ly successful. Oh, I know it sounds silly, but it is n't."

"Do you mean you like me less because I'm reliable and efficient and—well, I take your own word—on the road to success? Would you want to marry an irresponsible failure?"

The allusion was plain, and she did not like him better for it. None the less, she recognized that this man, standing there in the quiet arrogance of strength, had qualities admirable and worthy of great respect. He was master of himself and, so far as one can be, of his destinies. The cleft chin, the square jaw, the cold gray eyes so keen and steady, expressed character, and of a kind that would take him far. But it was a road she would not travel with him.

"No. But I'd like to know that I was a help to my husband in making his success. You can't understand, Justin. I'm not what you want—not at all. If you saw me as I am, you'd know it. I'd always be affronting your sense of the fitting thing. The right wife for you is one who would sit at the head of your table well-dressed, handsome, and charming, an evidence of your standing in the community. You know—a gracious hostess, good at teas and bridge and that sort of thing. You're really a city man. I'm not a city woman and never shall be."

To Merrick, clear-eyed in spite of his fondness for her, came a flash of insight that told him she had been wiser than he. He could never mould this wildling to his heart's desire. Some day he would look back on this episode and smile at it. But he had not reached that state of philosophy yet. His vanity was still engaged, and more than that—the last passionate flame of the boy in him that was being sacrificed to ambition. He craved inordinately the willful charm of this devastatingly sweet girl with the quick, disturbing eyes. She represented to him certain values he was deliberately trampling down, not because they did not seem to him good, but because they warred with something that he wanted more. He had impossibly

173

dreamed that she might stay what she was and yet become something different.

"Are you going to marry Hollister?" he asked.

She might reasonably have told him this was a private matter of her own. She might have evaded the question. Instead, she told him the truth.

"I don't know."

"Has he asked you?"

"No."

"But you will if he does."

"Yes."

"Knowing what he has been, what he may be again?"

"Knowing what he is," she corrected.

"Will girls never get over the folly of marrying men to reform them?" he flung out impatiently.

"I'm not marrying him to reform him—that is, if I'm marrying him at all, which is n't likely. He does not need reforming."

"How do you know he won't slide back into his vice?" He answered his own query. "You can't know. There's no way of knowing."

"He won't." She said it quietly, with absolute conviction.

Her attitude tremendously irritated him. It was a reflection on all the copybook virtues that had made him what he was. "Are you waiting for this tramp, this drug fiend, to make up his mind whether he wants to marry you or not?"

There was a spark of anger in her eye. She would not modify even his phrasing. It could stand as he put it.

"Yes."

"Sheer perversity."

"Is n't it?" she agreed, with dangerous sweetness.

He knew he was being punished for having indulged himself, as he rarely did, in a display of temper. At once he took himself in hand.

"I'm serious about this, Betty. A girl has no right to take chances of this sort. I grant you Hollister has qualities—splendid ones. But the damning fact remains."

Betty relented. He was human. He had cried out because he was hurt. "I don't think it remains, Justin. I'm absolutely convinced that it's conquered—what you call his vice."

"What I call his vice! Would n't every sane person call it that?"

"Not if they knew the circumstances. He was left with terri-

174

ble pains in the head after he was wounded. They gave him morphine—a lot of it. He got to depending on it. The habit grew on him. Then he woke up and shook it off. It's to his credit rather than the reverse."

"Even so. There's a danger that he'll go back to it."

And again she denied it, with the certainty of one who does not need evidence to bulwark an absolute assurance. "No danger at all."

They were standing in front of the porch. Reed came toward them from the stable. Both knew that the last word had been said.

Justin Merrick struggled with himself a moment, then held out his hand. He did not want to be a poor loser.

"The best of luck, Betty," he said.

Gladness gleamed in the soft eyes through which the eager spirit seemed to yearn to comfort him.

"You, too, Justin," she whispered.

CHAPTER XXXV

BIRDS OF A FEATHER

THEY sat on opposite sides of a table, the food and dishes not yet cleared away after their supper. A cheap kerosene lamp lit the room insufficiently. The smoke from a ragged wick had entirely blackened one side of the glass chimney. One of the men had cunningly utilized this to throw the face of his companion into the light while his own remained in shadow. His bleached eyes watched the emotions come and go as they registered on the twisted, wolfish countenance of this criminal on the dodge. He was playing on his evil instincts as a musician does upon the strings of a violin.

"Me, I said right away, soon as I seen you, 'This Cig's no quitter; he'll go through.' So I tied up with you. Game, an' no mollycoddle. Tha's how I sized you up."

"You got me right, Prowers. I'll say so."

The little man with the leathery face watched his victim. In the back of his mind a dreadful thought had lodged and become fixed. He would use for his purpose this vain and shallow crook, then blot him out of life before he turned upon him.

"Don't I know it? Cig ain't roostin' up here for his health, I says to myself. Not none, by jiminy by jinks. He's got business."

"Business is right," agreed the New Yorker. "An' soon as it's done, I ain't stickin' around dis dump no more. I'm duckin' for 'Frisco. But get it straight, Prowers. I taken all de chances I'm gonna take alone. See? An' it'll cost you two hundred iron men for my share of de job."

"Not that much, Cig. We've both got our reasons for wantin' to pull this off. Clint Reed an' his foreman ain't exactly friends of yours. You got yore own account to settle. But I'll dig up a hundred. That'll take you to 'Frisco."

Cig looked at his mild vis-à-vis sullenly. This harmless-looking old fellow was his master in villainy, more thorough, more ruthless. There were times when his bleached eyes became ice-coated, when the New Yorker had sensed back of them the crouched threat of the coiled rattlesnake. If he had known what Prowers was thinking now, he would have shuddered.

"Some generous guy, youse are," he sneered. "An' how do I know youse won't rap on me—t'row me down when de rubes make de big holler after de job?"

The old cattleman was at his suave mildest. No malignity showed in his smile. "I don't reckon I can give no written guarantee, Cig, but I never sawed off trouble yet on a fellow takin' the trail with me. Those who have rode with me could tell you that."

The crook from the East was uneasy. He did not know why. His restlessness drove him to the door of the cabin from which he looked out upon a cynical moon riding high above the tops of the pines. He shivered. This bleak world of white appalled his city-cramped spirit. It had been bad enough in summer. Now it was infinitely worse.

"Looks like there's a hoodoo on me," he growled. "It's de Gawd-forsaken country that puts a jinx on me. I'm losin' me noive. Every job I tackle is a flivver. After dis one, it's me for de bright lights."

"That's right. A getaway for you, pronto."

"When do we get busy?"

176

"To-night," Prowers answered. "Merrick has left two watchmen at the dam. One of 'em lives at Wild Horse. His wife's sick. He got a call half an hour ago sayin' she was worse. He's hittin' the trail for town."

"Leavin' one guy on de job. Do we bump him off?"

"Not necessary. A quart of bootleg whiskey reached him this afternoon. Time we get there, he'll be dead to the world."

"You sent de booze?"

"Merrick did n't," Prowers answered, with his impish grin.

"Sure he ain't on de wagon?"

"Dead sure. He can't leave it alone."

"Looks like a lead pipe," Cig admitted. "But de jinx on me —When I gunned dat Tug Hollister I'd 'a' swore I got him good. Nothin' works."

Jake could not quite forbear sarcasm. "You'd ought to take one o' these here correspondence courses in efficiency. It'll be different to-night, though. I ain't used to fallin' down on anything I go after."

"Meanin' that I do?" Cig demanded sourly out of the corner of a drooping mouth.

"Meanin' you ain't been lucky lately. Let it go at that."

Prowers moved about making his preparations. The dynamite and the fuses already made ready were put in a gunnysack. The tools were packed. Beneath his coat Jake put on a gaberdine vest, for it was possible that the weather might turn cold.

Presently both men were ready. The cattleman blew out the light and they passed from the cabin into the starry night.

They did not go direct to the dam. Prowers had in him too much of the fox for that. He would not leave tracks in the snow that might later take him to the penitentiary. Their footsteps followed the beaten trail that ran from the cabin to a road meandering down into Paradise Valley by the line of least resistance.

Half a mile from the point where they struck it, another road deflected from this one, leading to Merrick's camp at the Sweetwater Dam. Into this they turned. The snow had been beaten down by scores of passing feet. The top crust did not break beneath their weights, so that no evidence would be left written there as to who had made this midnight trip of destruction.

Cig's eye took in the ghostly white hills and he shivered. "Gawd, what a dump!" he groaned. His vocabulary was as limited as his emotions. He could never get used to the barren grandeur of the Rockies. They awed and oppressed him. They were too stark and clean for him. He struggled with a sense of doom. In cities he never thought of death, but premonitions of it had several times shaken his ratlike courage since he had been here. Twice he had dreamed that he was being buried in these hills and had wakened in a cold sweat of horror. He made up his mind to "beat it" for the Pacific coast at once.

They came down into the bowl where the dam was, skirting the edge of the timber to attract as little attention as possible in case a watchman should be on his beat. No sign of life disturbed the stillness. They crept to the tents and made a hurried survey. In one of them a man lay on a cot asleep. He was fully dressed. His arms were outflung and he was breathing stertorously. A bottle, one third full, stood on a small table close to the cot.

"Like I said, dead to the world," Prowers commented.

He turned away. Cig swiftly snatched the bottle and slipped it inside his coat. He wanted a drink or two pretty badly, and, like enough, Prowers would n't let him have them if he knew.

The two men crossed the dam-head to the gates.

"It'll be here," the cowman said as he put down the gunnysack.

Before they set to work, Cig concealed his bottle, but in the course of the hours that followed he made frequent visits to the spot where he had hidden it. Since Prowers was neither blind nor a fool he became aware of what the other was trying to keep from him. He said nothing. The bulk of the work fell on him. No complaint came from his lips. There was a curious smile on them, ironic, cruel, and unhuman.

Cig was in turn gay, talkative, maudlin, and drowsy. His boastings died away. He propped himself against the cement wall close to the gates and swayed sleepily. Once or twice he cat-napped for a few moments.

The old man continued to prepare the charges. Once, watching his accomplice, he broke into a cackle of mocking mirth, so sinister that Cig would have shuddered if he had been alive to impressions.

The tramp slid down to a sitting posture.

"Done up. Shleep a li'l 'f you don' min'," he murmured. Presently he was in a drunken slumber.

Prowers finished his work and lit the fuses. He looked at the

178

weak and vicious instrument he had been using, a horrible grin on his leathery, wrinkled face.

"You comin' or stayin'?" he asked squeakily.

The doomed man snored.

"Suit yoreself," the little devil-man said. "Well, if I don't see you again, good-bye. I got to be hittin' the trail right lively."

He moved briskly along the great wall of the dam, climbed the steps at the far end, and followed the road leading out of the basin. Once he turned to look at the deep lake lying placidly behind the rampart Merrick had built to hold it.

A great flash and roar filled the night. Even where Prowers stood, he felt the shake of the earth. Masses of torn concrete, of rock and sand, were flung into the air. The echoes of the explosion died, but another sound reached the anarchist on the hillside. He listened, with the diabolical grin on his lips, to a murmur of rushing waters.

The Sweetwater Dam was going out.

"The Flat Tops are liable to be irrigated good an' plenty, looks like," he murmured. "Well, this is no place for sight-seers."

He shuffled along the trail, the Satanic smile still on his leathery face.

It would have vanished promptly if he had known that a pair of eyes were looking down on him from the shadow of a pine above the road.

CHAPTER XXXVI

A STORMY SEA

BETTY, about to return to the Quarter Circle D E, found herself importuned by her small sister to take her along.

"I'll be the goodest, 'n' not bovver you, 'n' go to bed jes' the minute you say to," she promised.

The older sister hesitated, then turned to her father. "Why not? I'm staying there only one night."

"Fine. Take Little Nuisance along," Reed said, and poked a forefinger into Ruth's softly padded body. "I've got to go to town, anyhow, an' won't be back till late."

It was nearly two weeks since Betty had shaken hands with Justin Merrick and closed in good-will a chapter of her history. She had not seen Tug Hollister since then, but word had reached her that he had gone back to work in the hills. Merrick's men were on the Flat Tops running the lines where the ditches were to go.

She was waiting for Tug to come to her. Surely he did not intend to let things end between them as they were. He would ride up some day and tell her that he had been a stiff-necked idiot who had at last seen the light. Every day she had looked for him, and her eyes had moved up the road in vain.

In the pleasant sunshine R— prattled cheerfully of puppies, dolls, gingerbread, Sunday   ol, her new pink dress, and warts. Betty came out of a brown reverie at the name of Hollister.

"I fink he might come an' see us. I'm jes' as mad at him," the child announced. " 'N' I'm gonna tell him so, too, when he comes."

"If he comes," Betty found herself saying with a little sigh.

She knew that if he did not r   e the first move she would take the initiative herself. A little point of pride was not going to stand in the way of her happiness. But she believed he ought to come to her. It was a man's place to meet a girl more than halfway.

It was, of course, some fantastic sense of duty that was holding him back. She had not very much patience with it. Why was he not generous enough to give her a chance to be generous about this fault he magnified so greatly? He did not seem to appreciate her point of view at all.

On Betty's desk at the Quarter Circle D E an unopened letter lay awaiting her. She had never seen Hollister's writing, but at the first glance after she picked up the envelope her heart began to hammer. She knew who the message was from. The postmark was Wild Horse. Evidently the mailman had delivered it an hour or two earlier.

She tore the flap and read:

Ever since I saw you last I have been close to happiness in spite of my distress. You love me. I tell myself that over and over. I cling to it and rest in it. For this is the greatest thing that ever came into my life.

I wish, dear, dear friend, that I could show you my heart. I wish you could understand how great is the temptation to throw away discretion and accept this wonderful gift. A thousand times I have been over the ground, trying to persuade myself that you are right and my caution a coward's fear with no basis in reason. But I can't. I can't. Before I dared to take your life into my keeping, I would have to be sure. And how can I be? How can I *know* that this horrible thing won't rise up some day and throttle your happiness?

Why did I not meet you before I had given hostages to this destructive menace? I keep asking myself why. I can find no answer that is not born in bitter mockery.

If you could know what you have done for me, how you have rebuilt my faith in good, in God! No man ever had so wonderful a friend.

That was all, except the signature at the bottom. But it made her heart sing. Her doubts were at rest. He loved her. That was all she wanted to know. The difficulties in his mind would vanish. Her love would beat them down. What scruples, what fears could stand against this joy that flooded them both?

She longed to tell him so, to pour her heart out in what was to be the first love-letter she had ever written. Yet she was not impatient of the delays forced on her by ranch details, by Ruth's imperious demands for attention. She could attend to these competently and without irritation because subconsciously her being floated in happiness. Life had always given Betty what she wanted. It was unthinkable that there should be withheld from her that which was the crown of all her hopes.

Alone at the desk in the living-room, after everybody else on the ranch had retired, Betty gave herself up to the luxury of dreams. She felt very wide awake. It would not be possible to sleep until she had written an answer. There was no hurry about it. She wanted to take plenty of time to think out what she wanted to say before she even started on it.

When she began to write, her thoughts flew fast. They kept busy the flashing finger-tips that transmitted the messages to the white page on the carriage of the typewriter. The sentences were short, impulsive, energetic. They expressed the surge of eagerness in her.

181

She knew she would copy it in long hand, would go over every word of every sentence. The other side of her, the shy-eyed maiden of dreams who must be the wooed and not the wooer, would insist on deleting, trimming down, making colorless the swift and passionate staccato of the words. The letter she would send to Hollister would be pale and neutral compared to this cry of the heart she was uttering.

The little glass-cased clock on her desk struck two. Betty was surprised. She had been here alone with her thoughts for four hours. The fire in the grate had died down and the room was beginning to chill. She gathered the live coals and put upon them two split lengths of resinous pine.

For a few minutes she sat before the blaze warming her hands. That was the obvious reason for her staying. A more compelling one was that she saw pictures in the coals, dream pictures of the future in which two figures moved to the exclusion of all others. These had the texture of fiction, not consciously, but because our conceptions of the future must always be adjusted to a reality affected by environment and human character.

Betty lifted her head and listened. What was that rushing, swishing sound? She rose, startled, affected instantly by a sense of insecurity and danger. Something crashed heavily against the wall. The floor seemed to weave.

She went to the window and looked out into the darkness. A river, swift and turbid, was roaring past where the lawn had been a few minutes before. The girl stood terrified, her mind caught in the horror of unknown disaster. Even as she stood there, she saw that the waters were rising.

Again there sounded a rending crash of timbers. Like a battering-ram the end of a telephone pole smashed through the side of the house, crossed the room, and came to rest in the fireplace. With it came a rush of water that covered the floor.

Betty screamed. Her panicky heart beat wildly. Was the world coming to an end? She looked out again. What she saw was appalling—a swirl of rising waters tossing like the backs of cattle on a stampede. She noticed that the barn, plainly visible a few moments before, had vanished from sight.

The sloshing tide in the room was rising. Already it reached the bottom of her skirts. There was no longer any doubt that the floor was tilting. The house had been swept from its foundations. Built of frame, it was tossing on the face of a rough sea.

182

Betty waded to the stairway, climbing over the telephone pole. Except Ruth and the old colored woman Mandy there was nobody in the house with her. Both of these were sleeping on the second floor. In the bunkhouse were three men employed by her, but she realized that it, too, must have been carried away.

The girl flew upstairs from the pursuing flood. She knew now that it must have been caused by the breaking of the Sweetwater Dam. The Quarter Circle D E ran along a narrow valley down which must be pouring all the melted snow and rainfall impounded in the big reservoir.

Pounded by the impact of the descending waters, the house rocked like a boat. The lights had gone out when the wires had become disconnected, but Betty groped her way into the room where her sister lay asleep in the moonlight. She was running to pick up the child when Mandy's voice stopped her. It came in an excited wail.

"De day of judgment am hyeh, honey. Oh, Lawdy, Lawdy, we're sure come to de River Jordan!"

The greatest bulwark of courage is responsibility. The old woman's helpless collapse steadied her. A moment before she had known no sensation but terror. Now there poured back into her the sense of obligation. She had two children on her hands, one old and one young. She must be a rock upon which they could lean.

Betty stepped out of the room and closed the door in order not to waken Ruth. She noticed that the two lower steps of the stairway were already submerged.

"The dam's gone out, Mandy. We're caught in the flood," she explained.

In despair Mandy threw up her brown palms. She was a short, fat woman with an indistinguishable waistline. A handkerchief was knotted round her head for a nightcap.

"This am shore de night of Armagideon when de four ho'semen of de Epolipse am a-ridin'. Oh, Lawd, where am you at when pore black Mandy am a-reachin' fo' you-all?"

A lurch of the house flung her against Betty. She clutched at the girl and clung to her. Her eyes rolled. She opened her mouth to scream.

Betty clapped her hand over it. "Stop that nonsense, Mandy! I'll not have it!" she ordered sharply. "You'll waken Ruth. We're all right so long as the house holds together. I'll not have any of your foolishness."

The old woman's mouth closed. The words of Betty were

183

astringent. They assumed leadership, which was all that Mandy wanted. Her voice obediently abated to a whimper.

Betty did not open her mind to the colored woman. There was no use in filling her with alarms she had not yet conjured up. But the girl knew their situation was desperate.

At the lower end of the rock-girt valley was a gateway where the hogbacks on either side of it came almost together. There was room enough for a wagon to get through and no more. Out of this gap all the water rushing into the narrow basin would have to pour to the Flat Tops below. If the Sweetwater Dam had gone out—and of that Betty had no doubt—the floods would race down for hours much faster than they could escape to the mesa. The churning stream would grow deeper instead of subsiding. The house might waterlog and sink. It might turn over. It might be rammed by trees or rocks. Or it might be beaten by the waves until it fell apart.

"I'm going in to Ruth," Betty said. "If you're coming, too, you'll have to behave, Mandy. I'll not have you frightening her by any silly hysterics."

"Yas'm," assented Mandy meekly.

Ruth was still asleep, though the roar of the sweeping waters came through the open window and occasionally a drench of spray. Her sister went to close the casement. Above, the moon was shining placidly; below, the current boiled and churned. The depth of the stream, Betty guessed, must be eight or ten feet. It was still rising, but the force of its downward rush was terrific.

The house pitched like a boat. What was worse, it had tilted so that water was pouring in at the lower windows. If the stream continued to rise, it would probably either sink or overturn.

The noise of crashing timbers and beating waves continued. Betty wondered how much pounding an old frame building like this could stand. It was built with an ell, the wing a later addition to the farmhouse. The binding beams connecting the two parts creaked and groaned under the strain put upon them.

Ruth woke. Betty sat down on the bed and put her arms round the child.

"What 't is?" asked the child, frightened.

"Some of the water got out of the dam and we're floating in it, dearie. Don't cry, Ruthie. Betty'll be here with you all the time."

There came a series of heavy bumps accompanied by the

sound of rending timbers. It was as though the floor was being torn from under their feet. Betty thought they were going down. The house listed sharply, then righted itself so suddenly that the girl was flung to the bed.

The house had been torn asunder, one wing from the other. Mandy and the child screamed. For a moment Betty was near panic herself. But she fought down her terror resolutely.

"See. The floor's level now." Her voice was steady and calm. "We'll probably be all right. Stop that noise, Mandy. Did n't I tell you I would n't have it?"

The housekeeper sniffled. "I'm ce'tainly scared to death, honey, I shorely is." She folded her short, fat arms and rocked. "I been a mighty triflin' nigger, but I aims frum now on to get shet uv my scandalacious ways an' travel de road what leads to de pearly gates. Yas'm. Glory Hallelujah! If de good Lawd evah lets me git outa hyeh alive, I'll shout for salvation at de mourners' bench mighty loud."

The situation was too desperate for Betty to find any amusement in Mandy's good resolutions, but it occurred to her to turn some of her fear into another channel.

"Let's sing," she suggested.

Above the booming of the wild waters she lifted her clear young soprano and sang "Safe in the Arms of Jesus." The first line she carried alone, then Mandy's rich contralto quavered in and Ruth's small piping treble joined.

With an impact that shook every timber the current flung the house against a great boulder. The building swung as on a pivot and was driven into the rocks again. Betty looked out of the window. They were wedged between two great spars of red sandstone. The furious buffeting of the racing tide lifted their frail refuge and dropped it upon the sharp edges of the crags.

"We're caught at the Steeples," the girl told the others.

If they could get out and climb the rock spires! But that was impossible. The house was submerged almost to the second floor in the swashing torrent which surrounded it and dragged at it with a violence they could feel.

Again the shipwrecked three sang. This time it was "Rock of Ages." They held one another's hands for comfort, and in their prayer, voiced through the words of the old hymn, they found a sustaining strength. Presently Mandy took up "Swing Low, Sweet Chariot," and the others came in with support.

Betty helped to wear away the long night with talk. She forced into her voice cheerfulness and courage, though there was not a minute of the dark hours not filled with alarms. It would be morning soon, she promised. Daddy would come and get them, or Lon, or perhaps Justin Merrick's men who were camping on the Flat Tops. Then they would have fun talking it all over and telling how brave Ruth had been for not crying (except just the teentiest time) like a silly little girl.

After what to those in peril seemed an eternity of waiting, light sifted into the sky with a promise of the coming day. The darkness lifted and showed them a valley of wild and turbid waters. The Quarter Circle D E ranch had become a furious and rushing river flung back upon itself by the hogbacks which dammed its free course.

In the darkness it had seemed that the menace of the flood had been tenfold increased by the unknown peril that lay back of the visible. But in the light they could see too much. The force of the torrent was appalling. It showed them to what a puny reed of safety they were clinging. At any moment the building might collapse like an empty eggshell under pressure.

CHAPTER XXXVII

HOLD THE FORT

HOLLISTER was wakened by a sound of lapping outside his tent. It was a noise feeble as the meowing of little kittens. At first he thought it must be a memory from his dream. When he had gone to bed the stars had filled the sky above the dry and arid mesa where they were camped. No rain could have fallen in sufficient quantity to make even a rivulet.

But the rippling continued. The source of it puzzled the engineer. He flung back the bedding and rose. A chill shocked through him. His feet were in ice-cold water an inch or two deep.

Rapidly he dressed and then stepped through the flap of the tent. A shallow sheet of water covered the ground except where there were hillocks. Apparently it was flowing toward the south, as though before the pressure of a greater volume not in sight.

Tug walked to the tent of his chief and called him. Merrick answered sleepily, but at the words, "trouble at the dam," he became instantly alert. Three minutes later he joined his assistant.

One glance satisfied him. "The dam's gone out," he said quietly.

Neither by word nor manner did he betray what a blow this was to him. That which he had given two of the best years of his life for, had worked and fought for with all the brains and strength he possessed, was now only a menace to the community instead of a hope. It was a staggering disappointment. He had builded so surely, so safely, yet somewhere must have been a miscalculation that had brought disaster.

"The water's probably coming through the Quarter Circle ranch," he suggested.

"Yes. We'd better rouse the men and get right up there. There may be danger if the valley gets flooded."

Tug did not wait for the others. His words had expressed only palely the alarm he felt. If the break in the dam was a serious one—and it must be to have reached the mesa so quickly—the Quarter Circle must inevitably be flooded. He knew Betty was at her ranch. One of the men had mentioned in his hearing that he had seen her and Ruth going up the afternoon before. He was worried—very greatly worried.

His long strides carried him over the ground fast, but his fears moved faster. Presently he quickened his pace to a run. Dawn was at hand. He was splashing through water five or six inches deep.

Swinging round a bend in the road, he pulled up for a moment in dismay. Through the gap in the hogback, beyond which was the Quarter Circle D E ranch, a solid stream of water was pouring. Its flow was as steady and as constant as that of a river.

Cut off from the road, he splashed through a deepening stream to the foot of the hogback. It was a stiff quarter of an hour's climb to reach the rock-rim below the ridge. He grudged the two or three minutes' delay in finding a practicable ascent up the twenty-five-foot rim, for he was in a desperate hurry. Hand over hand he went up the face of the rock, clinging to projecting knobs, to faults in the surface, and to shrubbery rooted in narrow crevices. Over the edge of the sandstone he drew himself to the level surface above.

One glance from the summit showed him a valley submerged. Most of the cattle had evidently escaped to the higher ground, warned by the first of the flood as it poured down. He could see the upper hillside dotted with them. The barn, the bunkhouse, the ranch house itself, were all gone. Fragments of them might be made out on the surface of the lake that had formed—if one could call a pent-up, raging torrent by such a name.

His eyes swept the valley in search of the ranch house. He found one of the eaves sticking out of the current. All the rest of the overturned building was under water.

The strength oozed from his body. He was terribly shaken. If Betty was in the house—and he had no reason to suppose that she was not—she must have gone down in the flood. He could not, he would not believe it. And yet—

Again his glance moved down the valley. His gaze stopped at some rock spires known as the "Steeples." Some part of a building, much battered by the waves, was caught there. Even as he looked, his heart leaped. For from a window a white flag was streaming. He could see now that some one was leaning out and waving a sheet or a tablecloth.

He hurried down the hogback, every nerve of him quivering with desire to answer that appeal for help. He must get to her —at once—before the smashing current tore down and devoured her precarious and doubtful haven. Even as he went leaping down the hillside to the shore, his mind was considering ways and means.

A swimmer could not make it straight through the tumbling waters to the Steeples. He would be swept down and miss his goal. From what point should he start? He tried to decide this as he ran up the valley close to the edge of the water.

Opposite the point where the pasture-wire fence ran up the hill, a spit of higher land extended into the flooded area. He found a cedar post flung up by the waves.

Tug took off his shoes and his coat. He waded out, pushing the post before him. Presently he was in deep water. The swift current was sweeping him before it. He fought to get farther out in the stream, but he saw that the fencepost was impeding him. It came to him that he would be carried past the Steeples if he could not make more headway across the valley.

He let the fencepost go and struck straight across with a

strong, long stroke. The drag of the rushing water was very powerful, and he had continually to watch out for floating planks and timbers racing toward the gap between the hogbacks.

The cold from the melted snow in the uplands chilled him to the marrow. He had not fully rebuilt his blood from the illness he had been through. Before he had been in the stream many minutes, he knew that the force in him was failing. The velocity of the flow was too mighty for him to resist. Tossed here and there by conflicting sets of the current, he drifted as helplessly as a chip in a rough sea. His arms moved feebly. His legs were as though weighted. Soon now, he had no doubt, his head would sink and the waters close above it.

Then, out of a clear sky, a miracle occurred. It took the form of a rope that dropped from heaven, descended in a loop over his head and one arm, tightened, and dragged him from the racing channel into an eddy.

Three men were at the other end of the rope. They were standing on the roof of a one-story building that had stranded on a submerged island. A group of three cottonwoods had caught the floating building and held it against the pressure of the flood.

The exhausted swimmer was dragged to the roof. He lay there, completely done, conscious, but no more than that.

"Where in Mexico you haided for, anyhow?" a voice drawled.

Hollister looked up. The speaker was the cowboy Dusty, who had once dragged him back to the Diamond Bar K ranch at the end of a rope. One of the others he recognized as the lank rider Burt, who also had been present on that occasion.

"Lucky you were here," the rescued man said. "I was all in."

"Tha's twice I done roped you," Dusty reminded him. "I sure got bawled out proper last time. Say, howcome you in this Arctic Ocean, anyhow?"

"I was trying to reach Betty Reed. She's in a broken bit of the house at the Steeples. At least some one is."

"It's her all right. We drifted down here 'bout an hour ago. She's been singin'."

"Singing?"

"Hymns. 'How Firm a Foundation,' an' like that. Her an' the kid an' Mandy. Say, fellow, it's been one heluva night if any one asks you."

Burt spoke. "Was you tryin' to swim to where Miss Betty's at? You've got guts. You did n't hardly have a chanct with all the water in the hills a-b'ilin' down."

"She can't be far from here if you heard her sing."

"Not fur. Mebbe a hundred yards. Mebbe twice that fur. But I would n't tackle that swim for a million dollars. I never claimed to be no fish," Dusty explained.

"Downstream from here?"

"Yep. Over thataway. See the Steeples through the trees?" The cowboy asked for information: "How much longer do you reckon the water from yore dam is gonna keep on comin'?"

"Not much longer now."

"Well, I've sure had a plenty. An' they call this a dry country."

"Wish you'd rub my arms and legs. I'm cold," the engineer said.

They massaged him till he glowed.

Tug stepped to the edge of the roof and studied the current. Presently he spoke to the others. "Much obliged for your help, boys. I'll be going now."

"Going where?" asked Dusty, mouth open from astonishment.

"To the Steeples."

"You darned son of a gun! What's got into you, fellow? You been drowned once to-day—'most. Ain't that enough?"

"I can make it there now."

"Never in the world." The puncher was emphatic. "We come through by the skin of our teeth, with a roof under us. This ain't no swimmin'-pool. If you know when you're well off, you'll stay where you're at."

Tug did not wait to argue the matter. His business would not wait. He waved a hand and dived from the roof.

The problem before him was a simple one. Whether it could be solved, he did not know. While being carried down, he must fight his way as far across the valley as possible. He might be swept close to the Steeples and yet not be able to make a landing. If he failed to do this, he was lost.

He did not stop to see what headway he was making. All his energy went into the strokes with which he cleft the water. With every ounce he had he fought to gain distance. Within a minute or two he would know whether he had won.

A log careened down. He stopped swimming, in order not

190

to be struck. The current flung him round. Just below him were the spires of rock for which he was making.

In another moment the current was driving him past. A long pole stuck out into the water from the wreck of the house and rose and fell with the swell. He caught hold of this and flung his body across it. Precariously he clung, several times almost losing his hold. He edged along it, carefully, until he had worked into the shell of the house. One wall was gone entirely. Another had been partially ripped out. Through these openings the river raced.

Tug let go the telephone pole to which he had been clinging and swam to the stairway. Here he found a foothold and sank down, half in the water and half out. Again the strength had gone out of him.

Then, marvelously, as he lay there panting, the icy chill clutching at his heart, there came to him a clear, warm voice raised in a hymn. Betty's voice! His heart exulted. He listened to the brave words, gallantly sung.

She was singing, "Hold the Fort."

CHAPTER XXXVIII

BEYOND A SHADOW OF A DOUBT

"Do you fink Jesus will come, Betty?" a small voice inquired anxiously.

"I think he'll send some one, dear—Dad or Lon or—some one."

Ruth considered. "Do you fink he'll send him in time for bweakfast? I'm offul hungwy."

Betty did not know about breakfast, but aloud she quite confidently thought so. Hope was resurgent in her heart. The worst of the flood was over. Its level had already receded two or three inches. She had just discovered that. Within the past hour its fury had beaten in and torn away one wall of the house. Another had been partially destroyed. The shell of a

191

building that was left could not much longer endure. But she did not believe that much time would pass before a rescue was attempted. A few minutes since she had heard Dusty's cheerful shout, and, though he was probably marooned himself, it was a comfort to know that her party was not the only one in the devastated valley.

"My fry-pans an' my cook-stove an' my kitchen are plumb scattered every which way. I reckon I nevah will see them no mo'," Mandy mourned. "An' las' week I done bought dem luminous dishes frum dat peddler."

"Aluminum, Mandy."

"Das all right. Luminous or luminum, I ain' carin' which. What I wuz sayin' is—"

Mandy stopped, to let out a yell of fright. A dripping figure, hatless, coatless, shoeless, was standing at the head of the stairs. The face was white and haggard. The body drooped against the door jamb for support.

Straight from Betty's heart a cry of joy leaped. He had come to her. Through all the peril of the flood he had come to her.

"Tug!" she cried, irradiate, and moved to him with hands outstretched.

He was profoundly touched, but his words reflected the commonplace of the surface mind. "I'm wet," he warned.

She laughed that to scorn, a little hysterically, and went blindly into his arms, a smirr of mist in her eyes. All night she had been under a strain, had carried the responsibility of facing peril for all of them. Now she cast that burden, without a moment's hesitation, on broader shoulders.

His lip trembled. "I was afraid," he whispered, as his arms went round her. "Horribly afraid till Dusty told me he'd heard you singing."

"Oh, I'm _glad_ you've come! I'm _glad!_" she wailed softly.

He held her close, as though he were afraid that even yet malign fate might try to snatch her from him. Beyond a shadow of a doubt he knew now that if they lived nothing could keep them apart. She had been right. The sin that had held him from her was a dead and shriveled thing. It was no more a part of him than are discarded horns part of a living stag.

Tug murmured, with emotion, "Thank God! Thank God!"

Into this stress of feeling Ruth interjected herself. She saw no reason for being out of the picture.

"Did Jesus send you?" she asked, tugging at his shirt-sleeve. He did not quite understand.

Ruth explained, with the impatience of superiority. "Why, don' chu know? 'Hold the fort, f'r I am comin', Jesus signals still.' Betty said 'f he did n't come he'd send some one."

"I'm sure God sent him," Betty said, her voice unsteady.

"Bress de Lawd," Mandy chimed in. "Now you git us off'n this yere busted house, Mr. Man, fer I don' like no rampagin' roun' thisaway on no ocean v'yages."

Betty explained that he could not get them off just yet. They would have to wait to be rescued.

"Whaffor he come 'f he ain' gwine rescue us?" Mandy sniffed.

The girl smiled into the eyes of her lover. She knew why he had come, and in his presence by some magic the fear had dropped from her heart. The current dragging at their tottering place of refuge could not shake her sure confidence that all was well with them.

Hollister looked the situation over with the trained eye of an engineer. He must get them to the rocks before what was left of the house collapsed. But how? He could not take them with him through the waves beating against the sandstone. It was not certain that he could make a safe landing himself.

But if he could reach the flat ledge above, he might contrive some kind of bridge out of the dead and down trees lying there. It would be a hazardous affair, but he was in no position to be choice about ways and means.

Briefly he explained to Betty his plan. She clung to him, tremulously, reluctant to let him go.

"Must you?" she murmured, and shuddered at the black waters rushing past. "Must you go in again? Could n't we just wait here?"

" 'Fraid not, dear. You feel how the house is shaking. It can't last long. We've got to reach the rocks."

"It's been pretty awful, Tug. When the wall was swept out, I thought—" She shook that appalling memory out of her mind and smiled at him, shyly, adorably. "I'm not afraid as long as you're here."

"Don't be afraid," he reassured. "I think I can do it, Betty."

"Can't I help?"

"Yes. Knot together two sheets to make a rope. I'll need it later."

He dropped from a window, found himself caught in an ir-

193

resistible tide that swept him away like a chip. It was all over in a moment. He was whirled round and dashed into the rocks. The impact knocked the breath out of him. He clung, desperately, to a jutting spar of sandstone, hardly conscious of what he was doing.

The life went out of him. When he came to consciousness, he lay on the shelf, feet and legs still in the water. He noticed that his head was bleeding and for an instant wondered what it was all about.

Betty's voice reached him. "Tug! Tug!"

She was leaning out of the window of the tossing house.

He rose and waved a hand. Strength flowed back to him in waves. The haze lifted from his brain. He visualized the problem of the bridge and set about meeting it.

The dead trees on the ledge were young pines. They had been broken off from the roots, probably blown from the crevices because they were insufficiently rooted. He dragged one to the edge of the sloping surface of the boulder and raised it till it was upright.

"Back from the window, Betty," he shouted.

Her head and shoulders disappeared. He balanced the tree-trunk carefully, measured the distance again with his eye, and let it fall toward the house. The end of it crashed through the window panes and landed on the casing.

Tug dragged forward a second pole, shouted a warning to Betty once more, and balanced the pine carefully. A second later it toppled forward, urged by a slight push, and the butt dropped into the casing beside the others.

On this frail bridge Tug crept on hands and knees toward the building. The house tilted down and back. The end of the logs slipped. Betty clung to them, desperately, while Hollister edged forward.

"I'll take that rope," he told the girl.

Mandy handed out the sheets. As the bridge swayed and dipped, he knotted the linen round the logs, tying them together in two places. It was a hazardous business, but he got through with it safely.

A few seconds later he was in the bedroom.

"Ruth first," said Betty.

Tug nodded. "Tie her to my back. She might get frightened and let loose."

The child whimpered as he crept out upon the logs.

"Betty's coming too in a minute," her sister called cheerfully. "Just shut your eyes, Ruthie, and hang tight."

The narrow suspension bridge swung dizzily with every lift of the racing flood. Tug inched along, his feet locked together beneath the water that reached for him. Once he lost his balance from a lurch of the logs, but he managed to recover himself. Ruth screamed.

"All right, dear," he told her, and presently was pulling himself upon the rocks.

Hollister left the little girl there and recrossed to the building. Betty crawled out on the bridge, the man close behind her.

She looked down, and was appalled. The pour of the stream that was so close carried the power of a mountain river in flood. Her body swayed. She could never get across—never in the world.

The voice of her lover came, strong and comforting. "Steady, Bess. We're all right."

His assurance went through her veins like wine. Tug was behind her. Of course, they would reach the rocks.

The logs dipped almost to the water at the middle. A monster that seemed to be alive dragged at her feet.

"Oh, Tug!" she cried.

"Keep going. We're almost across."

And presently they were, safe on the slanting sandstone shelf.

He returned for Mandy.

"I cayn't nevah git acrost on that there rickety rack," she moaned. "I'd bust dem poles spang in two."

Hollister was not sure himself that they would hold her weight, but he knew that before many minutes the house was going to break up. He coaxed and urged her to the attempt, and after she began the crossing he clung to the end of the bridge with all his weight.

How Mandy got across none of them ever knew. She stopped twice to announce that she could not do it, but after more exhortation continued edging along. To the very moment when Betty reached a hand to her, she insisted that she was going to be drowned.

Not three minutes after Tug had crossed to the rock shelf, the shell of the house shivered and collapsed. It went out with a rush, and presently was nothing but a lot of floating planks.

Betty watched it go, with trembling lips. "If you had n't come," she murmured.

195

His soul went out to her in swift response. "I had to come. It was n't chance. That's how it was meant to be. Why not? Why would n't I be near enough to come when you needed me?"

She caught his hand. "You dear boy," she breathed.

"There's nobody like you—nobody I ever met," he cried in a whisper, as lovers have done since Adam first wooed Eve. "Could any one have done more for me than you? Your faith rebuilt my life. If I'm ever anything, I owe it to you. And now—the greatest gift of all. Why to me? Why not to Merrick, far more worthy of you?"

In her smile was the world-old wisdom Leonardo has expressed in his Mona Lisa.

"Love does n't go by merit, does it? I wonder if Justin is n't too worthy. He's perfect in himself—complete. He does n't need me."

"God knows I need you, if that's a reason," he said humbly. "But it's not fair to you."

"Was it Justin who swam through the flood to save me?" she asked softly, her face aglow.

"He's doing a much more sensible thing—building a raft to get you ashore."

"Who wants her lover to do the sensible thing?" She turned to him impulsively, warm, tender, luminous, a rapt young thing caught in a surge of generous emotion. "I'd want mine to do just what you did—come through water or through fire instantly when I needed you. I'd love you now, if I never had before."

"And if Merrick had come?"

"He could n't come. It would n't be Justin to do that—to fling his life away on a thousandth chance. Don't you see, Tug? He does n't tread the mountain-tops—and you do."

"I see you're always giving. If I could only wipe the slate out, Betty—begin my life over again to-day," he said wistfully.

In her deep, soft eyes a dream lingered. "That's just what I want—to begin everything with you. It's silly, but I'm jealous of all those years when I did n't have you—of all the sorrows and joys you've had, of the girls and the men you've known—because I can't share them with you. I've got to know all you think and share all your hopes. If you ever think, 'She's just my wife—' "

"Never that. Always, 'She's my wife,' " he promised.

"As long as you say it that way, Tug," she murmured, and clung to him with a little feminine savagery of possession.

Ruth, impatient at being ignored, again claimed attention. "Talk to me, too," she ordered.

Tug caught her small hand in his. "Of course, we'll talk to little sister."

"Are you my big brother?" she asked.

Betty stooped and snatched the child to her. "He's going to be," she whispered.

Upon this Ruth set the seal of her approval. "Goody, I like him. An' he'll get me heaps 'n' heaps of tandy. More'n anybody."

CHAPTER XXXIX

THE TURN OF A CROOKED TRAIL

JAKE PROWERS had intended, while the work of destruction was under way, to return to his ranch and let it take its course. The body of Cig would be found, and the tramp would be blamed for the disaster. It would be remembered that he had already tried once to blow up the workers in the tunnel.

The cowman knew that public opinion would not hold him blameless. He would be suspected of instigating the crime, but, with Cig out of the way, nothing could be proved. There would not be the least evidence that could touch him. He had done a good job in getting rid of the New York crook. Moreover, he had not lifted a hand against the man. Was he to blame because a drunken loafer lay down and deliberately went to sleep where a charge of dynamite would shortly blow him up?

The wise course, Prowers knew, was to retire for a time to the background and to be greatly surprised when he was told that the dam had gone out. But there was in him a desire stronger than prudence. He wanted to see the flood racing through the Quarter Circle D E and its waters being wasted on the Flat Tops which they were to have reclaimed. Half his pleasure in the evil thing he had done would be lost if he could not be on the ground to gloat over Clint Reed and Merrick.

Before the night had fully spent itself, he was on his way to the Quarter Circle D E. The sun was almost up over the hilltops by the time he looked down from the rim of the little valley upon the havoc he had wrought. The ranch buildings were all gone, though he could see battered remnants of them in the swirling stream. Fences had been rooted out. A young orchard below the house was completely submerged.

The destruction was even greater than he had anticipated. It had not occurred to him that any lives would be lost, but he judged now that the men at the ranch had probably been drowned.

His interest drew him closer, to a point from which he could see the lower part of the valley. He made here two discoveries. Three men were out in the flooded district on the roof of a low building. Another group, on the shore line below him, were building two rafts, evidently with a rescue in mind.

One of the workmen caught sight of Prowers and called to him. Jake decided it was better to go down, since he had been recognized.

He glanced at the dam engineer and subdued a cackle. It might easily be possible to go too far just now.

"You move yore reservoir down here last night, Merrick?" he asked maliciously. "Wisht I'd 'a' known. I'd kinda liked to 'a' seen you bringin' it down."

Merrick said nothing. He continued to trim an edge from a plank with a hatchet. But though he did not look at Prowers his mind was full of him. He had been thinking about him all morning. Why had the dam gone out? Had it been dynamited? Was this the work of him and his hangers-on?

" 'Seems like you might 'a' let a fellow know," the cowman complained in his high, thin voice.

Black appeared, dragging a plank he had salvaged. He looked at Prowers, and instantly his mind was full of suspicion. He had known the old man thirty years.

" 'Lo, Don," continued Jake with an amiable edge of irony. "Always doing some neighborly good deed, ain't you? You'll be a Boy Scout by an' by if you don't watch out."

Black looked at him with level eyes. "Howcome you here so early, Jake?"

"Me! On my way to Wild Horse. Come to that, I'm some surprised to see you, Don."

"I been workin' for Mr. Merrick," the range rider said curtly. "That's why I'm here. But mostly when you go to Wild Horse you don't ramble round by the Quarter Circle, Jake. I'm kinda wonderin' how you happened round this way."

"Huntin' for a two-year-old reported strayed over thisaway. Lucky I came. I'll be able to help." He turned to Merrick unctuously, his bleached eyes mildly solicitous. "If the's a thing on earth I can do, why I'm here to go to it."

The men were carrying one of the rafts to the edge of the water. Merrick gave his whole attention to the business of manning and equipping it.

"This raft heads for the Steeples," he announced. "Two volunteers wanted to steer it."

Black stopped chewing tobacco. "How about you 'n' me, Jake?" he asked quietly.

For once Prowers was taken at disadvantage. "I ain't any sailor, Don."

"None of us are. But you offered to help. 'Course, if you're scared."

The cattleman's head moved forward, his eyes narrowed. "Did you say scared?"

"Sure. Last time I seen you, Jake, you was guessin' I had a yellow streak. I'm wonderin' that about you now. I'm aimin' to go on this boat. Are you?" The range rider's gaze bored into the eyes of the man he had served so long. It was chill and relentless as steel.

Prowers was no coward, but he had not the least intention of voyaging across the flood in so frail a craft.

"Too old, Don. I ain't strong as some o' these young bucks. You go on, an' when you come back we'll settle about that yellow streak for good an' all."

The raft set out on its perilous journey. A young surveyor had offered to go as the second member of the crew.

Pegs had been driven into the edges of the raft for rowlocks. The oars had been hastily fashioned out of planking.

The float drifted into the rapid water and was caught by the current. Black and his companion pulled lustily to make headway across stream. There was a minute of desperate struggle before the craft swung round, driven by the force of water tumbling pell-mell down.

A rowlock snapped. Black's oar was dragged from his hand.

A log crashed into the raft and buckled it up. Caught by a cross-tide, the two who had been flung into the water were swept into an eddy. They swam and clambered ashore.

It had not been five minutes since Black had embarked on this adventure, but, as he moved up the shore toward the little group of men he had left, he saw that something unexpected had developed.

Prowers was in the saddle and he had his gun out. It was threatening Merrick's group of rescuers. The cattleman's thin, high voice came clear to the range rider.

"Don't you touch me! Don't you! I'll fill you full of lead sure's you move an inch, Merrick."

Then, swiftly, he swung his horse round and galloped away.

Out of the hubbub of explanation Black gathered the facts. The man whom Prowers had lured from the dam with a message that his wife was worse had stopped for later information at a ranch house on the way down. He had telephoned his house and talked with his wife. He was perplexed, but relieved. After an hour's chat at the ranch, he had headed for the dam and reached the scene in time to identify Prowers as he left.

A minute ago he had arrived and told what he knew. The engineer accused Prowers point-blank of the crime. His men had talked of lynching, and Prowers had fled.

Black did not discuss the situation. He returned to camp, saddled a horse, and took from his roll of bedding a revolver. Five minutes later he was jogging into the hills. A day of settlement had come between him and the man who had deflected him from the straight and well-worn trails of life.

He knew the size of his job. Jake was a bad man with a gun, swift as chain lightning, deadly accurate in aim. It was not likely that he would let himself be taken alive. The chances were that any man who engaged in a duel with him would stay on the field of battle. Don accepted this likelihood quietly, grimly. He meant to get Jake Prowers, to bring him in alive if possible, dead, if he must.

The range rider had no qualms of conscience. Prowers had probably drowned several innocent people, very likely Betty and her little sister among them. The fellow was dangerous as a mad wolf. The time had come to blot him out. He, Don Black, was the man that ought to do it. If Jake surrendered, good enough; he would take him to Wild Horse. If not—

So his simple mind reasoned foggily. He was essentially a

deputy sheriff, though, of course, he had not had time to get Daniels to appoint him. That was merely a formality, anyhow.

Don rode straight to the Circle J P ranch. He swung from the saddle and dropped the lines in front of the house. As he did so, he noticed two buzzards circling high in the sky.

Prowers must have seen him coming, for when Don turned toward the porch the little man was standing there watching him. Black moved forward, spurs jingling.

His eyes did not lift from those of Prowers. At the foot of the steps he stopped. "I've come after you, Jake," he said evenly.

The skim-milk eyes in the leathery face narrowed. They were hard and shining pin-points of wary challenge.

"What for, Don?"

"For blowin' up the dam, you yellow wolf."

"Then come a-shootin'."

The forty-fives blazed. The roar of them filled the air. Across the narrow range between the two men bullets stabbed with deadly precision.

Black swayed on his feet. He knew he was shot through and through in several places, that he could count his life in minutes, perhaps in seconds. Through the smoke rifts he could see the crouching figure flinging death at him. Still firing, he sank to his knees. He could no longer lift the revolver, and as his body plunged to the ground the last cartridge was exploded into the sod.

Down the steps toward him rolled the shrunken form of his foe, slowly, without volition, every muscle lax. They lay close to each other, only their eyes alive to glare defiance till the film of dissolution shadowed them.

They must have passed out within a few seconds of each other.

CHAPTER XL

BETTY DISCOVERS WHY SHE IS YOUNG

FROM the house Tug had brought matches with him. He gathered pine boughs and lit a fire upon the rock slab. The warmth of it went through them and restored their diminished vitality.

"The water's going down fast," Betty said. "See the rock. It's several inches lower."

"Yes. Merrick will be here soon."

Except for Ruth and Mandy, the girl did not care how long he was. She was young, and in love. Beside her sat the man who was to be her mate. A flash of the eye brought happiness. A touch of the hand thrilled.

Even when she did not look at him, she was acutely conscious of his presence. Without turning her head she saw the line of the razor stroke where the golden down ceased on his tanned cheek, was aware of the gallant set of the fine head on strong shoulders. Oh, it was good to be near him, to know that out of all the millions of men in the world she had found her mate. There was in her a strange, a primitive, instinct to accept his leadership, a desire to be subject to his wishes and commands.

She smiled. This was not like her. Perhaps it was a merely temporary aberration.

"Are we really all alike?" she asked herself, trying to understand this love-complex that already was changing her point of view. "We want to be free, want to express ourselves. We're thinking of nothing else. And then—enter a man. Our house of cards comes toppling down, and we don't care a bit. Sometimes, of course, he is n't the right man. Then—tragedy, I suppose."

The young philosopher, looking at her hero, was very sure he was the right man. Her certainty went beyond evidence, beyond faith.

Merrick's raft reached them about noon. He was admirable in the rôle of rescuer. Efficiency showed in everything he did, even to the sandwiches, and coffee in a thermos bottle, which he had not forgotten to bring.

"Where's Dad?" asked Betty, between bites.

"He and Forbes were at First View last night."

"Does he know we're safe?"

"Yes. He's headed for home now."

Within the hour they were back at the Diamond Bar K. Clint drove up a few minutes later, Forbes beside him.

The cattleman took his children in his arms and held them close. He could not talk without breaking down. He dared not put his feeling into words. They had come back to him from the dead—these two. Inside of him a river of unshed tears flowed.

Betty left him making over Ruth and slipped into the next room where some one was waiting for her. Lon Forbes was telling Hollister some news.

". . . Jake's men found 'em there dead, not three feet apart. Both guns empty. Four bullets in Jake's body, five in Don's—an' most any one of 'em a fatal wound. They were that game they would n't quit. It takes a heap o' killin' to finish an old-timer, I'll say."

Tremulously, Betty moved forward. "Who?" she asked.

Lon told her. "I'm sorry about Black, but Jake sure had it comin'," he finished.

The foreman passed into the other room to tell Clint the news.

In a hushed voice Betty talked the tragedy over with Tug. The swiftness with which Nemesis had overtaken and obliterated Prowers was appalling to her. She had a momentary vision, vivid and amazingly sure, of God in the shadows passing judgment on the sins of men. It was as though they were back in the days of the old Hebrew prophets when the hand of the Lord stretched out and laid itself upon wicked men for their punishment when the measure of their time was full.

"He tried to stand above the law in this valley," Hollister told her. "He wanted to stop progress—said there should n't be any dam to reclaim the Flat Tops for settlers. Merrick will rebuild it. The land will be watered. Your ranch will be good as ever in three months. And he'll be buried and forgotten."

"And poor Don Black?" she whispered. "Poor Don, who

203

never had a chance in this world, or, if he had one, muddled it so badly?"

He could only hope that Don had gone to a better-ordered world where circumstances did not dominate good intentions.

Betty's sense of tragedy lingered just now no longer than a cinema picture. The life urge in her clamored for expression. No world could be a sad one with her and Tug in it.

"Shall I go in and tell your father now?" the young man asked.

"Soon." She made a rustling little motion toward him and found herself in his arms. "Is n't it splendid, boy? To-day's the best ever, and to-morrow will be better than to-day—oh, heaps better—and after that all the years forever and ever."

He looked into the deep lustrous eyes of his straight slim girl. What a wife she would be! How eager and provocative, this white flame of youth so simple and so complex! Her happiness now would be in his hands. The responsibility awed him, filled him with a sense of solemnity.

"Forever is a long time," he said, smiling, and quoted a stanza of magazine verse they had lately read together.

It began, "How far will you go with me, my love?"

Close-held in his arms, Betty answered without a moment of hesitation.

"She smiled at the stile with a sweet disdain;
 She scoffed at the bridge and the great oak tree;
 And looked me full in the eyes and said:
 'I will go to the end of the lane with thee.' "

The door of the inner room opened and Clint stood on the threshold. "Hello!" he said, surprised.

Betty disengaged herself, blushing. "He's decided to take me after all, Dad," she said demurely.

"Hmp! Has he? Kinda looks that way." Clint gripped Hollister's hand till it hurt. It was the best he could do just now to show the gratitude he felt for what this man had done.

"That's not quite the way I put it, sir," Tug said.

"Does n't matter how you put it, boy. It'll be her say-so from now on. Don't I know her? Has n't she bossed me scandalous since she was knee-high to a gosling?"

"Now, Dad, you're giving me a bad name," Betty protested, hugging her father.

"If he ain't man enough to stand some bossing, he'd better quit right now before he says, 'I do.' "

"*He* likes being bossed, Dad," Betty announced, and the imps of deviltry were kicking up their heels in her eyes. "Don't you, Tug?"

Hollister looked at the girl and smiled. "I'll say I do," he admitted.

William MacLeod Raine, hailed in his later years by reviewers and contemporaries alike to be the "greatest living practitioner" of the genre and the "dean of Westerns," was born in London, England in 1871. Upon the death of his mother, Raine emigrated with his father to Arkansas in the United States where he was raised. He attended Sarcey College in Arkansas and received his Bachelor's degree from Oberlin College in 1894. After graduation, Raine traveled throughout the American West, taking odd jobs on ranches. He was troubled in his early years by a lung ailment that was eventually diagnosed as tuberculosis. He moved to Denver, Colorado in hopes that his health would improve, and worked as a reporter and editorial writer for a number of newspapers. He began writing Western short stories for the magazine market. His first Western novel was *Wyoming* (Dillingham, 1908), that proved so popular with readers that it was serialized in the first issues of Street & Smith's Western Story Magazine when that publication was launched in 1919. During World War I, Raine's Western fiction was so popular among British readers that 500,000 copies of his books were distributed among British troops. By his own admission, Raine concentrated on character in his Westerns. "I'm not very strong on plot. Some of my writing friends say you have to have the plot all laid out before you start. I don't see it that way. If you have it all laid out, your characters can't develop naturally as the story unfolds. Sometimes there's someone you start out as a minor character. By the time you're through, he's the major character of the book. I like to preside over it all, but to let the book do its own growing." It would appear that because of this focus on character Raine's stories have stood the test of time better than those of some of his contemporaries. It was his intimate knowledge of the American West that provides verisimilitude to all of his stories, whether in a large sense such as the booming industries of the West or the cruelties of nature—a flood in *Ironheart* (1923), blizzards in *Ridgway of Montana* (1909) and *The Yukon Trail* (1917), a fire in *Gunsight Pass* (1921). It is perhaps Raine's love of the West of his youth, the place and the people where there existed the "fine free feeling of man as an individual," glimmering in the pages of his books that will warrant the attention of readers always.